INTO
THE
SUBLIME

Also by Kate A. Boorman

INTO THE

THE

SUBLIME

KATE A. BOORMAN

HENRY HOLT AND COMPANY
New York

Henry Holt and Company, *Publishers since 1866*
Henry Holt® is a registered trademark of Macmillan Publishing Group, LLC
120 Broadway, New York, NY 10271 • fiercereads.com

Our books may be purchased in bulk for promotional, educational, or business
use. Please contact your local bookseller or the Macmillan Corporate and
Premium Sales Department at (800) 221-7945 ext. 5442 or by email at
MacmillanSpecialMarkets@macmillan.com.

Library of Congress Cataloging-in-Publication Data
Names: Boorman, Kate A., author.
Title: Into the Sublime / Kate A. Boorman.
Description: First edition. I New York : Henry Holt Books for Young
Readers, 2022. I Audience: Ages 14–18. I Audience: Grades 10–12. I
Summary: Four girls from a defunct thrill-seeking group descend into a
dangerous underground cave system in search of a subterranean lake that
local legends claim has the power to change things for those
who can confront their deepest fears.
Identifiers: LCCN 2021046004 I ISBN 9781250191700 (hardcover) I
ISBN 9781250191694 (ebook)
Subjects: CYAC: Fear—Fiction. I Guilt—Fiction. I Caves—Fiction. I
LCGFT: Novels.
Classification: LCC PZ7.B64618 In 2022 I DDC [Fic]—dc23
LC record available at https://lccn.loc.gov/2021046004

First edition, 2022
Book design by Michelle Gengaro-Kokmen
Printed in the United States of America

ISBN 978-1-250-19170-0 (hardcover)

1 3 5 7 9 10 8 6 4 2

INTO
THE
SUBLIME

The body appears on a crisp October morning, breaking the glassy surface of the lake like a soft bubble of air escaping from the depths. There's a moment of stasis, several seconds where the corpse is still, framed by an apple-pink sunrise, autumn sweetness in the air. Then it begins a languorous drift toward shore.

Auto forward: DrkLegnds
From: AsphyxiA
Subject: Surfacing

I'm using the contact form on your site, which is probably weird but also my only option: They're monitoring my email. I'd give you some space, except I can't stop thinking about it, and I need to ask the one person who can explain it:

The surfacing.

I don't know how it happened exactly, but I have ideas about how it looked. How *she* looked.

You probably know all about it by now. You probably know that it took three months for her to appear out of nowhere, like an ember sparking to life in the ash. You know some backwoods local found her, a surprisingly long way from the caves, changing that particular corner of Colorado's woods forever.

You probably weren't surprised.

I haven't messaged the other girls; I think they need more time. Three months isn't very long—no time at all, really—to move past what happened down there. The dark changes things. But you know that.

I sent you all the details, like you asked, even though you already knew them. Everyone already knew—my testimony wasn't public, but these things get around. People love tragedy.

I guess I do, too; I'm a little obsessed with the moment of her surfacing. I like to tell it like a story, in honor of Sasha and her way of looking at things. I have a habit of trying to emulate her storytelling. But of course you know that, too.

I can picture it in my mind's eye, clear as day:

> The body appears on a crisp October morning, breaking the glassy surface of the lake like a soft bubble of air escaping from the depths. There's a moment of stasis, several seconds where the corpse is still, framed by an apple-pink sunrise, autumn sweetness in the air. Then it begins a languorous drift toward shore.
>
> One of the locals, a boy, is organizing himself for one last fishing trip—maybe illegal, this late in the season—at the pier. He glances up, sure the prize-weight pike he's been after all summer is giving him a final chance. Pikes are known to sit on the surface like that when they're hungry. He dials his brother in his excitement—*get down here quick*—but pauses when he looks again. No. Not a pike. No fish at all. *Call dad.*
>
> In a half hour all of Upward Junction, population

thirty-eight, is gathered at the water's edge. The body has come to rest against the wooden pilings: faceup, bobbing like a sunseeker on a pool floatie in mid-July. Hair drifting like a silken, seaweed-colored cloud, skin luminescent in the morning sun.

A shape-shifter morphing from the grotesque to the sublime.

The crowd is perplexed. She isn't one of theirs, isn't from around here. And with one road into Upward Junction and no visitors in days, there's only one way she could've arrived: the confluence—the hidden source that feeds their lake. She's emerged from that underground river, which means she's been beneath the mountain and traveled a long way—miles, maybe—to grace this shore.

They call the cops. And wait. No one dares touch her. No one dares disturb that . . . repose.

When a white patrol car finally crunches across the gravel it's a quarter to noon. Deputy Vargas didn't receive the message for the better part of an hour, and Meeker is a twenty-minute drive down the mountain.

She steps out of her cruiser, shading her brow against the Colorado sun, and eyes the residents of Upward Junction on the shore. Her small, strong frame moves with purpose as she starts down the bank. She stops shy of the crowd, a pressed-lip nod indicating she has, unfortunately, been waiting for this.

She takes a breath to ask them to disperse,
give her room. Upward Junction isn't nearly
as remote or unlawful as the spot the girl
disappeared, but authorities aren't common
around these parts. These people are bound to
linger, gossip. Maybe even give Vargas a hard
time on account of her being an outsider.

But the resignation on Vargas's face—*young
girl, go on home now, I'll handle this*—cracks
when the residents step back to give a view
of the body. Her eyebrows knit as she leans
forward to peer closer, then shoot skyward.

Her face drains of color.

Disbelief. A stunned pause.

And then she fumbles for her cell phone.

At least, I like to imagine it that way. Vargas is the deputy
who handled the investigation, and my arrest; it makes
sense for her to be there. She's there, and she's rethinking
everything I told her that day.

But I can't quite picture what happened after that.

It's ghosting around my thoughts, slippery and unformed. It's
there, waiting for me to catch hold, see it. Understand.

I don't blame you for anything; I made my choice, and I take
responsibility for that. I see, now, how alike we are . . . and
how very different.

But I do want to understand.

Help me understand.

What happened when she surfaced?

—Amelie

3 MONTHS EARLIER

WEDNESDAY, JULY 26, 1:02 P.M.

THE GIRL WAS A BLOOD-SPATTERED WOOD NYMPH, A TINY figure dwarfed by tall pine trees, splash of sunlight filtering through the boughs above, dappling her slight shoulders and dark cap of hair with white-gold. Blood had dried on her pale arms in a lattice pattern—dark-crimson, elbow-length lace gloves. Gore and particulate speckled her face and neck. Her T-shirt—a six-inch-long rip near the hem—jeans, and tennis shoes were coated with a chalky substance, like ghastly fairy dust. She was perched on one of three giant rocks placed in a line across the trailhead, feet on the boulder, wrists resting on her bent knees, gaze fixed on the ambulance.

Behind her, a weathered wooden sign sported a sun-faded, lacquered map, an uninspiring masthead, detailing the hiking paths in the dense forest beyond. Next to the trail sign sat a steel box, holding the emergency phone she'd called from an hour ago. Her voice was hoarse and halting, giving only the most pertinent information: *My name is Amelie Desmarais. We're at the White River National Forest, staging area number fourteen. Come quickly.*

She'd been mute since the first responders arrived, answering the paramedic's questions—*does this hurt? How about this?*—with a head shake, outright ignoring the deputies.

Uninjured, the paramedics had confirmed, everything intact, fully conscious, and space in the ambulance was tight, so . . .

So she was now the temporary charge of two deputies, dispatched from Meeker.

Vargas ended her call and tucked the phone away. "Cheyenne got her mother," she said to Draker. "We'll take her with us, meet them at the station."

Draker jerked his head toward the dusty red Toyota Echo sitting at the far end of the parking lot.

Vargas shook her head, raked three fingers along her scalp to smooth the wispy curls that were escaping her bun. "No keys and not her car, apparently. I mean, even if it was—"

"Parents are coming from where?" Draker had a bad habit of cutting her off when he knew what she was going to say. In this case: Even if it was her car, there's no way she could drive after this.

"Some retreat facility in Colorado Springs? Didn't catch the name. They were halfway to Denver." Vargas had offered the girl her phone to call her parents herself. The girl had keyed in the number, handed the phone back. The call, plagued with static, had dropped twice. Vargas finally radioed the station, had their clerk call.

Halfway to Denver meant hours away. "We've got time. We should get her talking," Vargas said.

"Here?" Draker slapped a mosquito on his arm, looking impatient. Probably because it was hot and buggy. Or maybe because Cheyenne was collecting for the next round of Powerball drawings—the station had a lottery group—and if they weren't back by four, he'd wouldn't get his twenty-six bucks in.

"I don't want to miss something."

"Search and rescue can handle it."

"Handle what, Dray?" They had no idea what had gone on here. This scene was hardly procedure. "Hey." Vargas peered at him. "You okay? You look a little green." She shaded her eyes against the sun to peer at him.

Truthfully, she wasn't feeling great herself. Not because of the amount of blood everywhere, the barely coherent babble of the one wild-eyed girl, and the ashen color of the other, who'd been drifting in and out of consciousness. Vargas hadn't attended a ton of accident scenes—she'd only been with the Rio Blanco County Sheriff's office two years, and Meeker wasn't exactly a hotbed of crime—but she'd seen enough accidents to know how to compartmentalize, shut the horror into a corner of her mind and focus.

It wasn't that. It was this place.

There were spots in the wilds of Colorado where law enforcement didn't fit, places that operated foremost on the laws of nature and second on their own, self-made law. Locals out this way never requested police presence.

Draker straightened up. "I'm good."

"Okay." She let him go first and lingered, falling several steps behind as they approached the girl. No good appearing as though they had an agenda, better to look casual.

"Your parents are on their way," Draker announced. Vargas stopped several feet away, giving the girl space, but Draker moved in close. "They'll be a little while." Like she'd gotten a flat tire on her bike and needed a ride.

Behind them, the paramedics sealed the back of the

ambulance, hopped in, and peeled out. The light flashed eerily without the siren as they turned onto the highway and disappeared behind a row of tall pines, leaving the white-and-black patrol car and the Echo the only vehicles in the parking lot.

The girl's gaze had followed the ambulance to the highway. She stared at the spot it had been, a strange expression on her face. Not relief. Not fear.

Haunted was the word Vargas would've used. She shifted her stance, moving into the girl's line of vision. "They'll take good care of them, don't you worry."

"We've got some time," Draker added, like it was his idea. "We'd like to talk a bit"—he glanced at his phone, the transcription of the SOS call, like he hadn't already memorized her name—"Amelie. If you don't mind? Get a handle on what happened here."

The girl nodded wordlessly but didn't shift her attention.

"You might be feeling a bit out of it," Vargas said. "That's okay. We're here to help. And when you don't want to talk anymore, you say."

Another silent nod. A dragonfly landed on the girl's shin, its iridescent wings and jeweled body an incongruent bit of sparkle on her filth-crusted jeans. She took no notice.

"You want to sit somewhere more comfortable?"

The staging area wasn't a campground; there were no picnic tables or benches. That left the back of the patrol car. The girl straightened her legs, displacing the dragonfly, which whizzed off over the trees and into the cloudless sky. She shook her head.

"No problem." Draker settled himself on the rock nearest

her, affecting a casual lean, one hand on his knee. "Can you walk me back a bit? Tell me why you're out here?"

"Where are they taking them?" First words since they'd arrived twenty minutes ago. Her voice was a rasp.

"The hospital in Rifle," Vargas said. "Their parents are on the way. Like I said, they'll take good care of them."

"Amelie," Draker said again. "Can you tell us what you were doing out here?"

The girl pulled her gaze several feet closer, to the middle of the parking lot, her brow knitting. It was like she was trying to figure that out.

"Or a bit about you?"

Her brow furrowed deeper. She looked up at the cops.

"You wouldn't tell the paramedics that one girl's name," Draker pressed. "The one with no ID."

She glanced up. "I don't know it." She sounded surprised—as though she'd just realized this.

Draker exchanged a look with Vargas. "You mean you can't remember?" Vargas clarified.

"I mean that I don't know it."

"Because you met on the trails?"

"No. We came together."

Draker looked at the red Echo, shared another glance with Vargas. "But you don't know one another."

"We just met."

"At school or something?"

"Dissent." Pause. "It was a . . . meetup. For thrill seekers. In Denver."

"And you came out here for a . . . hike?" Draker glanced

at the girl's dirty tennis shoes—hardly adequate footwear for the backcountry.

Now she was looking at her feet as though they were a new addition to her body.

Draker leaned in. "Amelie, you on something?" Vargas shifted, put her hand to her side—a go-easy signal. Draker ignored her. "Molly? Weed?"

"I . . ." The girl seemed at a loss.

"You've been through something," Vargas interjected. "So how about you start at the beginning. Maybe . . . in Denver. Is that where you're from? You could start—"

"One of your friends had a bad wound," Draker persisted. "A laceration on her thigh—"

"I didn't stab her."

1:07 P.M.

THE GIRL STATED IT AS A MATTER OF FACT, NO EMOTION.

Draker and Vargas didn't look at each other, but a moment passed between them. A stab wound was exactly what it had looked like, though the paramedics hadn't had time to confirm. Both deputies had witnessed the girl babbling "She did it. Amelie did it" as they packed her into the ambulance. She'd been looking at her wound, though at the time Vargas couldn't be sure she'd been referring to it. Now . . .

"No one said you did." Draker's tone wasn't accusatory, but it was hardly neutral.

Then, he wasn't a subtle man: a by-product of his authority never being questioned? Vargas wouldn't know. "The wounded girl said there were four of you," Vargas said carefully.

"There were."

"So, where's the fourth?" Draker, again.

A long silence. It was hardly absolute; in the distance a crow was calling—a constant garbled refrain—and the radio in the patrol car was crackling sporadically through the open passenger window, but the girl's stillness had a strange muting effect on the scene. Her eyes were clouded with thought, as though she was listening to some internal monologue. Her mouth twitched. She seemed conflicted, wrestling with something. A slight shake of the head and her eyes hardened. *Decision made.*

She drew her head up. "There are no beautiful surfaces without a terrible depth."

The crow called again, clear and shrill, punctuating the silence that followed. Draker stood, a muscle working in his jaw. Vargas kept her face blank. It was a bizarre non sequitur, but also familiar. Draker gave Vargas the signal for a quick sidebar.

She hesitated, catching hold of the memory. "Friedrich Nietzsche," she said. She looked at the girl. "Beautiful surfaces."

The girl nodded.

"Nietzsche," Draker repeated. His brow wrinkled. "'God is dead'? That guy?"

"Yeah, but it's not . . ." Vargas paused. "You need the context."

"It's important," the girl said, though for some reason Vargas didn't think she was referring to "context." She didn't have the chance to clarify. Draker was jerking his head again, looking impatient.

"We'll be right back," Vargas said.

"Where are you going? I thought we were going to talk."

"We will," Vargas assured her. "Just going to check in with the hospital." As she turned to follow Draker, Vargas cataloged the change in the girl. Her strange detachment had been replaced by a palpable nervous energy. Was that typical, post trauma?

They moved to the far side of the patrol car, out of earshot.

"I know psychos come in all shapes and sizes," Draker muttered. "But a pint-sized pixie psycho is a first, for me."

"Maybe she's in shock."

"Her vitals were perfect, and shock victims don't quote dead philosophizers."

"Philosophers."

Draker squinted at her. "About that—"

"I took a philosophy course in college, okay?"

A resigned frown. He drew a breath. "Well, we should Mirandize her."

"Because we're charging her with . . . ?"

"Nothing, yet. But I'd rather anything she says be admissible."

"That Nietzsche quote really weirded you out, huh?"

"*She's* weirding me out. The whole thing is weird."

"Agreed. But I don't want her to shut down again; we just got her talking." And she seemed suddenly keen to continue. "Give me a few minutes with her. You're making her nervous."

He sighed loudly.

"Dray. You're trying to."

He glanced at the girl, back at Vargas. Relented. "Fine. I'll radio and see if Soustracs is at the hospital yet. When those girls are able to talk, we need someone ready to listen."

"Okay." Vargas nodded. "And hey, if it gets crazy, I'll make sure it can go on record."

"It's already crazy," Draker muttered as she turned away.

Vargas approached the girl again. She had her head bent

in thought, one foot tapping a rhythm on the boulder. Her initial distracted demeanor had vanished; now she was present. She was thinking. Vargas took up Draker's perch, sweat beading on the back of her neck. "Amelie, I know this is overwhelming. Anything you can tell us about what happened here would be helpful."

"Right." Amelie nodded as she chewed her upper lip. "Yeah."

"We left off talking about the fourth girl?"

"We left off talking about Nietzsche," she corrected. She recited: "The devotion of the greatest is to encounter risk and danger, and play dice for death."

"And that's relevant?"

"Well, yeah. That's how we know one another. It's exactly why we came."

"Nietzsche is why you came for a hike in the woods?"

"We didn't come for a hike." The girl shook her head, twisting her small body to look at the forest. She stared into the dense rows of trees, cocking her head, as though she was listening for something.

Or *to* something.

When she turned back, she regarded Vargas earnestly. "We'd heard about a subterranean lake."

Bingo. "An underground lake?" Vargas clarified. "Part of the Spring Cave system?" It was the most well-known of the systems in this part of the national forest.

"Maybe. Maybe a new system entirely. It was just a rumor. The Sublime."

"Sorry?"

"That's what they call it: the Sublime."

"Right. Okay." Something about the way the girl said it bothered Vargas, though she couldn't put her finger on why. She smiled encouragingly. "And you came out here to find it."

"We wanted to be the first."

"And were you?"

The girl shook her head.

"You didn't find it."

"We weren't the *first*," the girl clarified, tapping one blood-caked finger on the inside of her opposite arm. "But we found it." Her finger paused. "That's why three of us came back."

Vargas felt a cold sensation sluice through her. She reset, affecting a casual stance, both hands on her belt, trying to emit confidence. *She did it. Amelie did it.* "Can you tell me what happened?" The girl was a sprite of a thing, hardly a physical threat to anyone. But she was covered in *someone's* blood.

"Yes," the girl said. "But I need to tell you the whole thing. From the start." She looked at Vargas intently, dark eyes searching Vargas's face, seeking understanding there.

Or was it forgiveness?

"I'm listening."

The girl's brow knitted, as though she was thinking back. "Gia picked us up at the places we'd told our parents we were going to be. For me, that was home."

Vargas waited.

"We all pitched in money for gas, packed what we thought we'd need for a trip to the Sublime." A soft, rueful smile. "We had no idea."

SEARCH

THE GIRLS IN THE CAR WITH ME WERE A MIX OF NERVES AND hope—I could see it on their faces. The nerves were a good thing; it meant that they were into this. The hope, well, the hope was making me a little uncomfortable. For one, I didn't want them to blame me if this whole thing turned out to be fake. For two, it was contagious, and I was trying not to get mine up *too* high.

"How much further?" H, in the passenger seat ahead of me, squinted at Gia's phone, which was clamped to the dash, maps app open.

"A half an hour? An hour?" Gia guessed, drumming the steering wheel. Her eyes met mine in the rearview mirror.

I shrugged and nodded, like that would've been my guess, too, like there was no possibility this place *didn't* exist. "Probably not long."

The trip had required no small effort on everyone's part: lying to four different sets of parents and juggling part-time jobs (H and Devon) and extra goalkeeper training sessions (Gia) to free up this one day we could all scream out into god knows where . . . They wanted it to be worth the hassle. I wanted the Sublime to exist, too, though the possibility I was wasting time I didn't have was the least of my concerns. I had lots of time.

Fortunately, the directions had been legit so far. That was a good sign.

H went back to playing a crossword on her phone, black nail polish tapping at the tiles. "What's a seven-letter word related to 'awe, elevate consciousness, power.'"

"That's the clue?" Devon, beside me in the back, frowned. "Two verbs and a noun?"

"Could be one verb and two nouns. They're 'adjacent words'; it makes it more difficult."

We thought for a minute.

"Impress?" I suggested just as Devon said, "Deceive."

H craned her neck to side-eye Devon.

"I mean, anyone who tells you they can elevate your consciousness . . ." She shrugged.

"Hmm. It does end with an *e*," H admitted. "But maybe it's not a verb."

Gia tilted her head. "Sublime?"

H's eyes widened. She looked back at us, excitement sparking on her face. "That would be a crazy coincidence." She peered at her phone again. "Oh. No." Her face dropped. "*S* is the third letter."

"Boo," Gia said. Devon lost interest and noisily opened a package of red licorice.

By *coincidence* H had meant omen. Of course she was looking for one. I'd told them about the lore—just enough to pique their interest, answer their "How come we've never heard about this place?" query. I'd told them stories about the Sublime were hard to find if you didn't know where to look. The only mentions of it cropped up in old peoples' recollections of their childhoods, scary stories that were passed around the remote communities living out this way. That was because the Sublime wasn't just any subterranean lake; it was a local legend, complete with supernatural activity and, wait for it, a body count.

It's a subterranean lake in the White River park system. Finding the Sublime changes something important for those who dare to seek.

The location of the cave entrance was secret, known only to certain locals, so finding it would be nothing short of a miracle without directions.

But I had directions.

"Is that all you brought to eat?" Gia asked, glancing in the rearview. Devon was annihilating the bag, one string of fluorescent-red candy at a time.

"Of course not," Devon replied. "I have Skittles."

Unsurprising. A picture of Devon at Dissent flashed into my mind: standing with arms crossed, blowing a bright pink bubble of gum, looking bored as some kid scrambled onto the tracks on the Sixth Street bridge, between trains, and lit his designated firework. She was the only one of them I remembered clearly from those nights, mostly because of that lack of concern. And the candy.

Dissent was not the place for serenity. Or snacks, for that matter. It was an "elite gathering of thrill seekers" doing borderline-illegal challenges to "create chaos and control reality." Which Sasha had said sounded ominously frat-house-ish, but it actually wasn't some amplified version of truth or dare, where some idiot is pressured into doing something disgusting in front of everyone, or a girl gets slut-shamed for answering honestly about her "wildest night." It was about finding interesting thrills, something visually spectacular and exhilarating. The suggestions for the challenges were anonymous—fed to the organizers via DM.

All four of us had been participating in it for months, before the police investigation. Then Dissent shut down—a voluntary thing by the organizers, done out of respect for the victim, not on account of any police action. What could the police have done? Dissent was secret. The gatherings occurred in different locations every time, and the only way you knew where, was if you were pinged by the organizers. The only way you could post about them after the fact was secretly, using blurry, indistinguishable shots with hashtags only other Dissenters would understand (#beautifulsurfaces, #terribledepths).

It took about a month after the accident for another forum to crop up—no ghost of tragedy haunting this one—and I rejoined because I needed backup for this trip. There was no way I could do it alone. These three were the only ones who'd responded to my cryptic post about a major thrill out in the wilds of Colorado. We'd taken it to DM, exchanged info. That's when I realized these girls were true thrill seekers. I'd combed their socials and found out that none of them had been using the hashtags; they weren't there for the insiders' club. I didn't know if that was good or bad, I was just grateful

I hadn't ended up with some skeevy weirdo looking to hook up. I would've been okay with a non-skeevy weirdo looking to hook up, but that wasn't likely. The truth was, I had no experience with either scenario.

"You won't get carsick?" H asked Devon.

Devon shrugged, but I wasn't worried. She seemed too— was the word *controlled?*—for something as dramatic as throwing up. She had wild auburn hair that contrasted sharply with her cool but understated clothes and weird, ever-present calm. She could raise one eyebrow effortlessly—something I'd never been able to do—but it was one of the few indications of an emotional response. She never filled dead air with chatter; she spoke when she wanted to, paid attention when it interested her. It would've made me envious if I hadn't been a little unnerved by it all.

"It's just that I have a kind of vomit phobia." H—which is how she introduced herself and was also her username for every account (thankfully she'd mentioned her high school so I could track her down online)—was also weirdly intriguing. She had these isms that she was unapologetic about; the vomit phobia was new to me. Her socials had been full of posts about her "parasomnia," which manifested as night terrors. She'd told us that Dissent had been "medically necessary": *My doctor said I should elevate my adrenaline levels. It increases melatonin production, which helps you sleep.* She also had flawless skin and an amazing RBF that dissolved into a wide grin at surprising moments, which was strangely charming. "Like, vomit makes me vomit."

"Um, I just had my car detailed?" Gia said. "No one is vomiting in it."

Gia was easier to dislike. She was an early-acceptance-to-Duke, skipped-a-grade, elite-club-soccer-goalie with perfectly straight teeth and glossy black curls and—by the looks of her lavish quinceañera last year—a doting family. Not that I disliked her. She was a bit extra, but she wore it well. The fact she'd been at Dissent added an unexpected layer to her perfect veneer.

"I'm good," Devon said, eating another piece of licorice.

They had to have remembered me. I was frail, pale, and looked completely out of my element at Dissent, which is why it was always such a big deal when I'd complete a challenge. Word had gotten around about my childhood health issues, so everyone knew how much I was overcoming by being there. I was a bit of an anomaly.

What they didn't seem to know: I was the cousin of the girl whose accident had shut Dissent down. Probably because they'd never noticed Sasha. She was quiet around people she didn't know. She wasn't one to put herself out there, talk too loudly, or insert herself in conversations. And she also wasn't one to complain; she had a kind of stoic determination. Maybe because she was from a small town or something. She completed the challenges, sure, but she wasn't memorable like me. Plus, it was always dark, and there was always a crowd.

I wondered when I should tell them.

H went back to her crossword, and Devon turned to stare

out the window at the trees rushing past. I pretended to scroll through my messages.

Sasha was the only reason I knew about the Sublime. She'd been obsessed with the idea of a trip out here ever since she'd found an urban legends website graffitied on the back of a No Trespassing sign at one of the Dissent gatherings. She'd contacted "Henrik"—the owner of the website—and started making plans, insisting this was the perfect trip for us.

I'd told these three I'd stumbled on his site in some dark, thrill-seeking corner of the interwebs. Because, you know, we were just four thrill seekers . . . seeking a thrill.

I shifted in the back seat.

This trip wasn't about finding a new thrill, for me; it was about Sasha. It was *for* her. But that wasn't something I was going to explain to three complete strangers.

"Absolve!" H said suddenly, startling us. Right. The crossword. "It's *absolve*."

"That is the most random collection of adjacent words," Devon observed.

"It's supposed to be difficult," H said. "It's more satisfying when you win."

Exactly the kind of energy this trip needed.

"Hey, my maps app isn't working anymore." Gia squinted at her phone.

"Yeah," I said.

We'd driven another ten minutes into the middle of nowhere, and the landscape looked exactly the same, but this was an expected development. When I'd followed up on Sasha's plan, contacted this Henrik for directions, he said it was likely we'd end up in a dead zone. He admitted he wasn't sure because *he* never checked out the places he researched and posted about—something about bad karma. But all he needed from me in exchange for his directions was an honest account of what happened in the caves. It seemed like a fair trade. An honest account didn't need to include the fact that, deep down, I was harboring a tiny, wild hope that the lore was real. "I don't think our phones will even have service once we start hiking in."

"That's not ominous," H said, but she sounded good with that.

"We're going the right way to the staging area, though, right?" Devon asked.

"I mean, I followed Amelie's directions exactly?" Gia said. She slowed then, squinting at a cluster of buildings coming into view on our right. We peered at a wooden sign that had been repainted recently at the side of the road: WELCOME, FRIENDS.

"Want to stop and ask?" H gestured to the buildings we were approaching. "We are welcome, apparently."

Gia slowed further. "Is that a . . . summer camp?"

The buildings were intersected by a narrow dirt road. A large, ranch-style building sat to the left. Behind it, across an expanse of lawn, were several log cabin structures with tin roofs—they seemed to be part of the same outfit, which was either deliberately rustic or super run-down. There were antlers attached to the front door of one of the cabins. A hummingbird feeder full of sickly looking red liquid hung on a pole in a tidy flower bed.

"Looks deserted," I said, even though the landscaping was pristine.

"Looks haunted," H said.

Gia brought the car to a crawl but didn't turn in. We peered at the eerily still scene.

"Um, is the tune from *Deliverance* running through anyone else's head?" H asked.

"What's *Deliverance*?" Devon asked.

"A hillbilly horror flick from 1972," H said. "There's a famous banjo refrain."

Banjo. Yes. I was definitely getting a backwoods-and-proud-of-it vibe the last little bit. We'd taken 70 out of Denver, turned north at some nothing town called New Castle, and had been following a country road for at least an hour. The backwoods were everywhere: from the battered, tin mailboxes that fronted the occasional drive, to the cobbled-together houses with additions built from a variety of materials—one had a plywood roof that extended to incorporate an actual RV—to the privately constructed billboard proclaiming IT'S ADAM AND EVE, NOT ADAM AND STEVE in a field of bored-looking cows. The rolling hills had been getting steeper, the rows of spruce denser, the farther west we drove. This resort seemed to be the frontier of the absolute middle of nowhere.

"I think I see someone," Devon said.

"What? Where?" H craned her neck, and Gia slowed further. We were practically parked, though with the amount of traffic we'd seen in the last hour, which was exactly zero cars, it didn't feel particularly dangerous.

Devon pressed a finger to the window. The cabin nearest the road had two identical windows on either side of its door, obscured with white lace curtains. "On the right," she said.

Okay, there was a shadow behind those curtains. Maybe human-shaped, maybe . . .

"It's a zombie," H said decisively. "It's a zombie lair."

"It's a bunk bed," Gia said. "It's a summer camp."

"Zombies like summer camp," H protested.

"I think we're good," I said. "No need to disturb the campers."

Gia accelerated, peering into the rearview and scanning the scene behind us. "Seriously. Who comes here for vacation?"

"I already told you," H said. "People from Rifle."

"You said zombies."

"Yeah."

Gia hid a smile, refocused on the road. "Pretty quiet for

high season." Was she unnerved by that? Gia didn't seem the type.

"Well, maybe they took a field trip to the Sublime," H suggested. "Maybe we're going to find them down there. And maybe they've been down there so long, searching for the lake, that their flesh is opaque and their eyes don't work. And maybe they've resorted to cannibalism to survive."

"I thought they were already zombies?"

"I'm talking a different kind of mutant humanoid. There are several."

Gia glanced at us in the rearview, her brow wrinkled comically.

"Some are faster than others."

"Should've brought a pickax," Devon remarked.

"Or a flamethrower," H said.

"Or a sandwich," I said. "Throw it, and while they're fighting over it, run away."

"I think I'd be all right mano a mano," Gia said, rolling her neck. Her curly ponytail bunched against the collar of her Adidas jacket. Yeah, that didn't surprise me. She looked strong, capable.

"Not me," H said. "I definitely need something better than my Swiss Army knife."

"I don't think we need to worry about mutant humanoids," Devon said. She paused. "We'll be enough."

H turned around again and eyed her. "Enough, like we'll have no trouble, or enough, like we *are* the trouble?"

Devon tilted her head. "Guess we'll see."

H stared at her.

Something about the weighty silence that followed struck me as kind of funny. I pressed my lips together and swallowed the urge—I'd told a weak joke; no need to look unhinged—until I locked eyes with H.

There was a sudden sparkle of amusement there. I saw her mouth twist as she cleared her throat, which became a sort of half laugh, half cough. Gia glanced at her like she was concerned, which made her burst out with a loud guffaw. Gia snorted, and then all three of us were laughing. Devon watched with a bemused smile as our voices filled the small car in a cacophony of glee over flamethrowers and pickaxes and mutant humanoids. Over whatever awaited us below.

Hilarious.

It would never have crossed my mind at the time that our irreverence would end up being horribly ironic. I was too content with the idea that something unseen and unspoken connected us to realize that fact, itself, was the omen.

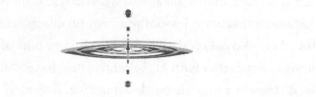

THE PARKING LOT WAS DESERTED; IT DIDN'T LOOK LIKE THERE were any other hikers in the area—at least none who'd entered the trails here. After the weirdness of the zombie summer camp it was a bit unnerving, but if it felt that way to the other girls, they didn't show it. So I didn't mention it.

We piled out of Gia's little red car and collected our things from the trunk, looking around at the dense woods, the faded trailhead sign. It was already three in the afternoon. The hike to the cave entrance was supposedly an hour, and the lake itself was another half a mile, but since we didn't know for sure, they'd built in contingency overnight excuses so their parents weren't expecting them at any particular time. H was "marathoning Romero"—whatever that meant—at a friend's house. Gia was having a sleepover with a girl from her soccer team. Doing the math with the best-case scenario, we'd arrive back in Denver before midnight, and they'd sneak into their respective sleepovers. Devon was in the clear; her mom was out of town with her younger brother. Vacation or something.

My parents were also out of town and, unbelievably, unreachable. After everything with Sasha, you'd think they might've decided leaving me alone and going "off the grid" in Colorado Springs was a less-than-stellar parenting decision.

But the shock of all of that had worn off, and they were back to being preoccupied with their own problems. Namely, saving their marriage. They'd recently joined one of those hip new churches that meet at rec centers and have young pastors in distressed jeans on headset mics encouraging you to be confident and live your dreams, and had paid a lot of money to attend a several-day retreat for "uninterrupted connection." It was pretty obvious their marriage was in its death throes, but I guess they wanted to make sure by hanging out with a bunch of people who'd given Jesus the wheel. The only upside was there was no way they'd know I left town.

"Okay," Gia said, shouldering her backpack. "Ready to play dice for death?"

That was the Dissent mantra, a Nietzsche quote we had to intone at the start of every challenge.

"It *is* the greatest devotion," H said ironically, but she definitely looked ready. She had on actual hiking boots and had slipped into a Gore-Tex jacket that must've been sweltering—she even had a CamelBak attached to her backpack. It was all a bit incongruent with the sparkly tights, nail polish, and cropped tee, but she looked prepared.

Devon, who was carrying her water bottle in her hand, was not. She was in a vintage cargo coat that had about a billion pockets, suede Blundstones, and boyfriend jeans—like she was headed out shopping at the consignment stores on South Broadway or something.

My tennis shoes and messenger bag probably weren't ideal for this, but at least I'd dressed in layers. That was a thing, wasn't it? The truth was, I hadn't given it a lot of thought—a

side effect of being helicopter-parented most of my life, probably. Or maybe I'd been preoccupied with the why of this
trip, instead of the how.

But we'd be okay. Between us we had water, flashlights,
some food, H's backpack of "survivalist crap," plus Gia's
obvious overachiever-ness, which had compelled her to pack
a first aid kit, rope, and, by the look of her bag, a billion other
"just in case" items.

Gia glanced at her phone. "I barely have a signal." She
turned it off, opened the passenger door, and put it in the
glove compartment. "Any other valuables?"

I pulled my phone from my bag, switched it off, and
handed it to her.

The car beeped twice as Gia locked it. She glanced over
at the trail, looking perfectly capable of anything you could
throw at her: a woodland hike, a caving expedition, killing a
wild animal with her bare hands . . .

I watched H tuck a squishy rubber octopus into the top of
her pack and pull the pack on.

It was a nice day; blue sky was visible through the top of
the forest, and the air was fresh.

Creak. Pause. *Creeeeak.* The trees shifted slightly in the
unseen breeze, rubbing against one another. The sound was
like rusted hinges, or a knife scraping bone.

"All good?" Devon asked.

Gia pulled a piece of paper from her jacket pocket, which
reminded me:

"I have directions," I said hastily, digging into my back
pocket for a printout of my conversation with Henrik.

Gia waved her paper. "I printed out what you sent me," she said.

Right. I'd sent her a different screenshot, containing the driving directions as well as directions to the cave. "I guess we don't need two?"

"Nope. I've got it." She was already turning away, pocketing her instructions. She seemed the type who was used to being in charge. I'd wanted to lead—I mean, it made sense that I would—but I also didn't want to look desperate.

"Let's do this."

I got rid of the paper and hurried after Gia, past the trailhead sign and into the trees, where the path rose in a gentle incline and the earthy smell of pine and moss deepened.

The surrounding trees were suddenly, monstrously tall. They dwarfed us, blocking out the sun and dropping the temperature by degrees. I was used to being aware of my size, but it was different in this context. I had the sudden image of us as a line of ants, picking our way through a forest of grass, unaware of the surrounding larger world. Oblivious of forces beyond our control.

I stepped carefully. Gnarled tree roots emerged from the earth now and again, like bulging veins from lumpy skin, crisscrossing the path in a kind of grotesque and hazardous hopscotch.

We continued for several minutes before I realized that the soft creak of the trees had gone silent. Everything was still. The only sound was our trudging feet, navigating the root-veins, heading for the heart—

"Yuhbear!" H yelled suddenly, stopping us dead and

sending my heart rocketing into my throat. Gia whirled, and H, still walking, ran into her. She stopped and drew back like she was surprised at Gia's reaction.

Gia flung her arms wide. "What the hell?"

"You're supposed to make noise on forest trails." H gestured around. "To ward off bears and stuff."

"Could you give a little warning?" Devon asked.

"Or, like, a lot?" Gia scowled. "And does it have to be a Tarzan scream?"

"Um, it was a banshee howl, thanks."

"You're really supposed to make noise?" I asked, still thinking about the unsuspecting ants. "Seems like letting bears know we're here is a bad idea."

"It's a good idea, actually. They don't like surprises."

"Neither do I," Gia said.

H shrugged. "We should make some kind of noise. I don't know about the rest of you, but I want to stay alive long enough to see the Sublime."

"We can talk," Gia said.

"Talking's not enough. We should clap our hands once in a while."

"Are you, like, a wilderness expert or something?" Devon asked H.

"Hardly."

"You look like one," I observed.

"This?" H picked at a loose thread on her sleeve, which had the crest of a pterodactyl or something. "I googled 'hiking' and ordered the first outfit that came up."

"For real?"

We started off again.

"No. My sister used to do outdoor-pursuit-y things, which is how I know about bears. I borrowed this crap. She'll never know—she's at university in Austin." H clapped her hands together three times. "I mean, unless I don't come back. Then she'll know."

"You'll come back," Devon said. "You'll just be changed." She looked at me. "Right?"

"The lore says *something* will change," I qualified. I hoped it sounded casual; my pulse had skipped with the thought.

"That *something* will need to be my underwear if I end up fighting mutant cave humanoids," H said.

Gia rolled her eyes. "Those don't exist."

"You sure about that?" H asked.

Gia answered something I didn't catch. A memory with Sasha was pinging in. We were in my parents' car, driving back from that meetup in the woods.

"What are you afraid of?" she asked.

Blood was thrumming through my ears.

"Seriously, Amelie—"

"Peeling wallpaper," I said sarcastically. "Creatures behind the walls."

"I didn't mean that kind of fear." Something flickered in her eyes. Resentment?

"—fear?"

"Hmm?" I snapped back to the present.

"Spiders? Clowns? What?"

I tried to reset. Focus. H was trying to get me to be specific about what scared me.

"Fears aren't always literal," Devon said.

Gia frowned. "They aren't?"

"No. What you're scared of is usually a reflection of what you fear in yourself."

"Hmm," Gia said, like she didn't care to follow that thought any further.

"You should spend some time in my nightmares," H said to Devon. "You could analyze me." She looked at me. "Hey, speaking of weird shit, I think it's story time."

I blinked.

"You said you'd tell us the lore when we got here?"

Right. I had said that. I'd held it back on purpose. It wasn't because I thought it would scare them off; they hadn't seemed the sort, from our DMs. And now I felt like I'd gotten that right: Gia was too focused and logical, Devon too unflappable, H too . . . much of a horror-phile. None of them were going to be deterred by the story. The real issue: Info was the only thing that made me a critical part of this little operation. I had no spelunking skills; I'd never even hiked before. I'd acquiesced and given Gia the directions before we even left Denver. I couldn't do this alone, and I needed *something* that made me a part of the team.

"Okay," I said. "Story time. I'll warn you, though. It's pretty messed up."

"I'm good with messed up," H said. "So long as it's not 'old Indian burial ground' or 'ceremonial cave' messed up."

"Ugh, yeah," Gia agreed. "No 'good white people disturbing the ancient, non-white evil' please."

"Uh, it's not . . . that." It wasn't, was it? I'd honestly never thought about scary stories that way before. "It's more like an . . . outsider tale?" I added: "With mysterious disappearances, possibly murder."

We hit a wide, flat part of the trail where we could walk next to one another. I hurried to keep up with their strides.

"I like outsider tales," Devon said.

"I like murder," H said. We looked at her. "In my *fiction*, obviously."

Gia waved a hand. "Okay, so . . ."

"So," I said. "The legend is that decades ago, before this was a national forest there were small communities living out this way. People who preferred the edges of society."

"Think we passed by their summer camp?" Gia glanced up at the trees, half-interested.

"Right. So anyway, there was this woman living alone in the forest out here. A witch. She hung wards around her property, talked to things that weren't there, had a scar where one eye should've been."

H looked sideways at me, unimpressed.

"Cliché outsider stuff, I know," I said hurriedly. I increased my pace; they all had half a stride advantage on me. "But she was strange, even by backwoods standards. It seemed like she'd been around forever—no one could remember when she arrived or where she came from—but she never seemed to age. People would tell stories about her; kids would draw pictures of her to scare one another—one scarred eye, long stringy red hair."

"Red hair is terrifying," Devon said blandly.

I forced a smile. I didn't want to look like I was trying too hard. I thought back to my DMs with Henrik, the wording he'd used. "One day some brave soul went to see her and reported back that she claimed she'd lost her eye in a cave nearby. It was the price for her survival, because, as it happened, the cave was some dangerously mystical place. Deep in the cave was a lake that had the power to change things for those who dared to find it."

"Ah yes, the wishing-well part of the lore," H commented skeptically.

"It's not a wishing well," I said. "You don't make a wish. It's more like: Whatever you want deep down to change will change if you find the lake."

H wrinkled her brow. "It *sounds* like a wishing well."

"What changed for the witch?" Gia wanted to know.

"Apparently she was dying before she went into the cave. Then she found the Sublime and . . . well, remember that 'never seemed to age' thing?"

"So now it's a fountain of youth?" H sighed. "This isn't getting better."

"It's not a fountain of youth, either," I said. "Obviously she wanted the 'dying' part to change, right? It would be unique to . . . whoever finds it."

"How does the lake know?" Gia asked. "Like, do you say a thing? Do some ritual?"

"Maybe *you* just need to know." Devon looked at me to corroborate.

"Yeah, maybe."

"Oh, I get it!" H said. "The witch had cancer. Sarcoma in the eye. That's why she needed to pluck it out—"

"Ew?" Gia wrinkled her nose.

"Just spitballin' on this 'unique to whoever finds it' thing," H said. "That's good news. That means there isn't an eyeball-gouging admission fee we all need to pay—"

"Eyeball gouging aside," Gia cut her off. "What's the dangerously mystical part?"

"Oh. Well, supposedly you have to, like, face yourself—your darkest fears."

"One and the same, usually," Devon commented.

I squinted at her.

"This is pretty tame so far," Gia commented. "You said it was messed up."

"Yeah, well," I said. "The messed-up part is the murdering-people bit."

They quieted.

"So, at first the locals chalked all of this up to crazy witch talk and were determined to ignore her. But then people got curious and started visiting her. And then people started disappearing." They'd fallen into step with me. No more ironic glances; they were definitely paying attention now. "Some families were sure the old woman had taken them to this lake. Others started to believe the woman was murdering them and hiding their bodies in the forest."

We stopped, gathered into a small circle like playground girls sharing secrets. "But no one knew for sure because the bodies were never found." The tops of the trees above us rustled with some unseen wind.

H was rapt. "How many people?"

"Half a dozen or so? Enough to make people pretty panicked."

"Enough to create a legend," Gia observed.

"By all accounts—newspapers and stuff—people *did* go missing."

"Who went missing?" Gia asked.

"I don't know names," I said. "But—" I paused for effect. "It was all young girls."

There was silence.

H blinked. "This is the part in the horror movie where people shout at the screen for us to turn around."

"Young girls," Gia repeated. "Maybe they ran away?"

I shrugged. "Maybe." I looked at H. "Are you turning around?"

"Are you kidding? Turning around is for B characters."

"Perfect."

H grinned. Gia seemed a little nervous. Devon looked impressed with my delivery of the whole thing.

"There's more," I said.

They waited. I drew out the moment, making it look like I was trying to find the words because it was *that* scary. They leaned in, anticipating, and I drew a breath . . .

"But I'll tell you when we find the cave."

They broke apart with exclamations of protest.

"Why can't you just tell us now?" Gia demanded.

"Trust me," I said. "It's better this way."

"There *is* an eyeball admission fee, isn't there?" H said, looking at me.

"Will you stop?" Gia grumped.

"Hey," I said to her. "It's just an urban legend."

"I know," Gia said a little defensively. "I just . . . need both eyes." She gestured to herself. "Goalie?"

"Fair enough."

We started off again, H and Devon more animated, Gia noticeably more reflective, and me feeling satisfied I was, clearly, a critical part of our trip. I needed their buy-in; I couldn't do this alone, and I needed to do it. And if there was any truth to the lore . . .

There isn't.

But if there was? If finding the Sublime—the place that could change something you really needed changed—was possible, then some descent into a damp cave was definitely worth it.

We reached a fork in the path. There was a wooden signpost that indicated Elk's Peak (7.2 miles) one way and Braden's Ravine (3 miles) the other. The woods had gone from rows and rows of tall, spindly trees to denser brush and thick pine.

The silence of the woods was more noticeable when we weren't moving. Practically deafening, actually.

Gia unfolded the directions and scanned them. "Pretty sure this is it."

"It's going to rain," Devon said. We looked at her. "You can't smell that?"

We inhaled. Okay, yes. The air was denser, and the forest smelled moist.

"I hate that smell," Devon said.

"Seriously?" H said. "Everyone loves the smell of rain."

"It's ozone, not rain." Devon dug in one of her various pockets and pulled out a handful of candy. "Jolly Rancher?" I shook my head no.

Gia pocketed the paper again and pointed off the path into the trees behind the sign. "It's this way."

The forest was formidable; there was some bushwhacking in our immediate future for sure. I wanted to pull my hoodie on, but I was sweating from the hike in. Scratched arms it would have to be.

"That's actually coming in fast," H noted, jerking her chin toward the patch of sky above the treetops and the dark clouds that were crowding in.

"Then let's not get soaked," Devon said, sweeping an arm ahead of her.

Gia reclaimed her place at the front, and we started off, leaving the path and heading into the unmarked woods.

For the next twenty minutes or so we pushed aside branches and wove around trees. Gia had a small compass in her hand that she was checking regularly; I'd never known anyone who could read one of those things. The directions were a little vague at this part, as I recalled. They indicated that if we walked northeast for long enough, we'd find an important marker.

I glanced around. Everything looked the same in here, the rows of trees indistinguishable from one another. A pang of anxiety hit me. What if this was all bullshit? What if I had dragged them all out here—three *actual* thrill seekers who'd rearranged their Saturday plans—and there was nothing to see? I would look like the biggest idiot. But way, way worse than that: This thing I was doing for Sasha would mean nothing at all. No cave, no gesture. And, as far-fetched as it was to even hope for it, no chance at something changing.

I caught a branch as it whipped back at me and held it long enough that Devon was able to grab it. The next one came faster than I anticipated and caught my bare forearm like a bee sting. I sucked in a breath. That was going to leave a mark. A bruise.

An uneasy feeling appeared in my chest. I tried not to think about it, tried to shut it out, but the image of porcelain skin appeared in my head. Pockmarked with purple blue.

I ducked as another branch came at me.

When Sasha was found, fresh bruises were peppering the insides of her arms. Bruised skin, bloodied skull.

I forced myself to breathe, to push the thought away.

"This forest looks like something from *The Wailing*," H commented.

"Do I want to know what that is?" Gia asked over her shoulder.

"A stellar Korean horror flick," H replied. "And I'm not saying that because I'm Korean. It's fact that Korea has some of the best horror. We're talking deep political commentary. Although there are also some really good Spanish-language ones—"

"I'm not watching a horror movie in any language," Gia cut her off.

"Too scared?"

"Too busy." Right. Gia was headed to Duke on some soccer scholarship in the fall and, from the sounds of how tricky it was to free up time for this, was spending every spare minute studying and practicing. Her life was intense, but she'd made time for Dissent. Was that weird? It was a little weird.

We continued in silence for another few minutes. Then Gia started to slow, scanning the forest.

"How much further?" H wanted to know.

Gia threw her a look. "You were that kid, weren't you?"

"I just wonder how you even know where we are."

"I know what I'm doing," Gia said. "We're only supposed to go as far as—" She broke off, pulled up short, and looked down. She glanced back triumphantly. "This."

We reached her and realized the continuation of the forest beyond was an optical illusion. The row of trees and scrubby brush continued, but on the far side of a gap in the earth, the edge of which Gia was standing on. Rock walls plunged steeply downward; we were looking at a kind of vertical cave.

"We follow this ravine thing to the entrance," she said.

I craned my neck, trying to see the bottom, but shelves of rock stuck out, obscuring the view.

"How far down is it?" H asked.

"Far," Gia said, looking at the paper. "But don't worry—there are 'stairs, sort of.' There's a marker . . ." She scanned the ravine. Her eyes widened. "Look." She pointed. There was something hanging from a tree about twenty feet away.

We followed as she crossed over and reached up to touch it: a strange little sculpture made from sticks and bound with bright orange twine. Like a charm or a ward or something, but it looked like a person.

"Damn," Gia murmured.

"The Blair Witch says hello," H remarked, staring at it.

"What?"

"*The Blair Witch Project.* That found-footage horror film from the nineties?" H looked at our blank faces. "Oh come on! It's another cult classic!"

Devon pushed at the marker with one finger, setting it to sway. "*Someone's* saying hello." That idea didn't seem to bother her.

Gia glanced around again, all business. "So, then the way down is going to be right . . ." She ventured close to the edge of the ravine again, putting a hand on the trunk of a tree clinging desperately to the cliffside and peering around it. "Here!"

We crowded in and steadied ourselves to look. About five feet below us was a moss-covered rock shelf. There was another tree growing out from the side of the craggy decline, and then a second shelf to its left. After that, the path dropped out of sight.

"Omigod," H said.

"These are the stairs?" Devon looked skeptical.

"Stairs, *sort of*," Gia said, grinning. She sat and dangled her legs over the edge, then pushed off and landed gracefully on the shelf below. She hopped to the next shelf and peered down. "Come on!"

We watched as she disappeared to the next part of the path. I was trying not to feel anxious that she was the one fearlessly leading the group—they were my directions after all—but the truth was I'd never been a leader.

H's face split into that wide smile, and she followed. She made the first landing effortlessly, then hopped to the next shelf and peered down after Gia.

I went next, navigating the first bit with far less grace. The drop was practically my height, so I turned over, preparing to slide on my stomach before I dropped. My messenger bag got caught between me and the ground, and I writhed awkwardly, freeing it so I could move, straining with my toes for solid ground. Devon watched me impassively. She didn't offer a hand.

When we got to the edge of the landing, we found Gia and H making their way, hugging the cliffside and traversing a path that was peppered with a series of dubious-looking steps, basically craggy chunks of rock that allowed them to stop and regroup and not slide all the way to the bottom, which was visible now, a moist-looking ravine littered with leaves and boulders.

There was a small pool of water at the bottom that began to dance with raindrops. We were under the canopy of overhanging trees and hadn't noticed the rain arrive. Thunder rumbled in the distance as it came harder, breaking through the shelter of the boughs and hitting my bare arms. I cursed. My hoodie was in my messenger bag, and I needed at least one hand to hang on to the cliff.

Gia looked back at us. "This is going to get slippery. We should hurry."

We picked up our pace, spidering down the cliff as quickly as we could manage. I knew I was holding Devon up in places—the parts where the gaps from one footfall to the other were too wide I'd have to sit and stretch a toe and grasp at whatever was solid in the cliff wall for balance—and my center of gravity was constantly thrown off by my messenger bag.

But surely she remembered I might struggle. Everyone at Dissent knew that.

I slipped and threw out a hand to steady myself against the cliff. H looked back. "You okay?"

I nodded. "Yeah. I just . . ." I took a breath. Gia had stopped and was looking back at me. "Compromised lungs," I explained. "Preemie birth."

"Right," H said. She tilted her head. "I always wondered how you managed the confined-spaces challenges at Dissent."

"By being a little psychotic, I guess," I said. "Childhood asthma will do that to you."

"Did you bring an inhaler?" Gia's brow creased.

"I haven't used one in years," I said, waving her off.

She looked at me reproachfully, unconvinced.

"Seriously," I said. "I'll be fine." I straightened up, breathed normally. "See?"

She studied me, and there was a flash of something in her eyes—admiration?—that sent a small thrill through me, since Gia seemed so perfect. She turned and continued down the cliff face.

I followed with renewed energy.

"So you were sick as a kid?" Devon's voice came from behind me. Had she not remembered that from Dissent?

"Yeah," I said. "The first six years of my life were pretty dramatic."

My preemie birth had resulted in jaundice and undeveloped lungs, complications that had necessitated intervention: incubator, respiratory machine, UV mask. Managing the repercussions had been a full-time job for my parents.

"There were a lot of impromptu hospital visits," I said.

There was that time I'd wandered into our under-construction basement where a crew was sanding the drywall, and my parents had dashed me to the hospital for inhaled particulate. Another time I'd gotten the air knocked out of me falling out of a tree, and my mom had been sure I'd collapsed a lung.

"I spent time in the hospital as a kid, too," Devon said. "Denver Children's?"

"Uh, yeah." I gripped a protruding root from the cliffside as I jumped a small gap.

"They had lime Jell-O."

"Yeah? I don't remember." My parents probably would've insisted on something more nutritious. They'd fussed over me that way. And the kids at school had treated me like some rare bird—I'd gotten physically carried around by the older kids at recess.

I labored down the cliff behind H.

It was a temporary affliction; I had, like the doctors hoped, aged out of it. I'd say "grown out of it," but the reality was that I stayed small, like "still buying clothes from the kids' section of Old Navy at sixteen" small. It was a side effect I could've done without.

There was also a side effect of getting better no one had anticipated. As it turned out, Project Keep Amelie Alive had been a kind of glue holding my parents together. By the time I hit junior high, things were looking better for my health and worse for their marriage. By high school, things had shifted dramatically: from obsessing over my life to obsessing over how Jesus could show them how to live theirs, together.

Not like I wanted parental supervision, but the truth was I had nowhere to be and no one to be with in my newfound freedom. Until, that is, Sasha moved to Denver.

Standing in the hospital corridor. Antiseptic smell, squeaky shoes.

"What was this gathering?" My dad.

My mom's wide eyes. Scared, but grateful I hadn't been part of it.

Behind her, my aunt, sobbing in my uncle's arms.

I left my parents standing there, went down the hall to the vending machine, and bought a package of cherry-flavored gummies. Sasha's favorite.

I'd always hated cherry-flavored gummies. But I ate the whole package right there, poking in one artificially fruit-flavored piece of gelatin after the other. Ascorbic acid burning my tongue, cherry coating the inside of my mouth, goo sliding down, blocking off my urge to sob—

"Watch your step!" Gia called back to us.

I pushed the memory away, focusing on the fact that the path was dwindling, narrowing into nothing. There was another large rock surface looming on our right—a boulder, maybe a chunk of the cliff that had collapsed years ago. It was covered in vegetation and seemed permanent enough for us to trust as a place to gather. There was a space of about four feet to clear to get to it, which Gia and H did easily.

I followed with effort, my heart lodging in my throat as my messenger bag swung and threw me sideways. I stumbled, and Gia threw out a hand to steady me. Devon landed beside us.

"Nice." Gia looked at us like we'd all made the cut for her soccer team.

"That was intense," H said. "But cool." She looked at me. "This is cool."

I felt a rush. It was cool. And the whole thing had been my idea.

Sasha's idea.

"Now what?" Devon asked.

We began searching for the path from the boulder, but a quick look revealed there was nothing but a sheer rock face that dropped about forty feet to the ground. Out of reach, and about ten feet below, the path reappeared on the cliff wall we'd been following, winding to the bottom.

"Um . . . ," H said.

"What are you thinking?" Devon asked Gia.

"I mean, I have rope," Gia said.

"But what do we tie it to?" H asked, looking around. "Besides one of us? And then how does the last person get down?"

We stared at the drop.

There was no way, save throwing ourselves from the cliff face and hoping we sprouted wings.

"Huh," Devon said. "Maybe this ends here." She looked at us, disappointment creasing her features. "Maybe we're not meant for the Sublime."

No. I didn't say it aloud, but my pulse skipped with a panicked beat. No. This couldn't be a dead end already.

"The directions don't say anything about this." Gia frowned, scanning the paper again.

"Can I see?" I asked, and Gia reluctantly handed it over.

"Let's look again," H said. "There has to be some way."

"It says here the stairs are to the right of the marker," I said. "You went left."

"No I didn't." Gia frowned.

"Yeah, you did," Devon said. "I mean, whatever; we were supposed to descend. But there's probably a more direct way."

"So should we retrace?" I asked. Rain streamed under the collar of my tee and down my back.

"Like, climb back up and start again?" H looked dismayed. I couldn't blame her; the path was dangerously slick now. It wouldn't be easy.

"There has to be a way down." Gia sounded defensive.

I pulled my zip hoodie from my bag and put it on over my damp T-shirt, watched her venture to the gap we'd jumped over.

"Look." She pointed.

We crowded in and peered down. About six feet below,

the gap narrowed as the boulder we were standing on widened to touch the cliff wall again, creating a crevice that was big enough for a person to stand sideways in.

"If we lower ourselves into that space and shuffle to the edge, we can jump to the path on the wall," she said.

"Okay, that looks dangerous," H remarked.

"And tiny," Devon added.

Gia rolled her eyes. She sat on the edge and gauged the space in the gap. "It can totally work. We'll need to lose our bags, is all."

"Um, we need them?" H said.

"I *know* that. We'll throw them from here." Gia got to her feet, shrugged out of her pack, and moved to hold it over the side. "Bombs away." It dropped from her hand. She pointed to my bag. "Anything breakable in there?"

I shook my head and handed it over. It disappeared over the edge.

H pointed at Devon's water bottle.

"Sure," Devon said, handing it to her.

H pulled her bag open, losing a few of the contents. "Damn it." She gathered up the items hurriedly and, along with Devon's water bottle, zipped them inside. She gave it to Gia.

Gia dropped it, her attention already back on the little gap she was going to navigate. We watched as she thought a moment, then began her descent: spidering her body into the crack, bracing herself against the walls until it got too narrow, then turning sideways and dropping. A curse rang out.

"What?" H called.

We leaned over to look.

"Nothing. Banged my chin." Gia was already continuing, squeezing along in a side shuffle to the edge. She reached her arm out, grabbed a root emerging from the cliff face, tested its weight, then used it to leap-scramble to the path along the wall. She steadied herself and turned to look up at us. Rain peppered her face, mixing with a river of blood that was streaming down her chin.

"Are you okay?" I asked.

"Piece of cake." She pressed the back of her hand to her wound.

H went next, complaining loudly about how "pinch-y" it was.

For once, my size was useful—I dropped in no problem and moved along the space easily. The leap to the cliff wall was less doable. When I landed safely, I realized my jaw was sore from clenching it.

Devon came last. She squeezed along the crevice with more difficulty. When she got to the end, she froze and her eyes widened.

"Are you stuck?" Gia called.

Devon didn't answer. She tried to continue but was held fast. She pulled backward but didn't move. Yeah, she was stuck. She squirmed again, futilely.

"Omigod," H said.

Devon stopped moving. She closed her eyes, and her mouth formed a circle as she blew out a breath. Then she shifted her shoulders a fraction . . . and was free. She continued to the edge, cool as a freaking cucumber.

She leapt for the wall, landed beside me, and peered ahead to Gia as if wondering what we were paused for.

"How did you do that?" H asked.

"I would've panicked," I added.

Devon shrugged. "I blanked my mind."

H grinned impishly. "Like, *elevated your consciousness*? You said that was bullshit."

"It is," Devon said. "Panic is a biological response. Biological processes can be controlled."

Gia studied Devon, looking intrigued.

Then H said, "Turns out that crevice *was* tiny."

A flicker of annoyance in Gia's eyes. "She's fine."

"I'm fine," Devon agreed. "Are we doing this?"

Gia turned, and we continued behind her, traversing the now treacherously slick path to the ravine floor. We gave ourselves only a couple of seconds of rest before we started to scour for our bags.

Gia found hers immediately and shouldered it, smearing mud against the arms of her baby-blue track jacket, which was stained pink at the collar from her bleeding chin.

Mine was lying nearby, next to the pool of water we'd seen from above. As I pulled it over my head, a flash of lightning lit up the patch of sky. Thunder rolled, not far behind.

"Let's go!" Gia urged.

"I can't find my bag!" H called. She was clambering over rocks and fallen logs near the boulder. I scanned the area, hoping to see something out of place in the landscape. My gaze traveled the chunk of boulder and rested on a crevice in the cliff face to the left. And stopped there. Stairs?

Yes, definitely there were stairs hewn into the rock there. They disappeared into the crevice above.

"Check it out." I pointed.

Gia and Devon looked.

"Right," Devon said. "To the *right* of the marker."

Gia's jaw tightened.

"Hey, no big deal," I said to her. "Now we won't have to climb back up."

"Assuming we return at all," Devon said.

Gia didn't smile. She turned away and joined H in her search. Devon looked unconcerned at Gia's reaction, but my stomach flipped.

The rain was a roar now. But as we stumbled about, getting drenched and muddy, we couldn't find H's bag anywhere.

Devon disappeared behind the boulder but returned empty-handed. She gestured up at the ledge. "Maybe it got caught on something?" she called over the storm.

I squinted up into the rain. If it had, there was no way we were retrieving it.

"We need to go!" Gia shouted again, moving backward along the ravine. "We'll find it on the way back!"

H lingered, still scouring. By the time she gave up and joined me, Gia was far ahead.

"Thanks for not abandoning me," H said.

"I'm not really feeling Dissent tonight." I gestured at the door. *"You go."*

"I don't want to go without you. I'm sorry, okay? I didn't mean—"

"Get. Out."

I blinked. "What was in your backpack?" I asked. We'd caught up to Devon, who seemed to be hanging back. Or perhaps she was unwilling to match the furious pace Gia was setting. She'd turned a corner where the ravine twisted and was now out of sight.

"Oh, nothing I'd ever need," H said ironically. "My water. Devon's water. My Swiss Army knife. Rope. Flares. My lucky Octo squishy."

"Well, whatever you do, don't tell Gia it's her fault." I glanced at Devon for commiseration, but her face was unreadable.

"Queen I Know What I'm Doing?" H said. "Yeah."

Around the bend, Gia was waiting for us impatiently. She turned and continued before we reached her, forcing us to hurry. The rain had let up, fortunately, but I was freezing, and as we trudged along, mud began to seep through the sides of my tennis shoes.

No one looked excited anymore; they looked cranky, a little resentful. Gia was stalking ahead like we were tagalongs, not part of her team. If the Sublime didn't actually exist, this trip was going to be a colossal failure. On several levels.

We slogged on.

"WHERE *IS* THIS PLACE?" H COMPLAINED.

It was exactly what I'd started wondering. We'd been stomping through the soggy ravine for the better part of an hour. The ravine was twisting regularly now; the walls were squeezing in on us, getting narrower with every turn.

Worse, the rain had started back up. We were soaked.

"These are garbage directions," Gia muttered, wiping a strand of hair back from her forehead.

"Hey," I said, trying to keep my voice light. "They've been right so far."

"Then where is it?"

I didn't respond. The truth was I couldn't shake the feeling that the ravine was going to narrow into nothing pretty soon. And then, like the terrain had read my mind, it did.

We rounded a small turn, the walls close enough to touch on either side, and found ourselves at a dead end. A rock face stretched up into the curtain of rain. It was sheer; there was no way to climb it.

"Fuck!" Gia raged.

H's shoulders drooped. "Seriously?" she said. "We came all this way for nothing?"

My face heated. "Maybe we were supposed to go the other way after we climbed down that—"

"There was no other way, Amelie!" Gia snapped. She brandished her compass. "Plus, the directions said north. We've been going north!"

She was super pissed. Worst of all, there was no cave. No cave.

No.

"What's this?" Devon asked, pointing to her left.

A crevice full of bramble marred the smooth cliff face, a mess of rotted tree limbs and withered leaves. Maybe there had once been a waterfall that had since run dry, leaving behind the debris.

"Um, dead plants?" Gia barely looked her way.

Devon leaned over, stood on her tiptoes, and peered through it. "There's a way through here."

"Really?" H crowded in next to her. "Omigod!" She looked back at us. "It's a passage!"

"How did you even see that?" Gia asked Devon, irritation lacing her voice. Probably because she'd missed that on the directions, too.

Devon pulled a gnarled branch aside, making the space behind it obvious. "It's almost like someone hid it on purpose."

H looked at us, excited. My pulse sped.

"Little help?" Devon asked.

We joined Devon, pulling branches and bramble from the space until it was wide enough for us to squeeze through.

"Sorry for freaking out," Gia mumbled to me. "I just . . . hate it when stuff is a waste of time."

"No worries."

Devon stood back, waiting for Gia to lead, which she did without hesitation. We pushed through the passage, traversing a short tunnel and heading for the daylight on the far side. We emerged into a huge, circular space about the size of an indoor skating rink. Tall rock faces stretched toward the gray skies. At the center was an enormous pool of water, boiling with raindrops.

"Holy. Shit." Gia pointed.

It looked like a large streak of . . . rot on the rock cliff across the pond.

Cliffs don't rot.

I stared harder. It was an opening; the black was the absence of light inside. An entrance.

"Omigod." H's face was elated. "It *does* exist."

Relief washed over me. It *did*.

A cloud of white mist appeared at the entrance. It wafted out and dissipated. "Oh wow," I said. "It looks like it's . . . breathing."

"It's a biochemical reaction," Devon said.

"Yeah, right," H scoffed. "There's obviously a dragon inside."

"That means there's treasure," Gia said. Everyone's moods had lifted significantly.

We skirted the pool, taking a soggy, sandy path to the mouth, where we halted.

We stood, considering the low sliver of dark space before us, about six feet across and three feet high. Devon pulled out another candy, unwrapped it, and stuck it in her mouth.

Gia extracted a headlamp from a pocket on the outside of her pack and put it on, switching the light to high before she got down on her hands and knees to peer inside. "It looks like it gets bigger, past this overhang."

The entrance was unimpressive, just a crack in a rock. Nothing to suggest it was some portal to a dangerous, mystical world.

Then, you never know what lurks beneath the surface.

"Hold up a quick second?" I asked. "I'm . . . feeling dizzy." Dizzy wasn't quite the word.

Gia looked back, alarmed.

"It's no big deal," I said. "My lungs are super sensitive to oxygen levels; they're still adjusting to the level in this ravine." I held up a hand, anticipating her next comment. "They'll get used to the cave, don't worry."

Gia extracted herself from the rock and stood. I leaned back against the cave wall, taking a deep breath. The sun darted out from a wash of gray and splashed across us.

"You sure you're okay?" H wanted to know.

I felt a ping of reassurance at their concern. "Totally," I said, and took a deep breath to demonstrate. "Just give me one minute."

Their attention was drawn away by a butterfly that appeared, flitting haphazardly. It landed on Devon's arm.

"You ever heard of this ninja butterfly?" she asked, raising her arm and inspecting its green wings.

"A butterfly that is also a ninja?" H asked.

"I forget its real name. It's this blue butterfly, and when it's in the larval stage, it gives off a pheromone that tricks ants. Instead of eating it like they normally would, they bring it into their nest and care for it—they even feed it their own eggs sometimes."

"The hell?" Gia wrinkled her nose.

"Then it undergoes metamorphosis and flies away."

"Wild," H said. "Tricking something into destroying itself by caring for you?"

"That is messed up," Gia said. "The ants think they're acting instinctually, but some outer force is controlling them."

"I don't think the ants think," I said, feeling a pang of discomfort.

Gia flapped a hand. "You know what I mean."

"It's actually genius," Devon said. "It's nature." She said *nature*, but it sounded like she meant *natural*. "The butterfly and the ants aren't the only organisms that do it."

My skin felt hot suddenly. Why was I flushed?

"That's so true," H said. "My halmeoni, my dad's mom, comes to visit every summer. And she's weirdly manipulative—she drives my mom crazy."

The butterfly took flight. "Free will is an illusion anyway," Devon said. "Biological processes—hardwired behaviors—are responsible for our decisions. We just think we're in control. It's called determinism."

Gia frowned. "What does that have to do with brain-washed ants?"

"Well, what's the difference if some other organism's biology controls us or our biology does? Either way, we aren't actually making decisions."

"The difference is that something wanting to control me is creepy," Gia said flatly.

Devon tilted her head. A small smile played on her lips.

"I don't get it," H said. "What you're saying is that I didn't actually choose to come on this trip? My . . . body . . . did?"

"My mouth is deciding to call bullshit on that," Gia said. "Life would be pointless."

"You'd never have to take responsibility for your actions," H agreed. "You could murder someone and not be responsible because it was in your DNA."

"Determinism isn't fatalism," Devon countered. "Our actions still have consequences we need to reconcile."

"Why should I take responsibility for something I didn't choose?" Gia frowned.

Sasha's face swam into my mind. I took a couple of deep breaths.

The butterfly was back. "There's also this wasp that eats the ninja butterfly's larvae," Devon said, turning her head to trace its flight path. "But of course, the larvae is safe under the ant hill, protected by the army of ants. So the wasp emits a chemical that makes the ants fight one another, and while they're at war, it goes into their nest and eats the larvae they've been protecting." The butterfly flitted over the pond and up the cliff face.

"Wow," H murmured. "So it's all for nothing."

"I wouldn't say nothing," Devon said. Drops began to fall again. Across the pond, a curtain of rain was approaching.

"I'm good now," I ventured.

"Great. Moving on from psychotic bugs." Gia got down

on her hands and knees again. She moved forward, immediately getting her backpack caught on the rock overhead. She cursed and dropped lower, not quite to an army crawl.

H, backpack-less and unhindered, followed.

I had a flashlight in my messenger bag but wasn't sure how to crawl and hold it, so I followed H, heading for the blue light of Gia's headlamp.

It's actually genius.

It was an interesting choice of words, but that was about as much thought as I gave it in that moment. There was something different needling at me: the butterfly effect. The idea that small decisions could have major, unintended consequences. As I crawled into this cave in the middle of nowhere, that felt significant.

And I was too wrapped up in parsing out how to realize Devon had been trying to tell us something.

THERE WAS A PAUSE AS THE GIRL'S BROW FURROWED. SHE looked up at Vargas. "Sorry," she said. "I didn't mean that last part."

"You didn't go into the cave?"

"Not that. I meant the bit about Devon. That was just . . . I was being dramatic."

Vargas looked at the girl, fascinated. Dramatic. Yes. From the sounds of it, that had been her MO on the way to the cave: reminding the girls about her maladies as a child, making them wait for the story about the witch. She had a calculated way of releasing information, that was for sure.

"So she wasn't trying to tell you something?" Draker's voice rang out from a few paces away. He'd finished his call by the time Amelie had started her story and was leaning against a nearby tree. He was giving Vargas the space she had asked for—physically, anyway.

"No, she was. She was trying to tell us why she was there. Why she came."

"And that was . . . ?"

The girl folded inward again—not literally, it was an emotional burrowing—and Vargas watched the girl wrestle, again, with something. She looked up at Vargas. "I'm getting ahead of myself."

Ahead of herself. Ahead of the way she needed the story to unravel? "That's okay," Vargas reassured her. "You just tell us all you can, and we'll worry about assembling the pieces later."

The girl nodded, but something about it felt false, like she was humoring Vargas. Like she had no intention of doing that. "I told her I'd tell it from the start."

"Her?"

The girl shifted. "Devon." She met Vargas's eyes. There. That look again. It was . . . beseeching. *Understand me? Forgive me?* If Vargas didn't listen carefully, she'd miss something—she could feel that.

Keep her talking. "Well then, let's keep going," she said. She felt Draker shift in irritation and ignored him. "You'd found the entrance. Then what? Did you go inside?"

"Yeah." The girl nodded, looking relieved. "We went inside." Her eyes grew distant, like she was remembering. "We started down."

DESCENT

I PULLED MYSELF TO STANDING IN THE DARK, SURPRISED AT how warm it was. The beam from Gia's light flitted around as she swiveled her head, showing parts of the cave in frustratingly brief snippets. I fumbled for my flashlight, but Gia's light was suddenly erased by a white glow.

Devon was in and had pulled her phone from somewhere in her jacket of many pockets. She moved it in a steady circle, revealing that we were in a small but surprisingly spacious cavern. The ceiling was twice my height, and the four of us had room to move without running into one another.

The rain outside was muffled, and all around us was a distinct, thick silence. The faint smell of artificial cherry candy lingered. I fought the sudden urge to gag.

Then Gia and Devon zeroed in on something in the corner at the same time: a large tunnel that extended back into the earth and out of sight.

"So," Gia said.

"Yep." That was Devon.

More silence. No one moved.

"Do you think it's very far . . . from here?" H asked, peering into the gloom. She cleared her throat. "I wish I had my backpack."

"Hopefully not too far," Gia said. "I mean, I don't have a ton of water to share."

"The lake is made of water," Devon reminded her.

"Sure, if we can find it, it's an option."

"Um, getting giardia from some stanky lake is not an option," H disagreed.

Gia laughed, though it sounded strained. "Wow, it's dark in here."

We contemplated the tunnel entrance, which sat like an open mouth, waiting to swallow us into the depths of the cave's innards. A cool breeze wafted from it.

"I'm roasting," H said, even though we were soaked. She unzipped her jacket and flapped it.

"Candy?" Devon said, offering a handful of Jolly Ranchers around.

Gia waved her off, but I grabbed one.

H unwrapped one and put it in her mouth. She grimaced. "Sour apple."

"That's the worst one," Devon said. "Take another."

H pocketed a second, retrieving a thin cylinder from her coat in its place. She held it up and twisted it. A tiny beam of light flicked on. "Penlight," she said unnecessarily.

I felt a spike of anxiety. They were stalling. I wasn't in any great hurry to head off down that pitch-black tunnel, either, but I just needed a minute. It seemed like they were having doubts.

That wasn't good. I wasn't going to go alone, with one stupid granola bar and a handheld flashlight. But I needed to go. An image of Sasha rose in my mind. Standing in my bedroom that night, reading off her phone:

"'It's a subterranean lake in the White River parks system. Finding the Sublime changes something important for those who dare to seek.'" She looked up, her face illuminated with the red from Henrik's website. For the first time in weeks, she looked animated. Excited, even. "We need to go."

"We do?"

"Yeah. It's, like, physically challenging—which you are all about these days, clearly—and it's . . ." She trailed off. "It's perfect for us."

"You don't even like the challenges at Dissent," I said. "Why would you want to do this?"

"Just . . ." She flapped a hand. "The lore is cool. Don't you think?"

"The dare thing?"

"The change thing."

I squinted at her. What would Sasha need to change?

"Besides," she pressed on. "The stuff at Dissent is too . . ." Pause. "Performative. This trip would be something just for us."

I stared at her. Performative. "I don't get it."

She pocketed her phone. Looked at me, like she was trying to decide something.

"Amelie," she said. "What's the real reason we go to Dissent?"

"Well?" H's voice.

I blinked, pulling my focus back into the dark cave. "What?"

"The rest of the story about the witch. You said you'd tell us."

78

"Oh." I noticed Gia's shoulders hunch. They hadn't ventured any closer to the tunnel. If anything, they were crowding back toward the entrance. "Um, you sure you want to hear it now?"

"Why?"

"Well, I mean . . ." I gestured at Gia.

She frowned. "What?"

"You seem worried."

"About your ghost story? Hardly. I'm weighing the odds of us getting lost in here. Something we actually need to be worried about?"

"Well, that, and drowning," Devon said.

"Drowning?" Gia frowned at her.

"We're searching for a lake." Devon looked at me. "Lakes swell with the rain, right?"

"Uh," I said.

"What, like the cave is going to flood?" H asked.

"Depends on the terrain," Devon said. "If this area isn't absorbent, like if it's limestone or something, then . . ."

"We won't drown," I said, though my heart rate had accelerated a bit. "And we won't get lost. We have directions."

"Speaking of," H said. "How do we have directions to a place 'no one has returned from'?"

"That's explained in the story," I said, but I suddenly realized the problem with that. If they were already nervous, the story was hardly going to reassure them. "But that's not . . ." I hesitated. "Honestly, the story is sort of beside the point, for me." I needed to change the tone, the conversation.

"What do you mean?"

I had to tell them about Sasha. I took a breath. "Well, I didn't say anything before, because I didn't want it to be weird, but I'm . . ." I hesitated. "I'm actually here for my cousin."

Gia squinted at me. "What?"

"She really wanted to do this trip, together, but she . . ." I paused. "She was in an accident three months ago, so now I'm doing it for her."

There was an awkward pause. The muffled patter of rain outside intensified to a dull, steady drumming.

"Um, that's intense," Gia said, not unkindly. "What happened to her?"

Right. That part. "The, uh, the girl at Dissent? That was her. Sasha." H's mouth dropped open, and Gia blanched visibly. Shit. Was this the right move? Maybe they'd get spooked, or think I was bad luck or something.

"Wow," Gia breathed. "God, I'm sorry."

"It's okay," I said. "Like I said, I don't want to make this weird. But she was sort of obsessed with finding this place, and now I want to see it through. For her, you know?" I suddenly realized Devon was looking at me intently. "I know it's kind of dumb."

"It's not dumb," H said quickly.

"Not at all," Gia said. "I mean, everyone has their reason for—" she mumbled over the next word—it sounded like *being*—and corrected it to "doing things."

Had she been about to say *being here*? I hadn't given that much thought, honestly—the idea that they might have motives beyond thrill seeking. I filed that away to ponder later. "We were really close." My voice caught on the last word, hitching because it was the truth and also not the truth. We *had* been close.

Gia's eyes were round, liquid with sympathy. "I'm super close with my cousins. If something like that happened to one of them . . ." She shook her head. "I think it's cool, what you're doing."

"Yeah," H agreed.

I felt a twinge of relief. I wasn't *trying* to use the situation with Sasha, but a moment ago it had felt like I didn't have a choice. And besides, I didn't need to tell them *everything*.

"Your cousin had directions to the Sublime?" Devon clarified.

"Yeah."

"Huh." She tilted her head. And then she said something that threw me completely: "So did the police find who did it? They were looking for a perp, right?" She was referring to Sasha's accident.

H's eyes went wide, and Gia shifted, looking slightly mortified. The thrum of rain was punctuated by a muted roll of thunder.

"Uh, yeah," I managed. "Or no, I mean. They ruled it an accident."

"Huh."

"Anyway!" Gia clapped her hands. "We doing this?"

"Hells, yeah," H said, much more enthusiastic than she'd been a moment before. "Yep. Yeah. We're doing this."

"I'll lead?" Gia pulled on her backpack and tightened the straps.

H waved her penlight. "I'll follow."

I pulled my flashlight from my bag and flicked it on. "Me, too."

Devon was still looking at me strangely. I turned away, trying to push my discomfort aside and lean into my relief. They weren't bailing; we were doing this. It was what I wanted . . . no, it was what I *needed*.

Gia led us into the tunnel with cautious steps, like she was finding her way without sight, except that her headlamp was intense. In contrast, and sandwiched between our various light sources, the beam from H's penlight was invisible.

About thirty feet in, Gia picked up the pace slightly—probably realizing that it was going to take us a year to find the lake at that speed. The tunnel opened up for a little while, wide enough that we could walk in pairs, which seemed to relax her. The ceiling remained low, no more than a foot over Devon's head beside me; she was the tallest of us. An earthy, dank aroma surrounded us. It smelled a bit like when we'd used clay in art, but with a tinge of something metallic—like iron. Or blood.

The path started to decline, and the air became noticeably cooler. We were obviously heading deeper into the earth, and it occurred to me that, just like in the forest when the trees had dwarfed us, we were like clueless little ants. With every step, we were surrounded by more and more rock, pressing down and around us from all sides, but all we could see was the inky space in front of us.

Yeah, there was no way I could've done this alone. "The air is different down here," I remarked. H and Gia looked back at me, confused or skeptical, I'm not sure which. "My lungs. Remember?"

"Oh, right," H said.

"You going to be okay?" That was Devon, but she sounded amused, not concerned.

"I'm good."

"Tell me if you need to stop," Gia said, throwing Devon a look.

"Yeah," H said.

That was all I needed: A little reassurance. Not that I was going to get it from Devon, apparently. She didn't seem to care about making people uncomfortable; she was oblivious. But, I realized, observant at the same time. I thought back to her finding that overgrown path that led to the cave. If she hadn't noticed it, we'd be heading back to the car right now.

And I would've failed Sasha.

H's voice broke into my thoughts. "*Now* can you tell us the rest of the story?"

Ugh. "Are you sure you want to hear it?" The truth was, I wasn't really that excited to tell it anymore. Saving it for the cave was a decision I'd made in daylight, in the comfort of Gia's Echo. Down here, speaking it aloud felt like a bad idea.

"I'm fine," Gia said. "Seriously. I like to be prepared. I was just . . . preparing, back there."

"Tell it, tell it, tell it," H urged.

I didn't really have a choice. I'd built it up like this on purpose. To pique their interest, yes, but I think I was also trying to emulate Sasha. She knew how to build suspense when she told a story, and she was deadly with her punch-lines. Our lights danced over glistening cave walls, lighting up small portions of them at a time. Shadows darted away in our peripheral vision. Deadly, down here, was taking on a different connotation. I cleared my throat. "Okay." *It's just a story; tell it like Sasha would've.* "So, like I said, young girls allegedly came here with the witch, and then didn't return. There was no proof the witch was responsible for whatever was happening—no body, no crime—but the locals had their own law. And people took matters into their own hands."

"Mob-and-pitchfork style?" H interjected, already into this.

"Uh, sort of," I said. "They sent a young girl to ask the old woman to take her to this supposed cave, and then followed them into the woods. Turns out there *was* a cave. Which"—I gestured around—"we know."

"Yeah, we do." H grinned.

"Anyway, the mob was conflicted: A few of them wanted to search for the girls, but the rest were convinced the caves were deadly. They wanted to put a stop to all of it." I paused. "There was an argument. People were spooked and angry, and things got out of hand. Some of the mob attacked the witch, dragged her to the entrance, and stuffed her in and"—I had to clear my throat again—"sealed it shut."

Gia stumbled slightly.

"They *buried her alive?*" H's eyes were wide.

"I guess?"

"Shit," she said. She looked around reverently. "We're

walking in the Blair Witch's tomb." Her eyes sparked with excitement. "Omigod. We are totally going to find her corpse down here."

"Fantastic," Gia muttered.

"Well, actually, right before they trapped her here, the witch told the locals that their efforts were futile. She said that girls would continue to try to find the Sublime, and when they succeeded, they'd set her free. It was the last thing she said before they sealed her in."

"Damn." H was very into this. "Okay, so then what?"

"Well, everyone pledged to keep the cave's location secret. Probably so nobody else went missing."

"But the girl who had instructions into the cave—"

"Obviously told someone. And then they were passed down, over the years. It's how Henrik had directions."

"Who's Henrik?"

"My source."

"*Sasha's* source," Devon corrected.

"Uh, yeah," I said. "Originally. But I corresponded with him, too." Why would she feel the need to make that distinction?

"Wait," H said. "If nobody's been down here since, and we're the first, that means *we're* the ones who are going to set the witch free."

"We're not the first ones," Gia said. "The entrance wasn't sealed; *somebody's* been down here."

"Maybe there were two entrances," I suggested.

"Then she was hardly sealed alive, was she?"

H was having none of Gia's skepticism. She clapped her hands gleefully. "This is so cool! The 'setting free' thing has major *Oculus* vibes—you know, without the mirror? Actually, if we were in a horror movie, it would be a mash-up of two cave horrors: *The Descent*, with the wilderness and all? And then *As Above, So Below*, since this cave is so pedestrian-friendly. Of course, we're not under the streets of Paris, so it's just the vibe, not the premise."

Gia looked at her like she had no idea what she was talking about and also didn't want to. "We're not in a horror movie," she said flatly.

"But if we were . . ."

"If we were," Devon said, "Amelie would be the last one standing."

"Why me?"

"People love the unexpected." I thought she was referring to my size, how incapable of survival I looked, but then she said, "The last one standing is always the one with the most to lose."

A prickle touched my neck. I squinted at her. What did she mean?

"The last one standing always carries the evil out with her," H corrected.

"Wow," Gia said. "That's happy."

"That's horror," H said. "It's sort of the point."

The tunnel began to shrink again, and we were forced to move back to single file, effectively cutting off the conversation. I was okay with that; Devon was freaking me out, a bit. What I wasn't okay with: The walls squeezed in, closer and closer, until they were brushing our shoulders. I would never have described myself as claustrophobic, but then again, I'd never been in a cave. Navigating a shoulder-wide space with limited visibility definitely wasn't the most relaxing experience. We slowed our pace, pressing through carefully. I fought down a swell of anxiety.

"Think I had a dream about this," H remarked.

"For real?" Gia glanced back.

"I have several recurring nightmares. There's one where I'm getting squeezed so tight by something—well, many things, actually—that I can't see, so tight I can't breathe. So, yeah."

"Yikes," I commented, trying to ignore the fact that I was worried about the exact same thing currently.

"That's not the worst of them," H replied. Then: "Jesus!"

The tunnel had shrunk yet again. We were forced to turn sideways and move laterally so our shoulders would fit. I moved along okay, but Devon had to squeeze, and the sound of her jacket scraping against the stone was deafening in the silence.

"It's just for a bit!" Gia reassured us from ahead.

I closed my eyes, feeling my way along the rough stone. I was in no danger of getting stuck, but it was an intensely uncomfortable sensation. And then it was gone. We'd cleared the passage, and the tunnel opened up again into a long cavern, not wide enough to walk together, but not frighteningly narrow, either. We picked our way along, ducking under overhanging rock.

"So, what's your worst?" Devon asked H. She was tall enough to speak over the top of me.

"Nightmare?" H said. "Hmmm. Gotta be the one where there's this thing hunting me by smell—it's blind. And it makes this really wet-sounding growl as it sniffs the air."

"Blind," Devon repeated. "So, a cave would be its perfect habitat?"

"Stop freaking her out," Gia threw over her shoulder, sounding a little freaked out.

"It's okay," H said. "That's exactly the point: It would be its perfect habitat. It's an unorthodox form of therapy, but at two hundred an hour, how can my doctor be wrong?"

"Your parents send you to a shrink?" Gia glanced back again.

"Um, my parents *are* shrinks? So, yeah, they support the idea of therapy."

"I do, too!" Gia amended quickly. "But my mom would never. And she's a nurse, even."

"My mom thinks therapy is for criminals," Devon said.

"Well, obviously," H said, gesturing to herself.

"Does this kind of therapy have a name?" Gia asked.

H shrugged. "I've never asked. Extreme Self-Help for Parasomniacs?"

The passage was narrowing again. Great.

"Speaking of," Gia said. "Devon, how long did it take to learn that not-panicking thing? At the cliff?"

"I don't know."

"But you must have trained yourself?" She pressed. "You know, to 'clear a space in your mind'?"

"I guess," Devon said. "Panic is a biological feedback

loop. Your brain responds to a perceived threat by sending instructions to your nervous system, and your body's physical response reaffirms the idea that there is a threat. This loops over and over until you aren't in control."

"So you decided to take control," Gia stated, slowing to negotiate a tricky bit of footing. "Of your fear." She pointed. "Watch it."

"Not really." Devon was behind me, so I couldn't see her expression. "I'm not scared of anything to begin with."

"Nothing?" I peered down, stepping carefully over the broken bits of rock.

"That I can figure out."

"You don't have nightmares ever?" H asked.

"I don't even dream."

That wasn't possible. She didn't *remember* her dreams. Only insane people didn't dream. Or, not dreaming made you insane. One of the two.

The tunnel walls opened up again, veering away from us sharply.

"Oh, thank god," Gia said, inhaling loudly. Then she cursed. Her light jerked wildly as she slipped, throwing out a hand.

"Watch it!" H said, grabbing for her.

My foot lost purchase in something slick, and Devon let out a curse from behind as I skittered sideways.

We shone our lights at the ground. The floor of the cavern was covered in black mud.

"Wow," Devon said. "It smells awful."

It did. The dank earth smell had disappeared, masked completely by an acrid stench, like we'd walked into a giant litter box.

"Ew," Gia said. "There are bugs in that mud." Her light danced over a few skittering insects.

"It's not mud," Devon said flatly. "It's guano."

"What's guano?" Gia asked.

In answer, Devon shone her phone upward. Gia and I joined her with our lights to reveal a cavernous space. The cave had opened up significantly, to at least forty feet above us.

And the ceiling was squirming.

"What the hell is that?"

"Bats."

We froze. We were staring at a cluster of them. Like furry grapes, stippling the rock, they clung, shifting now and again. Yes, bats. Dozens of bats. Our lights framed the mass of them like some writhing, mutant deer in the headlights.

"What do we do?" I whispered.

"Let's go with 'not startle them'?" H suggested. "Devon's hair would not survive a bat attack."

Devon searched the space with her light. "How do they get in?"

"The same way we did?" H asked, shining her penlight back the way we'd come.

I protested, "But it's so low—"

"Who cares?" Gia hissed. "How about we get out?"

We aimed our lights down and continued until the ground was less sticky and the ceiling dipped, creating a low passage again.

Once back under the safety of the rock, Gia took off. We scrambled after her, moving fast—faster than was comfortable in a tunnel with jagged pieces of rock sticking out at random angles and an uneven stone footpath. We reached out our hands to propel ourselves along, and I banged my knuckles against the wall a half dozen times before Gia slowed.

The tunnel had opened up once again, and we filed into the space, grouping together in a circle, breathing loudly. Devon and I searched the low ceiling with our lights—no more bats. Now a wide high ceiling was less comforting than a cramped tunnel. You couldn't win, in this cave.

"Damn," Gia managed. "That . . . was . . . disgusting." It was weird; she was the most in shape of all of us, and yet she was the one having the most trouble catching her breath.

"Bats are a good sign," Devon said. "Their presence indicates a substantial oxygen flow."

Gia didn't seem to hear her; she was turned away from all of us, hands on her knees. Was she talking to herself?

"Oh, that's wonderful." H pulled the Jolly Rancher out of her pocket. "Now I can breathe in the smell of their guano freely." She unwrapped the candy and put it in her mouth, wrinkling her nose.

As H's complaint registered, it occurred to me that Devon seemed to know a lot about caves. Then she said, "But you should be able to tell that about the oxygen, hey, Amelie? You're our canary in the coal mine." Was she . . . mocking me?

"Hey, we should see how dark it is here," H said. The faint smell of artificial watermelon reached me. "We should be deep enough." She flicked off her penlight.

"Why?" Gia was upright again.

"I read that it's kind of incredible, experiencing pitch black. And when do you ever get a chance?"

"You don't," I said, grateful for the new direction in the conversation. I switched off my flashlight.

Devon shrugged and switched off her phone. Gia stood there a moment, indecision on her face. Then she followed suit.

The black was instant, absolute. I held my hand in front of my face and saw nothing, not even an outline. I half expected my other senses to sharpen, but those felt muted, too: my hearing, the feeling of the air on my face. It was like I'd disappeared and only the dark existed.

I chewed my lower lip, comforted by the sensation. No, I existed. And Devon's "canary in the coal mine" comment was still needling at me, dredging up a memory . . .

"I hope I don't hyperventilate," I said.

The forest floor was littered with leaves and debris. We were standing next to a junk pile that hadn't been used in a long while: rags, old tin cans, bedsprings, and the Dissent challenge: an old freezer. Sunset was an hour ago, and a chill was descending on the woods.

"You sure you're okay?" Some girl I vaguely recognized watched me climb in.

I turned to look at the crowd of Dissenters who'd gathered.

"Guess we'll see."

And then I caught Sasha's eye. She was standing at the back of the crowd. I tried to coax a smile from her, but I should've

known better. The last three challenges, it was like she was
trying to ruin the vibe. Her eyes were distant. She looked . . .
Resentful?

I shifted slightly, and the sound of my tennis shoe scraping
against a loose bit of rock was reassuring.

"Fucking amazing." A guy helped me out of the freezer,
twelve minutes later. "If I had bad lungs, I would've freaked."

Sasha was standing close now. She'd pushed to the front
of the group, obviously concerned about how long I'd been
in the freezer, which was a good thing, I guess. Everyone was
looking at me appreciatively, everyone but her.

"I think I need a cold compress?" I said. "I have a killer
headache. Oxygen levels, you know?"

I dug my toe into the solid rock.

When we were younger, Sasha had looked up to me. Back
then, they were living in that ancient farmhouse in Wyoming, Uncle Remy was the administrator at a dinky, boring
hospital, and her mom worked in the laundry there. Sasha
was, naturally, a little impressed with my life. I was from the
big city. My dad was building a career in financial manage-
ment; he wore a headset to take calls, threw around phrases
like "investment opportunity" and "return on equity." My
mom sold herbal products for some kind of lifestyle company, and Sasha thought the self-employed part was fancy.
But the most impressive thing, of course, was me. My constant brushes with death.

What she didn't know: She was the most interesting kid I
knew, too. Admittedly I didn't have a ton of friends to gauge

this by, but her strange way of looking at things, of finding a story anywhere, would've fascinated anyone with a brain. With Sasha, a spider on the windowsill became a tiny traveling silk salesman, a cloud became a portal to another dimension, a bowl of cereal became mad scientist pills that froze a part of her body, sequentially, as she ate breakfast. She could look at things and immediately see them for what they weren't. I wasn't imaginative like that; I envied it.

They used to come to Denver on vacation every year. My dad, serving up mojitos in Ikea cocktail glasses on the deck overlooking our small square yard, identical to the yards on either side of us ("The developers leave the landscaping a blank slate, but we haven't decided what we want yet"); my mom, bringing out a dip she'd bought at one of those home parties hosted by someone in the neighborhood ("Oh, Evie, you don't have Epicure in your town?"); and me, showing Sasha all the things in my room: inhalers, stickers from my many clinic visits. Hoping, secretly, that she'd craft a story that turned my oxygen tank into a spaceship to Venus.

As we got older, the vacations stopped—my parents were starting to fray and probably wanted to keep that quiet—but Sasha and I grew closer, messaging and texting. I was getting better by then, but it was easy to keep up some facade of a life she'd once admired. I didn't tell her about my parents.

But then they moved to Denver, and everything changed. Uncle Remy's work ethic got noticed by whoever notices these things, and he was offered a better position at an affiliate, bigger, hospital in Denver. They moved into a nice neighborhood with massive, landscaped yards and neighbors who bought their appetizers at European gourmet markets, not home parties. Sasha was put in a fancy private school; she had ambitious new friends and a bunch of freedom. Her life was infinitely better, way more interesting, and I knew that because she invited me into it. I was the one familiar thing in Denver, after all.

But a few months after her move, Sasha changed, too. She became distracted, stopped sharing her thoughts with me . . . and not just her wacky ones, either. She seemed *unsure*, started to be visibly reluctant at Dissent. She'd never loved it from the start, but she could joke about that, at least. Now it seemed to really bother her. And the silences between us were getting strained. I remember thinking that maybe her new life was too much pressure. That the change had been too much, too fast.

And then she started talking about the Sublime. How it would be the perfect trip for us.

But the way she talked about it—like it was real—was strange. She was fixated on the lore, the change thing. I guess she'd never truly grown out of that childhood tendency to seek out fantasy, escape reality.

I blinked in the black. But maybe that's exactly why she'd wanted to find this place. If her new life *had been* too much pressure, maybe she'd thought she could change it. Maybe she even wanted her old life back, their shitty house in Wyoming with the rats in the walls, her boring small-town friends. It didn't make sense, but Sasha had stopped making sense.

I swallowed. Getting her old life back would've been unlikely in the best of circumstances; it was impossible now.

My chest hitched with a breath. All I could feel was oily darkness everywhere. On my skin, in my hair, seeping inside with every inhalation.

A murmuring reached my ears, like a fly buzzing against a windowpane. It took me a few minutes to realize it was a voice, whispering. Muttering.

Gia again? I fumbled with my flashlight.

"Welcome to hell," a voice rasped. H's face appeared. She was holding the penlight under her chin, lighting up the contours of her face: sunken cheeks, hollows for eyes. She grinned. "That was amazing."

"Yes, it was very dark." Gia's unimpressed voice came from behind H. "Now come on." She switched her headlamp on, materializing, and turned to lead the way. A shape blocked her path.

"I saw a light." Devon was, inexplicably, ahead of us; she'd somehow moved without bumping into anyone or anything and was standing, pointing down the tunnel. The hair on my arms rose.

"Seriously?" H dropped her penlight from under her chin.

"Dead serious."

"Where?" Gia pushed in front of Devon and headed down the tunnel so quickly we had to scramble after her, flicking our lights on.

"What kind of light?" I asked, trying to keep up.

"A glow," Devon answered. "Didn't you see it?"

"I couldn't see anything," I said.

"Me neither," Gia said. "Are you sure it wasn't, like, spots on your retina or something? From the sudden change to dark?"

"Nah. It was coming from somewhere this way."

"What would make a glow down here?" Gia wondered aloud.

"Could be the lake," Devon suggested, a rare note of excitement creeping into her voice.

"But we haven't even seen the Crow's Foot yet." Gia started forward again, bending to get under a chunk of rock. "It's a landmark that tells us we're going the right way."

"Have we even been looking for that?" Devon asked.

"Yeah. I mean, I have."

"Maybe we all should?" Devon said, ducking. "If you told us what to look for—"

Gia stopped quickly and turned, causing Devon to pull up so short that I ran into her back. Gia's headlamp beam zeroed in on Devon's face. "Why?"

"Um, so we have a chance of finding it?"

Gia crossed her arms. "Are you talking about the stairs again?"

"The stairs?"

"Because the directions weren't exactly specific." Gia sounded defensive.

"I was making a suggestion that would improve our chances for finding this lake. Four people looking for a landmark is better than one."

Gia snorted, and I glanced back at H to share a "well, this is uncomfortable" look, but the beam from my flashlight lit up an empty tunnel. I moved it, searching the way we'd come.

"Hey." I threw the word over my shoulder at the other two.

"I don't need my hand held," Gia was saying. "I'm perfectly capable of—"

"Hey."

They looked at me.

"Where's H?" My flashlight darted about the dark space. No one.

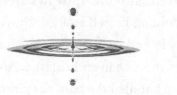

THERE WAS A LONG PAUSE. I GLANCED BACK AT DEVON AND Gia, who looked like they were trying to decide if I was playing a practical joke.

"She's gone," I said, turning back to the tunnel. "H!" I called, my voice echoing.

We waited.

Nothing.

"Huh," Devon remarked. "Unexpected."

"What the hell?" muttered Gia. "Why didn't she follow us?"

"She did," I said. "She was right behind me."

"H!" Gia tried calling this time, her voice resonating into the tunnel.

"When we—"

"Shhh!" Gia held up a hand to shut me up. We listened.

Silence.

"Wow," Gia said. "She freaked out and bailed."

"She's seen every horror movie made since 1970," Devon said. "That doesn't seem likely."

There was a pause as we looked at one another.

Then Gia said, "That was a front. She was talking too big. She was probably looking for an opportunity."

But I felt like that more aptly described Gia than H. Gia seemed to be forcing herself to lead, shoving away her reluctance, whereas H had only been momentarily hesitant. After that, she'd been more than enthusiastic. Also, the timing made no sense: H had handled the bats okay, then suddenly got too scared to continue because Devon mentioned a light? No.

"Maybe she got lost," I said.

"We walked a straight line here," Gia pointed out. "She's either standing back in that first cavern, or she's getting soaked outside."

Anxiety was squeezing my chest. "But maybe we should go see if she's okay?" *Thanks for not abandoning me.* She'd said that back at the ravine.

"You want to go back alone?" Gia asked.

I shifted nervously. I really didn't.

"I'll go," Devon said suddenly.

Gia let out an exasperated sigh. "You guys. It's a waste of time. There's only one way she could've gone, and that's out the way we came in. I don't want to go back; I want to find this lake."

I did, too, but . . . "It'll just take a second."

"I don't think splitting up is a good idea," Devon said.

"Agreed." I looked at Gia. "I mean, what if she has some other . . . health-ism she hasn't mentioned?"

Gia softened. "Fine," she said. "But I'm waiting for you on this side of the shitty bat cave."

We headed back down the tunnel, through the wider space we'd paused in to experience pitch black, and into the corridor toward the bat-riddled cavern.

I entered gingerly, planning to creep beneath the bats quietly, but as my flashlight searched the far side of the space it lit up a different portion of the wall that wasn't solid. To the right of our tunnel was a smaller one; when you entered from the far side, it was hidden behind an outcropping of rock.

I stopped, training my light on its depths. "This tunnel forks," I whispered. None of us had noticed it when we passed through; we'd been too preoccupied with the bats. Gia and Devon filed in beside me.

"You think she took the wrong one?" Devon asked.

"Well, she didn't have a very good light." Another reason it was weird for her to decide to turn around.

"We'd better go see," Devon said.

I started forward.

Gia grabbed my arm. "Can we think about this?"

"If H is in there, she's getting more lost by the second," Devon remarked.

"If H is in there, she'll figure out pretty quick that she's taken a wrong turn," Gia countered over her shoulder.

"Unless she doesn't." I said. Our whispers were rising in volume.

"You haven't even checked the entrance yet!"

"But if she went this way we're losing time—"

"Do we have to argue directly under the shitting bats?" Devon asked.

I shone my light at the smaller tunnel again, and the beam caught something shiny on the ground at its mouth. I crossed over and picked it up. A Jolly Rancher wrapper. I held it up and looked at them triumphantly.

"Huh." Devon moved in beside me.

Gia stared at us a moment. She sighed. "Damn it." She joined us, squeezing past to take her place at the front. She readjusted her headlamp and peered ahead, then let out a sudden "No way."

"What?" I craned my neck but couldn't see past her to where she was looking.

"It's the Crow's Foot."

"It is?"

"What the hell? There was no mention of bat shit . . ." Her voice rose in excitement with the realization. "This is the way!" She hurried forward.

Now that the passage was opening up, I could see a large symbol drawn on the tunnel wall: like an arrow with no tip, the three lines demarcating feathers. Ahead there was a slight rise. I touched my fingers to the drawing. "This looks weirdly new."

"Oh my god." Gia stopped suddenly. She turned. "Do you think H knew?"

"What do you mean?"

"Do you think she had directions, too, and knew we were going the wrong way and wanted to get there first?"

"Is it a race?" Devon asked.

"That little horror weirdo. She totally knew!"

"I don't think she did," Devon said.

But she *had* been prepared, gear-wise. Until she'd lost her pack, at least.

"She did." Gia moved forward, up the incline. "She probably found the same site you found, Amelie."

That was possible. She could've noticed the same graffiti Sasha had, that night. Though if that were the case, wouldn't she have mentioned it?

"Why would she need to get there first?" Devon pressed.

"To say she did?" Gia picked up her pace.

"But, like, this is good right?" I said, hurrying to catch her. We crested the rise. "We're going in the right direction at least, so—"

I heard Gia's intake of breath a split second too late. Her headlamp jerked wildly as she pitched off-balance, and by the time that registered, I was sliding. The path dropped sharply, a decline that created a veritable slip-and-slide of rock and shale. My heart jackhammered as I threw my center of gravity backward and my arms out, trying to find something to slow me up. The walls were too far away, and I fell, hard, onto my butt and continued to slide.

I was picking up speed, could hear Devon barreling down behind me. Ahead, Gia let out a yelp, and then the ground gave way completely and I screamed too, airborne for a heart-stopping second before my feet slammed onto the ground. I rocketed forward, directly into Gia. She'd somehow stuck the landing and was strong enough to absorb my impact, but then Devon arrived, crashing into us like a bowling ball scattering pins. My flashlight clattered out of my hand and winked out as I pitched forward.

Then I was hurtling through dark nothingness once more.

Hard rock hit my outstretched hands, and I slammed to the ground, banging my chin and losing my air in a painful rush. I lay, stunned, for a few long moments in the dark.

When my breath returned, I wiggled my legs, my arms. Nothing seemed broken. I listened for the others but there was no movement around me.

Silence. A sickly stillness.

Oh god. Were they okay?

"Gia?" My voice came out a whisper. No reply. I pulled myself painfully to my knees, stretched out my hands, and groped for something, anything. "Devon?"

Nothing. My hands stilled as I noticed the smell.

It was putrid, a slightly sweet aroma. Like rotting meat and decomposing plants mixed with some kind of drugstore perfume or shampoo . . . A skittering reached my ears.

Scritchscritchscritch.

Insects? Had I fallen in another mound of batshit? The thought was repulsive, but also weirdly comforting because, for a second, I'd been sure that smell was a dead animal. Something . . . decaying, nearby.

I heard movement beside me.

"Gia? Devon?" I reached forward, fingers groping until they touched solid metal. My flashlight. I fumbled with it, clicked it on.

The sound again, behind me this time.

I swung around, cutting the beam in a panicked arc. It glanced over a figure—a stutter-step, heartbeat in time—but my brain registered an image: a girl, standing, neck bent and blond hair obscuring her face. I recoiled, the flashlight clattering out of my hand, and opened my mouth to scream—

"Are you okay?" A light blinded me. Gia's voice: "Are you hurt?"

I threw a hand up to shield the glare and realized Gia and Devon were standing over me. I was flat on my back, my ribs complaining like they'd been crushed.

"You ended up underneath us." Gia tugged her headlamp to the side slightly so she could look at me without directing the light into my eyes.

I pulled myself to sitting and felt around. My fingers found my flashlight. "I'm . . . okay," I said, touching my head. I swung the flashlight around the space. My fear quelled, that initial bolt of adrenaline dying into a whimper as I realized it was just me and Devon and Gia. No girl. I'd gotten knocked out, briefly, maybe; hallucinated. I stood carefully. I felt okay, just a little squished. "Are you?"

"My wrist hurts," Gia replied. "But nothing's broken."

"Not even this." Devon held up her phone, intact. "That was lucky."

We were in a cavern double the size of the one at the entrance. A sizable tunnel was visible in the corner, disappearing into the depths.

"Shit," Gia hissed, tilting her neck so her lamp illuminated overhead.

Any lingering spookiness evaporated as I took in our very real situation: Lucky was hardly the right adjective. About six feet above us was the chute. We'd slid a long way; the start of our incline was beyond the reach of our lights.

Gia pressed the heels of her palms against either side of her head, staring upward. "Shit."

"Was that on the directions?" Devon asked.

"Obviously not!" Gia snapped. Then she looked at her

hands, patted her clothes, scanned the ground. "And I dropped them when I fell." We joined her searching the ground with our lights, but there was no sheet of paper. It was probably at the top of the chute. "Fucking perfect." She pushed through us to the back of the cavern, where she began to pace.

I looked at the chute again, contemplating the obvious: retracing our steps was impossible. Even if we could've boosted one of us—me—to the drop, there was no way I could climb back up; it was far too sheer, with nothing to hold on to.

Devon spoke, beside me: "I think we know, now, why no one's returned."

A kind of hissing reached my ears. I turned. Gia was talking quietly to herself, and she walked the length of the cavern and back. Jesus. Was she okay?

"Gia," I said, trying to quell my own swell of panic. Henrik hadn't mentioned an alternative way out to me, but that didn't mean there wasn't one, right? Gia continued to pace and generally look unhinged. "Gia." I tried again. "Maybe you were right, about the two entrances. There are obviously more tunnels down here than this one. Maybe we can get back to the one we were in before we doubled back?"

She stopped and fixed me with a glare. "Before you made us double back, you mean?"

"H—"

"H is back at the entrance!"

"But—"

"Do you see her here? Any trace? If she came this way, she'd be yelling for help."

"Maybe she's . . ." I trailed off. *Not conscious*. Like I'd been, a minute ago.

"What?"

I was sort of glad Gia was arguing with me. It was a normal response, at least, to the situation. Her muttering was getting super weird. "I don't know. But a second ago you were sure she was racing us to the lake—"

"Did you hear that?" Devon broke in.

"What?" Gia said irritably.

"I heard something." Devon held up a hand.

We listened. Nothing. Gia swung her light to the tunnel. "I didn't hear anything."

We waited another moment.

"Maybe it was a normal cave sound," Gia said. "Not like it's going to be totally silent down here, right?"

I nodded my agreement, though I had no idea what normal cave sounds were. My knowledge of caves started and ended with "underground."

"Okay," Devon said. "Now what?"

I looked around. Gia was right. There was absolutely no indication that H had been this way. But this wasn't my fault, was it? Gia was the one who'd rushed ahead.

"We keep moving," Gia said firmly. Whatever that moment had been before, it was gone. She was back to being in charge. "It's not a big deal. I practically memorized the directions." That was good; I hadn't.

"I feel like we're still on track," Devon agreed, though there was nothing, really, to suggest that.

I thought about the moment I'd landed. Unease crept

through me. I wanted to find the Sublime—of course I did. I just hoped I wasn't . . . concussed or something.

"I'm going to turn my phone off," Devon said. "I'm on fifty percent." She paused with her hand on the phone and looked at us. "What part in the horror movie is this, do you think?"

Gia rolled her eyes.

"I think it's the point of no return," Devon said, and her phone screen winked out.

We headed toward the tunnel, Gia first, Devon following, and then me.

Shadows danced in the beam of my flashlight, caught the edge of Devon's arm as she disappeared around the first corner.

What are you afraid of? Sasha's voice echoed in my head.

A muffled sound came from behind me. I swung around, catching something in the periphery of my flashlight—a shadowy shape, something darting past.

"H?" I called, swinging my light around the cavern.

Nothing. A cool breeze wafted from the chute overhead. The darkness beyond the beam of my light was resolute. Swollen with nothing. Lurking. Waiting.

No. The dark was freaking me out; the light was playing tricks.

"Are you coming?" Devon called from behind me.

I turned and hurried to catch them.

"HOLD UP," VARGAS INTERRUPTED. DRAKER HAD WANDERED away while Amelie was speaking and was over near the Echo now, rubbing his shirt like his chest was too tight. He looked pale.

Damn it.

"Hold that thought?" Vargas said. "Just need to . . ." Draker was headed for the police cruiser now. "I'll be right back."

"Can you ask him what he did with my hoodie?" the girl said.

"Hoodie?"

She held up her filthy hands, eyes skimming over her arms. "I was wearing it."

"Sure, yeah." Vargas was distracted, cataloging Draker's movements. He didn't seem to be in distress, but he wasn't likely to let her know. She caught up to him halfway to the car and drew close, keeping her voice low. "You going to call someone?"

"Sheriff—tell him we need search and rescue. Then Cheyenne."

"I meant about . . ." She gestured vaguely at his torso.

"I'm fine," he said, stopping and opening the passenger-side door.

Vargas stepped inside the open door, blocking his way. "You don't look fine."

"Goddamn hot out here is all." He jerked his head. "I'm sure you've noticed this girl is taking forever to get to the point. One girl didn't return, and she's not exactly in a rush to tell us why."

"She said she—"

"Yeah, yeah. She 'needs to tell the whole thing.' Well, the whole thing is weirdly specific."

Draker wasn't wrong. Facial expression, body language—it was all less important in detecting a liar than people thought. The truth, or lack of truth, was contained in the recollection of the events itself, the language used. Liars often gave away what they were holding back by including too many details to try to indicate they were holding back nothing. The girl's story was replete with details. Still . . .

"Details aren't difficult when you start at the beginning."

He shook his head. "There's more to this." He glanced over his shoulder at the girl, as if worried she'd overhear from this impossible distance, and Vargas noticed he was clutching a piece of paper in one nitrile-gloved hand. "Found this under the windshield wiper."

Vargas turned to dig in the console, pulled out nitriles and put them on. "What is it?"

"Directions."

Right. Amelie had mentioned she'd had her own printout

but hadn't wanted to look like she was challenging Gia's self-appointment as leader of the group so had left it behind.

"I wanted to see how accurate her memory was."

Check the accuracy of her storytelling was what Draker meant. Vargas took the paper—once soggy, now dried and warped—and unfolded it gingerly. The ink had been damaged at the creases but hadn't run badly, likely printed on a laser jet. Vargas scanned it. It was a screenshot by the look of things. An exchange with Amelie's so-called source:

> Henrik: That'll get you to the staging area.
> AsphyxiA: And from there?
> Henrik: From there it gets more difficult.

Here the line along the horizontal crease had blurred, evaporated.

> then north from the bottom of the ravine stairs
> until you find a passage in the rock that takes
> you to a small pond. On the far side is the
> entrance. After that, directions are vague and
> only mention landmarks: Crow's Foot, The

Another word blurred out on the vertical crease.

> The Eye, and then The Sublime.
> AsphyxiA: Doesn't seem too hard.
> Henrik: Yeah, but I mean, who knows? Nobody.

That's the whole point.

AsphyxiA: Obviously.

Henrik: One more thing: watch out for rain.

AsphyxiA: What do you mean?

Henrik: Rumor has it when it rains the caves

Here the ink had evaporated again.

ephemeral. It's part of what makes the caves scary.

AsphyxiA: Well, that and the lore about the witch?

Henrik: Sure, yeah. I guess I didn't mean scary: I meant dangerous.

Vargas read it a second time. She looked up at Draker, who seemed to be doing his best to block Vargas from the girl's view. "She knew," he said. "She knew it would be dangerous if it rained."

Vargas thought back. The girl had recalled Devon suggesting this very thing, but Amelie had, by her own account, downplayed it. She looked around. The parking lot was dry. According to the girl, it had deluged recently, though a quick search of the radar activity would confirm that. "Bad choices," Vargas said. "Teens are famous for them."

"Deliberate choices," Draker said. "Psychos are famous for them."

"This is why you're calling Cheyenne?"

Draker frowned. "No." He took the paper back from Vargas, folded it carefully. "It's this Sasha Desmarais thing."

"The cousin?"

"It's ringing a bell. The criminal-investigation kind."

"She said the cops were involved."

"Going to get Cheyenne to look into it." Cheyenne was also their resident Google genius.

Vargas studied him. "What are you thinking?"

"I don't know yet. I'll see what she digs up." He looked at Vargas expectantly.

Vargas stepped out of his way. "While you're at it, tell her to get the defib paddles ready."

"I said I'm fine." Draker frowned. "It's this . . ." He glanced around. "Heat."

Vargas had been sure he was going to say *place*. She had to admit that she was getting more uneasy by the minute, and it wasn't just the girl's story.

"Going to turn the AC on for a second." Draker folded himself into the seat, reached for the CB radio, and slammed the door.

Focus. Vargas turned back to the girl, assessing her.

Memories of events were fallible, so it was commonplace for truthful people to remember things after the fact. The girl hadn't backtracked at any point; she was telling it like a fireside story. So: one cousin involved in a mysterious accident a few months ago, and now this. Bad luck and coincidence were a thing.

Until they weren't.

Vargas approached the girl's perch.

The girl looked up. "Does he have it?"

It took a second for Vargas to realize she was referring to the hoodie. She'd forgotten to ask. "Uh, no. You sure you were wearing it?" The paramedics had been dispatched from Rifle and gotten here first—Draker had taken the wrong road at some nowhere place called Buford—and the scene was chaotic when they'd finally arrived. Vargas couldn't remember what Amelie had been wearing, although Draker was the first to question her and likely had it in his notes. "There's probably a foil blanket in the trunk." Draker had said she'd rejected the paramedics' offer of one.

"I'm not cold."

"Okay." Vargas settled herself on the adjacent rock. "We'll find it," she assured her. "Deputy Draker is just busy at the moment."

"Who is he talking to?"

"Oh, he's getting an update. Checking in with the station and the hospital, that sort of thing."

The girl nodded. "That's good."

Vargas thought about the note. It wasn't exactly incriminating, although Draker was clearly treating it like evidence. Her conscience needled at her. "Amelie, you don't have to keep talking if you don't want to." Vargas said. "You're free to go."

The girl looked puzzled. "Go?"

It did sound ridiculous. To where? "We're not detaining you," Vargas clarified. "And we're not interrogating you."

"Oh," the girl said. "Okay, yeah." There was a pause. "But I can keep telling you the story?"

The story. "Only if you want to." Vargas kept her expression neutral.

"Okay," Amelie said.

"And you can stop whenever you like." Vargas watched the girl's hand flutter up to rub at her chest, heard a sharp intake of breath. "Are you okay? Do you need some water?"

The girl looked down at her crimson-stained hand. Dropped it. A strange, self-deprecating smile crossed her face. "I'm fine. Sorry."

"Don't be sorry."

"I have a hard time—" She caught herself. Shook her head, almost imperceptibly. "I'm used to people looking out for me. Or, I was."

Vargas waited.

The girl bit her lip. "I just assumed the others would—" She caught herself again. "I mean, they all had their own reasons for being there."

"Oh?" Vargas made a mental note to pay close attention to the way the girl described the others. Projecting traits, seeding personality flaws—those things were effective if you were trying to deflect blame.

"I hadn't banked on that." She paused again, looking frustrated. "I'm not telling this properly."

Properly. Vargas decided a pointed question wouldn't hurt: "Your reason was Sasha, right?"

Amelie paused. "Yeah."

"Can you tell me what happened to her? You've mentioned an accident?"

"I mean, I don't love talking about it." She looked so

vulnerable, suddenly, that Vargas almost felt bad for asking. But then the girl frowned and shook her head, like she was admonishing herself. "Sorry. Yes." She took a breath. "There was a Dissent gathering at an abandoned farmhouse. She . . . fell down the cellar stairs. There were signs of a struggle. Bruises on her forearms. Sk-skin under her fingernails. But it was ruled an accident." Her voice was husky, and her eyes were getting blotchy, like she was holding back tears. This anguish, though, seemed genuine. "I wasn't there. I should've been, but I wasn't."

"Okay," Vargas said, her voice soothing. "It's okay."

"But you know?" She cleared her throat. "I think that's why I went looking for H."

"Because you didn't want to lose another friend?"

"I didn't want to bail again," she said. "But I was still telling myself that bailing was the worst thing I'd done."

Vargas leaned in. "And what was the worst thing?"

The girl looked at Vargas again, desperation on her face. Her voice dropped to a whisper. "I'm not a bad person," she said.

"Of course not."

"But I haven't always been good with the truth."

Vargas waited to see how this would connect to the girls' predicament in the cave, but Amelie circled back: "I loved Sasha. I would never want anything bad to happen to her. She was my best friend."

"Okay."

"I thought . . ." She chewed her lip. "I thought the Sublime might bring her back to us."

Vargas took a beat. Then realized: "The change thing. In the lore."

The girl looked miserable. "I know you think it's crazy."

"I don't think anything. All I know, right now, is what you tell me."

"The thing was, I was only thinking about myself. I didn't know H was hoping for something, too." She collected herself. "I didn't realize they all were."

Vargas was mystified. What did this have to do with Amelie's cousin? With the "worst thing" she'd done?

The girl said, "Sorry. Where was I?"

"You'd gotten into a part of the cave you couldn't get out of. And your fall scared you—you sort of hallucinated?"

"Right. That's what I thought." The girl tilted her head, her gaze flicking to the Echo, to the woods, back to Vargas. Was she remembering, or fabricating the story as she went? "But then Gia saw something, too."

NO EXIT

WE PICKED OUR WAY ALONG SLOWLY. GIA WAS CLEARLY unwilling to risk another potentially limb-breaking mistake, but she was leading confidently, like she was sure we were heading in the right direction.

They were both acting like everything was okay.

It could be true; I wanted it to be true. I wanted to find the Sublime.

But I also wanted to know we could get out.

What if that Crow's Foot symbol had been indicating we go the opposite way, or what if it hadn't even been a symbol? What if we were stuck down here?

I thought about the empty parking lot, the deserted resort. We'd gone to some serious lengths to cover our tracks. Even the alibis—Gia's teammate and H's friend—didn't know what they were doing. Both my phone and Gia's were in her glove box, but they were turned off. Devon's wouldn't work down here. Word of our disappearance would have to get out this far into the sticks for locals to notice and report Gia's car. Unless . . .

"Maybe H *is* back at the entrance," I thought aloud. That would be good.

"That's what *I* said," Gia said.

"Right, but I'm . . . I mean, she could go for help if . . ."

"We're fine," Gia said, but it sounded like she was trying to convince herself of that.

Because this could lead to a dead end. Or it could fork. We should probably have been thinking of a way to Hansel-and-Gretel our path, mark any decisions with—I thought of the useless contents of my bag—what? Not like I had bread-crumbs. But Gia's backpack: Surely she had something useful in there?

"We just need to find the Sublime," Devon remarked. "And then you can ask to get out of here. I mean, if there isn't another exit, that would be something you'd need to change pretty badly—"

"The lore isn't real," Gia shot over her shoulder.

"You sound sure," Devon said, but I couldn't tell if her tone was sarcastic or sincere.

"Sorry, you believe there was an immortal witch living out here who sacrificed girls to a cave?"

"No one said she sacrificed—"

"Oh, sorry: brought them here to die."

"Again, no. She didn't make them come here; she just showed them the way."

Gia waved a hand. "Same, same."

"Not really. In your version, she's responsible—like the locals thought. But she didn't make those girls come here."

"Look, I get what you're saying," Gia said, "But *we* wouldn't know about this place if not for Amelie, and just so we're clear: If H's mutant zombies show up, I can run faster than both of you, and I will." She said it jokingly, but also somehow not jokingly.

"Hey," I protested. "I probably weigh less than your backpack. You could carry me."

"Yeah, but I won't."

I forced a laugh. Would she really leave me behind, if it came to it? Would she blame me if we *were* stuck down here? That hardly seemed fair. I wanted to call her out but I didn't want to piss her off, so I settled for dismantling her logic: "So you *do* believe the lore?"

"Of course not," Gia said. "*If* girls disappeared here, it's probably because they got scared and disoriented, then made bad choices—"

"Choice being the operative word," I pointed out.

She sighed. "Whatever."

"Is everything perfect in your world?" Devon asked. A weird non sequitur, but that was Devon.

Gia frowned back at her. "What?"

"You don't believe the lore, so you're obviously not trying to find the Sublime because you want it to change something." Devon hadn't said it like she thought that idea was stupid.

"First, no, everything isn't 'perfect.' Second, change is something *you* have control over? Finding some lake isn't going to matter."

"Unless you confront something about yourself along the way."

"Right. I'm going to do a deep dive of my psyche in the next thirty minutes and have a life-shattering epiphany." Gia ducked under a rock. "I needed something more challenging than Dissent, okay?" She said it a little too forcefully, and for whatever reason, I felt like it was true, but also not the whole truth. Maybe she wasn't so sure she didn't believe the lore. Maybe there *was* something she wanted to change.

"That's why you came?" I asked. "A challenge?"

"Yeah." She looked back. "Didn't you?"

Gia clearly thought the lore thing was stupid; telling her what I was secretly hoping for wasn't really an option.

"Ugh, sorry," she said, remembering what I'd told her at the entrance. "I forgot. Sasha."

"It's okay." A bad taste filled my mouth. There was a distinct odor in this tunnel. Not bat shit. Antiseptic? Hospital hallway?

Hospital hallway, cherry acid burning my mouth.

My parents had been preoccupied, and Sasha's parents didn't suspect we were up to anything dangerous because they'd already raised one kid—her older brother, Daniel—and he was following in his dad's footsteps of hospital administration at Ohio State. Sasha was poised for something similar; what could possibly be happening beneath their noses that could compromise that?

I ran my tongue over my teeth, trying to rid my mouth of whatever I was tasting.

I'd only wanted something that leveled the playing field. Dissent was supposed to be that. It wasn't that Sasha was treating me differently because of her new life. The opposite, actually, which was sort of the problem. She'd ask me which coffee shops in LoDo she should invite her study groups to, where to shop for clothes, my opinion on the guys in her class—she just assumed I'd have the answers. She didn't seem to notice that her new life was very different, infinitely better, than mine.

I wanted to be the person she thought I was, but the truth was, my childhood hadn't exactly equipped me with skills for the social scene she'd instantly acquired. By the time my parents were no longer sheltering me from life itself, I had no idea how to insert myself in my peers' idea of it. And as Sasha continued to include me, it got harder to fake that I was the authority on . . . anything at all.

Dissent was something different—something for us to do that wasn't a house party I hadn't actually been invited to, or a hangout with Sasha's new friends that I'd flail through. It was new to both of us, so it was like a clean slate. I honestly thought she might like it. It was creative and weird . . . like her imagination. Sasha had been okay with it. At least, at first.

"That challenge was so . . . weird," Gia ventured, darting a look at me. She obviously wanted to ask about Sasha without asking about Sasha.

"I wasn't there," I said. Had that sounded defensive? I pressed on. "You mean, compared to the other ones?"

Dangerous was a more apt description for the other Dissent challenges. There'd been the "being led along the edge of a ravine, blindfolded" challenge, where some guy lost his footing and his partner had to save him from plunging over the side. There was illegal "fire sculpture" on the Platte riverbank: found-art sculptures of trash that we doused with kerosene and lit on fire, scattering before the cops arrived. There was the "retrieving flashing weights from the bottom of a reservoir" challenge: night swimming. And then that got taken to a whole new level with "drowning body bags": Players were zipped inside an easy-open body bag and thrown in a pond in a farmer's field. Oh, and the "locked inside a freezer" one: I'd needed a cold compress for a sudden blinding headache afterward, but I'd done it.

But it was the last one, for me. Dissent had been my idea, and getting an invite had been no easy thing, and it was supposed to be something for us—for Sasha and me. But by the last one, she'd been pulling away for a while, and the shine was off the thrill-seeking diamond. After the freezer challenge, we'd argued. And she'd gone to the challenge at the old farmhouse alone.

I ducked under an overhanging chunk of rock, a familiar sick pit appearing in my stomach.

"Well, yeah, compared to the others. It wasn't challenging at all. And then, afterwards, with the police looking for someone . . ." Gia trailed off.

"It was an accident," I said.

"You already said that," Devon said. "Did someone blame you or something?"

I snapped my head to look at her. "Of course not." My stomach tightened. "I wasn't even there."

"I tend to get blamed for stuff," she said. Her strange way of commiserating? "But that's why Dissent was genius— anonymous suggestions. No one could blame you if something went wrong. You know, like some kid wandering off a cliff?"

I stared at her. "That was your idea?"

"Ravine, reservoir, freezer . . . I had some good ones."

"Those were intense," Gia said carefully.

Devon shrugged. "Yeah?" Was she being sarcastic? It was so hard to tell.

"You don't think so?" I asked.

"I don't know." She tilted her head. "I told you before: I'm not afraid of things."

"Ever?" The thought of being potentially lost in a cave with someone who didn't recognize perils wasn't exactly comforting.

"Think maybe my amygdala's messed up."

Gia slowed. "Your what?"

"The part of the brain responsible for processing fear. Some people are born with a deficient amygdala. Maybe I'm one of those."

Gia brought us to a halt and turned to face Devon, exchanging a quick look with me.

I knew what she was thinking. We were deep under the earth with a girl who had, several times, put our safety at risk without seeming to know or care who *also* might have something wrong with her brain? Yes, we'd gone to Dissent willingly, knowing the dangers. But the lack of concern Devon was demonstrating was unnerving, to say the least.

There was a flash of uncertainty on Gia's face, but she made her voice light. "So you're saying we shouldn't let you make decisions down here."

Devon seemed amused. "Isn't making decisions your thing?"

Gia frowned.

"Hey, relax," Devon said. "Yes, don't look to me for decisions. Or any logistics, really. I'm just an ideas person."

Gia turned away. "Whatever." We followed as she continued on.

"Speaking of Dissent," Devon said, like the exchange hadn't happened. "You guys notice that the new forum was all talk? No one was making plans to do anything."

"Think the appetite for the challenges had sort of waned?" Gia said tersely.

"So, what was the point?"

"I guess they still wanted to be an elite group or whatever."

"I don't get it," Devon said.

"Actually, me neither," Gia admitted.

I did. I got wanting to be a part of something. Better yet, an integral part of something. It wasn't why I'd rejoined the forum, but I understood. I could see, now, that Gia had too much else going on in her life to care about something like that, though. And Devon, well, Devon was Devon: fully unconcerned with what people thought of her. Although that made me wonder . . .

"If Dissent wasn't challenging or exciting, why were you even there?" I glanced back at her.

"Testing that amygdala thing," she said.

"Like, trying to find something that scared you?" I asked.

"Yeah."

"And?"

"Nope," she said. "But maybe this trip will change that."

"Why would you *want* to be scared?" Gia asked, frowning back at her. She looked almost angry at that idea, but then, being fearless seemed to be a personal goal of Gia's.

"It's not so much that," Devon replied. "It's . . . I want to know what I'm capable of."

Which wasn't so far from Gia's reasoning, really. Or mine, before this trip. I'd been determined to complete the challenges at Dissent because of the fact that I was at a disadvantage. And okay, yes, knowing people were impressed didn't hurt. The look of disbelief on people's faces when I'd said I'd swim the reservoir. Amazed when I'd retrieved the flashing weights and was headed back to shore. Panicked when I'd cramped. Then relieved, and all the more impressed, when I'd made it to shore. I looked forward to that: their esteem.

But if I was honest, I was looking for Sasha's, too. We were best friends; of course I cared what she thought of me. And after years of her being fascinated with my life, losing that because I was no longer at death's door wasn't an option. I'd needed to go big.

But maybe Dissent had been a bit of a stretch. Maybe I'd been trying a little too hard.

"You want to be special." Sasha's *irritated frown dissolved into gentle trepidation—like she was telling me a hard truth—which was so much worse. "What are you afraid of?"*

My body felt heavy; the memory was clinging to me like a rotting second skin. Hearing Sasha say that—knowing she thought that . . . That strange smell had disappeared.

Now all I could taste was that sickly cherry on my tongue. I remembered the Jolly Rancher in my pocket and unwrapped it, smelling it first—lemon, thank god—before putting it in my mouth.

"Did you hear that?" Devon said suddenly.

Gia turned back. "What?"

"I keep hearing something."

"What kind of something?"

Devon shook her head like she wasn't sure. We stood there a moment.

Frankly, the silence was more unnerving. It felt unnatural, as though whatever had been making the noise Devon heard had quieted on purpose.

"Is this like that glow you saw?" Gia said. "Which turned out to be nothing?"

"We don't know what it was. We didn't go far enough to find out?"

"Oh yeah, I'd almost forgotten Operation Save H," Gia remarked, looking at me.

"It probably *is* H, trying to scare us," I said, sucking lemon through my teeth. I wasn't sure I believed that, but I needed to get Gia off the Blame Amelie train. And actually, the more I thought about it, that elevated-adrenaline-levels thing she told us seemed like total bullshit. What psychologist ordered you to scare yourself out of nightmares?

Gia raised her eyebrows.

"*You* were the one who said she had directions, too," I reminded her again.

"But how likely is that?" Devon asked me. "Didn't you

say you found Henrik's site in some obscure corner of the internet?"

"Well, yeah." I had said that.

"Who is this Henrik, anyway?" Gia asked me.

"Just some urban legend junkie."

"Is he from around here?"

"I don't know," I admitted. "He didn't exactly give me his résumé." Although his website had been graffitied at that one Dissent gathering, which meant he could, possibly, have been at Dissent. My pulse skipped. I'd never thought of *that*.

"Wait." Gia stopped abruptly and turned to face me. "Did you tell him we were coming here this weekend?" There was an accusatory tone there, but also fear.

My thoughts doubled back to the zombie summer camp. To that shadow in the window of the cabin. Shit. Gia was looking at me like I was some kind of dumbass.

I leaned into indignation instead of humiliation. I stuck the last bit of candy in a corner of my cheek, folded my arms across my chest, and spoke like I was talking to a child: "Did I tell some internet rando that I was going with three other girls into the wilds with no cell coverage this weekend? To a cave he told me about?" I tilted my head. "Is that what you're asking?"

She stared at me a moment. "Just . . . checking." The disdain on her face softened. "I don't always trust that other people think things through. I'm used to being the person that holds shit together, is all."

"I didn't tell him anything; I'm familiar with how creepy the internet is."

"Right. Cool. Sorry. I . . . don't want anything messing this trip up."

"A creepy internet rando would do it," I agreed, implying I accepted her apology.

"How about a lost hiking companion?" Devon reminded us, as though we might've forgotten about H.

"I meant for *me*," Gia said. She turned around and continued.

I followed, relieved we'd established I hadn't done anything truly stupid, but a little uneasy, rethinking my correspondence with Henrik. It was true: I hadn't told him anything about our plans. But what was also true was that I didn't know anything about him. At the time, I was too preoccupied with the idea of the Sublime—how to follow this through—to think too much about it. I'd contacted him through his website, which was pretty bare-bones. It was posts of urban legends organized by genre: abandoned buildings, strange figures, wild spaces, and so on. The favicon was, appropriately, a kraken. Or maybe it had been an octopus.

I slowed. "Gia," I said.

She turned again, squinting at the look on my face. "What?"

Before I could respond, something moved behind her. It darted from one bit of pitch black to the next, quick as an eyeblink. I sucked in a breath, jerking my flashlight in its direction. And then felt a breeze on my neck. Something brushed against my arm. I spun to the side, swinging my light wildly.

"What?" Gia demanded.

"Something touched me," I hissed.

"Amelie—"

"Wait," Devon's voice came, unusually hushed. "I heard it."

We bunched together. Or, Gia and I bunched backward toward Devon. I fumbled with my light, joining Gia in shining it into the corners, trying to get a picture, widen our sight. It was impossible. The dark was ever present, immediately occupying the place we'd last looked, so that it felt like it was creeping up on us, reaching for us.

"What was that?" Gia gasped.

"What?"

"It went behind that rock." Her headlamp illuminated a chunk of boulder we'd passed. It sat apart from the wall—as though it had fallen from the ceiling eons ago. "It, like, scuttled past."

"Scuttle is not a reassuring verb," Devon commented. But she didn't pull her phone from her pocket to help us look.

Gia swung her headlamp around in a wide circle, searching the crevices of the cavern. "I think there's something down here," she breathed.

"What kind of something?"

Gia didn't reply; she was staring at that boulder, back the way we'd come. It occurred to me, suddenly, that our lower halves were encased in darkness. Something about that felt wrong, vulnerable, and I jerked my flashlight to the floor, searching for—what? Something that crawled?

Scritch.

I froze. I'd imagined the sound, surely. I'd imagined it because I was thinking about rodents or insects or . . .

Scritchscritchscritch.

No. Something was down here. Something . . . familiar.

My stomach swooped, and my feet pinged, as if with electricity. I suddenly had the distinct sensation I was balanced on a precipice, even though that was impossible—I could see the cave floor, the path ahead. It had to be the dark, the swoop of our lights, disorienting me.

And then, all at once, I couldn't breathe. Something was choking me, sitting on my chest, cutting off my air. I panicked, my free hand flying to my neck but finding nothing—no fingers, no anything—and tried to suck in a breath. A wheezing, strangled sound escaped me.

Gia jolted and screamed, like she'd been touched by a live wire, and the pressure released. She lunged away from us, down the tunnel. The diminishing light from her headlamp relayed her velocity; she was moving as though her life depended on it.

I didn't glance back to see what had scared her. I sucked in a staggered breath and followed, scrambling after her. I heard Devon behind me, doing the same.

We plunged desperately, blindly, down the dark tunnel.

GIA'S RETREATING FORM FLICKERED IN AND OUT OF MY FLASH-light's sporadic beam—it was impossible to run and hold it so I could see where I was going. Every instinct in my body pro-pelled me forward—away from whatever was behind us—but inwardly I was recoiling, anticipating slamming into a sharp rock, plunging down into an unseen abyss.

I was glad Gia was leading, but damn, she was fast. I was barely keeping pace; I could hear Devon falling behind.

"Gia!" I wheezed. "Wait up!"

Gia stumbled and slowed.

"Gia!"

She was breathing hard. She was grabbing the side of the tunnel wall and practically throwing herself forward. She missed a step, wobbled, and dropped to one knee.

Devon arrived a second later. She was breathless, too, but not like Gia. Gia couldn't stand. The sight of her pulled me back to that strange precarious feeling, the lack of oxygen, just seconds ago.

"You're good," Devon said, shining her phone light behind her. "There's nothing following us."

Gia didn't respond. It seemed like she was struggling to keep upright. I grabbed her by the arm. Her face was an ashen color, eyes wide, and she was gasping for breath in deep wheezes. This was beyond exertion breathing.

"Are you asthmatic?" Maybe she'd asked about my inhaler because she had one.

Or needed one.

She shook her head, turning away and putting a hand to the ground. "No," she managed eventually.

"Are you sure?"

"I'm not. Fucking. Asthmatic!" Gia snapped. Her head was practically between her knees.

Then what was wrong with her? Disoriented, I shone my light back the way we'd come. Was Devon sure?

"There's nothing there," Devon said again, reading my expression.

I turned to Gia. "Just take a minute."

"Why did you run?" Devon asked her, though Gia was in no shape to answer, and it was bonkers that Devon couldn't see that. She tried me next: "What touched you?"

Gia's wheezes were slowing.

"Better?" I asked her. She didn't reply.

"Amelie?" Devon again.

"I don't know." *Scritchscritchscritch.* Now that we were no longer running and panicked, I couldn't be sure I hadn't imagined it. But that feeling of familiarity. For a minute, it felt like . . .

Impossible.

I met her eyes.

"Huh." Devon was spookily calm. "Well, I need to pee." She ducked into a corner.

I stared at her, stupefied by her weird shift in emotion. She said earlier that nothing scared her, so either it was true and she'd followed us for fun, or she was trying really hard to make it true. Either way—

"Do you mind?"

"Oh!" I pulled my light away quickly and turned.

Gia was preoccupied with her own situation. "I need water," she managed. She stood and pulled off her pack, fiddling to unclip the top. A rock clattered to our left, startling us both, and Gia fumbled and dropped her pack.

"My bad," Devon's voice came from the corner. "Hey, feel free to talk and cover the sound of me pissing."

Gia looked with annoyance at her spilled backpack. She grabbed her water bottle from the mess and took a drink.

"Are you okay?"

"I'm fine." And, weirdly, she seemed it. Whatever the moment was before, it was over. I was going to repeat Devon's question, but her eyes brightened as they focused on something behind me. "Hey," she said. "I think we found the Church."

I turned, shining my light with hers and revealing an enormous cavern beyond the tunnel we were standing in. We ventured a few steps closer.

"Look at those cone things."

Fifty feet above us, the ceiling bared vicious teeth; dozens of stalactites stabbed down. Here and again stalagmites emerged from the floor, stretching to gnarled pillars nearly my height. The dark mouth of a tunnel gaped on the far side of the space.

My pulse sped; the directions had described a cavern full of stalactites.

Our lights danced off the walls, which had initially appeared monochromatic but, on closer look, were glistening in places of moisture and sparkling where the stone was shot through with metallic-looking veins, like an other-planetary canvas.

"There's supposed to be an altar . . ." Gia pointed ahead. "Maybe that?" Two stalagmites that likely had started growing in tandem had met at the top, fusing together. The top surface had flattened to create a kind of table or, I guess, an altar.

"It's the Crow's Foot, the Church, then the Eye, then the Sublime?" I clarified.

"Yeah," Gia said, looking relieved. "This is a good sign."

It was. It meant we weren't lost. Even if we'd taken the wrong way to get here, we were going in the right direction. I felt myself relax.

But then Devon reappeared. "So, what was it?" she asked Gia.

"What?"

"Back there. What did you see?"

Gia chewed on the inside of her cheek, then turned away from the cavern of stalactites to face her. "An animal," she said.

My relief at finding the Church evaporated.

"What kind?" Devon asked.

"A canine kind." Gia looked uncomfortable.

"Like a wolf?"

"A dog, I think."

"But you're not sure?"

Gia shook her head.

Well, this was great. "You sure it wasn't a . . ." What? What other kinds of animals lived in caves? I remembered our hike in, how we were making noise deliberately. "Do bears hibernate this far into caves?"

"Bears hibernate in the winter," Devon said.

"It was wounded," Gia said. "It was bleeding—or at least, there was blood on its fur. I just saw it for a second."

We stared at her. So, this "dog" had gotten wounded and hid in this cave for safety?

Unless something wounded it in here.

I pushed the thought away. "Maybe it fell down that chute, like we did?"

Devon shrugged. "Sure. But regardless, it's probably not the friendliest cave companion."

We looked around.

"I think we should arm ourselves," Devon said.

Gia squinted. "With what?"

"With whatever you can." Devon dug in one of her pockets, drew out a red-handled Swiss Army knife, and pulled it open. The blade gleamed in Gia's headlamp. I stared. The knife had jogged the ghost of a memory I couldn't quite grasp.

I shook it aside and thought about the contents of my messenger bag. Two granola bars, an apple, water. Nothing that could be remotely used as a weapon. I searched the ground for a loose rock and found a jagged one the size of my hand, but then realized it was lighter than my flashlight. I tossed it aside. My flashlight would have to do.

Gia was rummaging around in her backpack again. She drew out a length of rope, neatly coiled, and hefted it in her hand.

"What are you going to do with that?" I asked.

"It should work." She flicked it forward. The loop hit the wall with a satisfying thud. "Like, beating someone with an electrical cord?"

"Which I'm assuming you've done before?" Devon asked.

"I've seen it done on TV." Gia hefted the rope again, feeling its weight.

"Okay, then," Devon said ironically. She jerked her head at the Church. "Shall we?"

"Hang on." Gia bent to gather the contents that had spilled our during her frantic search for a water bottle. My anxiety stalled at the sight of a small black cylinder.

"Is that a flashlight?" I pointed at it.

"Yeah." Gia shoved it back in.

"You have two flashlights," I reiterated.

"So?"

"So . . . H lost hers? When she lost her pack?"

Gia took another swig of her water and dragged her sleeve across her mouth. "If you're suggesting I should've lent it to her, she didn't need it. She was in the middle of us, and we had lights."

"But, I mean . . ." I shifted. "If she'd had more than a penlight, she might not have taken that wrong tunnel."

"How was I supposed to know she'd run away?" She pulled her pack on. "Come on."

Gia had a point. Still. She had two flashlights but had been saving one for . . . what?

I scrambled after her. "Devon's phone is dying," I pointed out.

"And I could lend a flashlight to her," she finished for me. I nodded.

"I could, except it's not my fault Devon came prepared for a backyard BBQ?"

Devon spoke. "I'm cool with the dark. Besides, you never know what else I'm carrying in my coat of many pockets. I could have a generator in here." She made a detour toward the altar thing.

I stared at Gia. The same could be said of her backpack. What else was she hoarding in there? "But H might not be lost right now if you'd given her—"

"I'm not H's mom, okay?" Gia snapped, picking up her pace. "Devon said people need to take responsibility for their decisions. Maybe her disappearance is her consequence."

A realization hit me: Gia didn't see this as a group effort. She was taking care of Gia first. She'd saved her second flashlight in case something happened to her headlamp. And what about her water? Food?

"Hate to interrupt," Devon's voice came from behind us. "But speaking of H . . ." She stepped completely out from the shadows. She was holding a Gore-Tex jacket.

I sucked in a breath, my thoughts about Gia evaporating.

Gia stepped close, took a sleeve, and examined it, her headlamp light tracing over the dinosaur-bird logo with the one loose thread. It was definitely the one H had worn in here.

"It was over there?" Gia asked.

Devon nodded.

"Wow," Gia said. "Okay, so. She *did* come this way."

I asked the obvious: "Why would she take it off?"

Devon shook it. "There's something in the pocket." She dug one hand in and withdrew an object: a Sharpie. "You were right, Amelie. That Crow's Foot did look too new." She uncapped the marker and sniffed it. "Sharpies aren't exactly survival gear."

Gia stared. "Oh my god," she said. "Are you serious?" She let out a word in Spanish that sounded like a swear. "She *did* have directions."

"She did?"

"How else would she know to draw a Crow's Foot?" Gia asked. "Oh my god, I am going to kill her."

"But how likely is it that both Amelie and H found the same obscure website?" Devon asked, looking at me. She wasn't convinced, and she'd said something similar earlier.

I chewed the side of my lip. Admitting it had been scrawled on a sign at Dissent meant admitting I'd lied about that initially. Although now that they knew the Sasha connection, maybe it was more forgivable? Or . . . a thought I'd had just before we got scared and ran back: "Maybe *she* is Henrik."

"What?"

"Henrik's avatar was an octopus, and H had an octopus squishy in her pack." Henrik's avatar had been, technically, a kraken. But maybe . . .

"Oh my god," Gia said. "Do you think?"

"Maybe? I mean, her therapy thing sounds completely fake, doesn't it?"

"Yeah," Gia said. "Yeah, it does. Plus, she was super into the horror element of this trip . . . She *wanted* it to be scary. Do you think she brought us here to mess with us?"

"Why would she do that?" Devon, ever calm, was back to examining the Sharpie.

"I don't know. Material for some amateur horror film she's writing?" Gia said.

"Or footage for a horror film she's *making*?" I added. "She's got hidden cameras somewhere?"

Devon raised an eyebrow.

"Okay, maybe not that," I admitted, a flush blooming on my neck.

"Jesus," Gia muttered. "*That's* why she was so intent on finding her stupid pack. She probably had a bunch of shit in there to scare us."

"Or, like, essential supplies," Devon said. "Handy when you're lost?"

Gia cut a glance at her.

"The good news is this means we're definitely not stuck down here," I said. "If H deliberately led us here, there's obviously an exit."

"Unless she's going full method acting," Devon remarked. "Then we're going to die."

"Okay, but wait," Gia said. "I saw a dog."

"Well," Devon said. "H shape-shifted, clearly."

"Would you stop?" Gia snapped. "It's not funny! None of this is funny. God, what a little psycho! All of that pretending to hear the lore for the first time when she probably made it up!"

I'd never thought of that. I tried to remember H's reaction when I'd told the story of the Sublime. If I recalled correctly, she'd seemed genuinely fascinated. She was obviously a better actor than we thought. Maybe her initial hesitancy at the cave entrance had been an act. But . . . if H made up the lore, the Sublime might not exist. And if it didn't . . .

"Better the devil we know, I guess?" Devon mused. She hiked up her green jacket, tied H's around her waist.

I thought back to that moment in the car, H asking Devon if she meant *we'd* be the trouble down here.

Gia squinted at her. Then she pulled on her backpack and gathered her coil of rope. "Come on," she said.

We started off again, making our way through the cavern. Gia was muttering to herself. Devon was a silent shadow behind me.

Devon, who'd anticipated trouble but seemed fully unconcerned at the prospect of it.

I squished my eyes tight for a heartbeat. Opened them to the dark. Was I relieved at the idea H was Henrik? Did I even believe that?

If I did, did that mean that this trip was for nothing?

If I didn't, then what had happened to her that she'd left her coat behind?

My pulse skipped wildly, thinking about that figure in the dark.

We headed deeper into the earth.

THE THING ABOUT THE PITCH DARK IS THAT THERE IS NO touchstone for time passing. One minute could well have been ten, or thirty. Or what felt like an hour might've been significantly less. I alternated between being sure time was standing still, stretching out forever like the black around us, and feeling like it was speeding by impossibly fast.

The disorientation made my mind wander weird places.

The dark was starting to feel like a living entity, one that pulsed and moved with us. And the more I thought about that, the more I could imagine it as something sentient, a kind of creature intent on keeping us disoriented—gaining something from our liminal state. In reality, the whole predicament was nothing a wristwatch wouldn't have solved. If only I'd had the sense to bring one.

"What time is it?" I asked Devon.

"I turned my phone off a while back," she said. "But it was seven thirty then."

Seven thirty meant we'd been down here a couple of hours already, which, now, seemed impossible. Worse, it would be dark outside soon.

There was a weird bit of relief mixed with resentment hanging in the air. Gia had said she was going to kill H and, sure enough, was stalking ahead like she was hunting for her. But she also looked reassured by the idea H was lurking around. She'd switched to that explanation for everything pretty damn quickly, which suggested that whatever she'd seen had scared her. Gia did not like being scared.

Scritchscritchscritch.

I pushed the memory away. I didn't need to legitimize it by thinking about it, especially if H was the reason for it. Besides, the more I thought about it, the more I realized both things could be true: The Sublime could exist, and H could be creeping around in the dark, being a weirdo.

It's just that the thing about H didn't feel right. I'd suggested it, yes, but the truth was I'd been deflecting.

The devil we know.

I would've had an easier time believing that about Devon. If she'd disappeared, I'd have assumed she was messing with us. There was her confession about Dissent, for one, and just her general . . . behavior.

I trudged on, feeling her presence behind me more acutely. Now I was thinking about how quickly she'd found the path to the cave. About how she seemed to know a lot about caves—their groundwater, what lived in them. About her weird questions about Sasha.

Stop it. None of that had anything to do with H's disappearance, or with our current predicament. How could it?

I was starting to lose it a bit, obviously. My fear was conflating reality with my perception of it. And what kind of view did you have on anything in the pitch dark? I needed to focus. All that mattered was finding the Sublime and getting out of here.

Eventually the tunnel widened into a small chamber, and Gia came to an abrupt halt. At the far side there was a rock wall with a small opening.

We ventured close, my flashlight and Gia's headlamp revealing an oval passage, about chest level for an average-height person and big enough to crawl through.

Gia stepped back. "It's the Eye," she said, confidently. "This is the last landmark."

Before the Sublime, she meant. I felt a wash of relief, excitement. Hopefully it wasn't much farther from here.

Gia undid a clip on the side of her track pants and looped the coil of rope through it, securing it to her side, then tightened the straps of her backpack. The muscles in her arms strained as she placed her hands on the shelf and pulled herself to her hips. She wriggled, finding purchase on the wall and scrambling up, then peered back at us, a satisfied look on her face. "It opens up again on this side."

My shoelace was untied. As I bent to fix it, Devon went ahead.

What she lacked in grace she made up for in height; she was able to pull herself all the way up easily.

I stared up at the little space and tucked my flashlight in my bag, leaving the hole dimly lit by Gia's headlamp on the other side. I knew from looking that there was no way I could do it myself. I tried anyway; Gia should know that I was, at least, trying. I took a couple of running steps, leapt up, and reached, hoping to dig my fingernails in for purchase. No chance: As soon as I placed my hands down, the rest of me slammed into the rock, and the impact sent me reeling backward.

Devon appeared above me, leaning through the Eye. "Give me your hand."

Her grip was strong. She pulled, deftly dragging me up and through the small passage. As I struggled to get my footing beside her, she reached out. Something caught my T-shirt, and as we pulled apart, I heard a ripping sound.

I recoiled farther and fumbled my flashlight out of my bag—Gia's headlamp was pointed the other way. I shone it down. There was a six-inch rip from the middle of my shirt to the hem.

Devon was holding the knife she'd pulled from her pocket earlier.

I stared at her in shock.

"Sorry. I forgot it was in my hand." Devon squinted.

How does someone forget they're holding a knife? How had she even climbed up with it in her hand?

She noticed my incredulous look. "I was trying to help." She folded the blade into the handle.

"Um, I always almost stab people when I'm trying to help them?"

Gia stepped back between us. "What's going on?"

"You think I meant to?"

Did I?

"Meant to what?" Gia demanded.

The annoyance clouding Devon's eyes was chased away

by a flicker of amusement. "Why would you think I wanted to stab you?"

"*What?*" Gia snapped her head toward me, alarmed.

I kept my light on the folded knife in Devon's hand, a different memory pinging in . . .

H, scrambling after the spilled contents of her bag up on that boulder. Squishy Octo and . . . a knife. That knife? It looked identical.

"Where did you get that?" I asked, pointing at it.

"From my jacket," Devon said. "Why?"

"Why are you flailing it around at people?" Gia demanded.

"I wasn't."

Gia pointed at my ripped shirt.

"I literally forgot it was in my hand," Devon said.

"Really. Interesting, for someone who's so quick to point out when others fuck up."

"Are you talking about the ravine stairs, again?" Devon smiled quizzically. "You can't let that go?"

But my mind was back there, too, thinking about the moment we'd searched for H's backpack in the rain. Devon had disappeared for a second. Had she found it, then lied? But . . . why? It didn't make any sense . . . unless she was trying to put H at a disadvantage down here. Though that didn't make sense, either.

"—to do with it."

"Well, I never said I don't make mistakes," Devon replied.

"Good thing, because that would be a pretty big one."

"Great. So we agree I *wasn't* trying to stab Amelie?"

I took a deep breath and tried to gather my galloping thoughts. The knife could've just looked like H's.

"I mean, Amelie doesn't even think so," Devon said.

I looked at her. "What?"

"You don't actually think I was trying to stab you."

I fingered my ripped T-shirt. "I guess I overreacted."

"Well, you got our attention," Devon commented.

"Pardon?"

Gia leaned close and peered at my shirt, fussing over me. "Are you okay?"

"Yeah." What had Devon meant by that?

Gia turned back to Devon, folding her arms across her chest. "An apology would help."

Devon stared at her. "Are you being serious?"

Gia lifted her chin.

"Why would I apologize?"

"To take responsibility for something you didn't choose?" Gia said pointedly. I realized, then, that her reaction was less about me and more about Devon. It was about the moments Devon had one-upped us with facts and philosophy, with her weird calm, with finding the path when Gia had lost it.

Devon, incongruently, smiled. "Hey, Amelie, I apologize for not trying to stab you but almost stabbing you anyway." She was looking at me expectantly, but for some reason I got the feeling that she didn't want an apology back; she was waiting for me to . . .

Make it a thing?

"It's whatever," I said, waving a hand quickly.

"Great," Gia said sarcastically. "Go team."

I shifted uncomfortably. "Should we . . ."

"Yeah, we should," Gia said. "Because before this, I saw a light."

"Was it blue?" Devon asked.

"Yeah," Gia said grudgingly. "It was, like, glowing."

"The lake," Devon said.

My heart skipped at the thought.

"Maybe."

"We could turn off our lights," Devon said. "To see."

"No," Gia said. "The last time we did that, one of us disappeared. No pitch black." She stepped away from us. "Come on. And keep your light on, so I know where you are."

Devon didn't hesitate to follow. She wasn't at all bothered by the exchange. And Gia, well, she was on her own mission.

I trained my flashlight on their retreating forms. The army green of Devon's jacket, her auburn hair; beyond that, Gia's baby-blue jacket and glossy ponytail disappearing out of range. I hurried to catch up, trying to push aside my unease.

I could ponder the incident with Devon later. More important right now: The lake was in reach.

Sure enough, there was a damp smell in the air. A drop of water landed on my brow and continued down the side of my face. I wiped at it, shining my beam on the ceiling. It was slick with condensation, glistening with moist teardrops. Was this what it ordinarily looked like, or was it damper, on account of the rain?

I splashed into a small puddle with the toe of my sneaker and tried to skip around the rest of it but lost my footing. I stumbled.

And then I was falling, pitching through a dark, damp space. I flailed, throwing out my hands, but instead of landing on all fours, I slammed flat on my back, my breath whooshing from my chest in a painful rush. Clouds of dust erupted around me, shuddering up from the floor with the impact and then slowly drifting down again. I gasped for breath and pulled myself painfully to sitting, waving a hand to see through the haze. How could I have landed that way? How could it be moist *and* dusty?

I squinted, shining my light, trying to find the other two. Had they even stopped for me?

That sweet, slightly rotten smell was back. It was intensifying, a cloying fruitiness, but more than that—decay. Bile rose in my throat.

Scritchscritchscritch.

A figure darted across the beam of my light. A shadow blur: silent, quick, one side of my light to the next.

I froze, swinging my flashlight in the direction it had gone. Rock wall, gleaming with moisture and tiny sparkling bits of rock. I searched the dripping ceiling, up and over and down, all over the craggy rock passage. Nothing.

Not nothing.

I'd seen something. Definitely human. Something that made a sound.

You know that sound.

Something that smelled sick.

You know that smell.

My throat closed off.

It's a subterranean lake in the White River parks system.

Finding the Sublime changes something important for those who dare to seek.

But the "dare to seek" part—that was because . . . *They must face themselves, their darkest fears.*

Panic closed a fist over my heart, gripped it tight.

"Guys . . ." I scrambled to stand. "Guys?"

The dust had disappeared. Ahead were two dark shadows, completely, utterly still. A spike of fear shot through me, but then they moved, and their shapes became discernible.

"Holy." Gia's voice. Her shadow was blocking most of the tunnel entrance, but there was a strange, blue hue seeping around the edges of her profile.

"What is it?" Devon asked.

Gia's voice came back, full of wonder. "We made it." She looked back at us, her eyes round and amazed. "We found the Sublime."

WEDNESDAY, JULY 26, 2:27 P.M.

"Vargas!"

Vargas tore her attention away from the girl to see Draker beckoning. She sucked in a breath, vaguely annoyed at the interruption, which she knew was irrational. There were two reasons Draker hadn't approached and waited for an opportune moment to interject. One, it was Draker, who had the finesse of a bull in a china shop. Two, much more forgivably, he was doing it on purpose: Interruptions tested a person's recall. The liar would continue where they'd left off, because they needed to hit certain story points to paint the right picture. The truth teller would end up skipping ahead or backtracking. It was basic Interrogation 101. Not that Vargas was interrogating the girl.

"Can you give me a second?"

The girl straightened up. "Did he hear from the hospital?"

"I'll check." Vargas got up, noticing with irritation that Draker was still gesturing, like she wasn't joining him fast enough. As she strode to the car, she realized he wasn't just impatient; he was excited.

He kept his voice low as she arrived. "You're not going to believe this."

Vargas raised her eyebrows expectantly.

"Two of these girls are already missing persons."

Pause. "Come again?"

"Gia Rodriguez's mother filed a missing persons Sunday night when she didn't return from a sleepover at a teammate's house. The teammate, apparently, had covered for her but didn't know why. Denver PD was prepping to issue a state-wide bulletin."

Vargas blinked. "Was there an Amber Alert?"

"No reason to suspect abduction. Her car was missing, and she'd been talking about visiting a cousin in Santa Fe, though her mother had told her she couldn't go. They chased down that way, searched Denver, but no leads. And then the Kim girl—this 'H'—was reported missing a day later."

"Monday." Vargas's thoughts were spinning.

Draker nodded. "Parents were traveling Sunday for a convention. They left before she got home from a friend's, got to their destination late, and didn't want to wake her. They phoned Monday morning to check in. Couldn't reach her. They've been pressing for an Amber Alert, but the friend admitted she'd been covering for her—so far, they're treating it like a runaway."

"So the last time anyone saw either was Saturday." Vargas glanced at the girl. "They've been gone almost five days." She looked at him. "And Amelie's parents?"

He nodded. "Got Cheyenne to call them back and clarify. Their retreat started Friday night, and they were unreachable until this morning. They didn't realize she was missing."

Vargas sucked in a breath. "Jesus." Vargas looked at the girl again. Five days. But surely they couldn't have been down there this whole time. It sounded as though they'd prepped for a day hike, but if they'd arrived Saturday, how would they have survived this long?

"Sheriff's mobilizing SAR," Draker said. Search and rescue, he meant. "Trying to keep it quiet for now. They want to get here before any media does."

"Okay."

"Right. Now for the rest."

"There's more?"

"Lots. Our victim with the knife wound is talking. Pretty incoherent picture so far—she's been jabbering on about a childhood pet—but Soustracs managed to get an explanation about her leg." He paused, tilted his head in Amelie's direction.

"She said 'Amelie stabbed me'?" Vargas asked.

"There another Amelie around these parts? Yeah. Soustracs double-checked."

She did it. Amelie did it.

I didn't stab her.

"Next thing: Cheyenne got details about this Sasha Desmarais case. There was some party at an abandoned property, a derelict house in north Denver. Victim was found in the cellar with severe head trauma. Initially they assumed she'd fallen down the stairs, but further investigation revealed signs of a struggle: bruising on her arms, scratches."

That squared with Amelie's story so far. Then Draker added, "She's been in a medically induced coma at Saint Joseph pediatrics in Denver since."

Vargas looked at him in shock. "She's alive?"

"Yep. But unavailable for questioning at the moment."

Vargas had assumed the cousin had died, but now that she thought about it, Amelie had never actually said that. It was a weird detail to fudge over, wasn't it? Well, no, that was the thing; it wasn't, for her. She was telling the tale exactly as she wanted—needed—to.

Another realization hit then: Amelie had insinuated she wanted to believe in the Sublime. But it wasn't because she wanted her cousin back from the dead; she wanted her out of her coma.

"There's more, still. Cheyenne got the list of names interviewed from the Desmarais accident scene, and Amelie wasn't on it." That, too, squared: Amelie had said she wasn't there that night. "But both Gia Rodriguez and a Devon Kirneh were."

"So, we have an ID on the fourth girl?"

"Looks that way. But they haven't been able to locate a parent or guardian."

Vargas's thoughts whirled. "Nobody was charged with anything?"

"Nobody admitted to anything but being there."

"How far did they chase the assault suspicion?"

"Far enough to collect DNA from willing participants and rule everyone there out."

She turned to look back at the girl, who had her knees clasped to her chest now, face tilted to the sun. Perched like some gore-spattered cherub. "Did this H corroborate the stabbing? What's she saying?"

Draker shook his head. "Still incoherent. Babbling about some monster."

"Monster."

"Yeah."

"And the girl with the lacerated thigh, Gia . . ."

"Deep wound in that quad, lost a lot of blood. She's pretty medicated right now. Her mom's talking legal action, depending on recovery prognosis."

Vargas glanced the girl's way again. "So she's covered in Rodriguez's blood."

"Maybe." Draker scratched at his stubble.

Maybe, because they still didn't know what had happened to Devon . . . except that she hadn't returned.

Draker shook his head. "Monsters, witches . . . this is all . . ." His next words were cut off as he winced.

Vargas watched him press a hand to his chest. She pulled open the passenger-side door and grabbed an unopened bottle of water. She offered it to him, but he waved her off.

"Damn hot out." He jerked his head. "But you could spill a little on her. See if she melts."

She was the witch, he meant. It was a stupid comment, but a prickle crept along Vargas's arms suddenly, as she remembered H's prediction: that Amelie would carry the evil out with her.

"I should probably check the woods," Draker offered. "See if I can find this place?"

An unseen breeze teased the tendrils that had escaped Vargas's bun, tickling her face. Why did that idea make her uneasy? Of all the stupid-ass things. Draker was right: It was hot out. She should've been sitting in the shade. Her abuelita would've given her hell; that woman avoided the sun like the plague, mostly for vanity reasons. Of course, her abuelita would've also told her not to go wandering into the forest to find a witch's cave. Vargas gritted her teeth. Witch or no, didn't these girls have any common sense?

"You don't want to wait for the search?" She inclined her head toward the girl. "She's on a roll now."

It was an understatement; the girl was practically consumed by her own storytelling. She seemed desperate that Vargas listen and understand, but she'd also been weirdly enigmatic, catching herself, rephrasing. Then, she was displaying no obvious "delight in deception," the term for the rush liars got from the act of lying.

But the way she talked about her cousin's ability to create fantasies, she clearly admired that. And, more to the point . . . five days.

"We should do a sweep." Draker glanced at his watch. "She's quite the historian. Let's see how she is on directions."

Vargas nodded, tamping down an irrational spike of unease. "Should I clarify how long they've been gone?"

"Think I'd let her offer up her version."

Vargas nodded. Amelie was either confused or lying, but there was no need to tip her off to what they knew to be impossible. Yet.

They headed back to the girl.

"Brought you some water," Vargas said as they approached. She offered the bottle as Draker continued toward the trailhead sign. "Deputy Draker here is going to look around the area. Do you know about how far up the trail you went before going off of it? You said there was a crossroads."

The girl looked between them, her expression conflicted. "You don't want to hear what happened?"

"How about you just skip to the part where you tell us where Devon Kirneh is?" Draker said.

Bright spots appeared on her gore-smeared cheeks. She blinked. "I'm trying to."

"Well, we're losing time. The sooner you tell us, the sooner we'll be able to help her."

The girl looked at Vargas, spread her hands like she was being asked something impossible.

"You can keep talking to me," Vargas assured her. "But Deputy Draker needs to go. So, was it about a ten-minute hike?" She watched the girl's expression carefully, hoping to detect something that would indicate her guilt.

It hadn't changed; there was that desperate need to be listened to. Vargas had seen this look before, but never with a perpetrator. Only when she was talking with victims. *I am trusting you with this.*

But that glimmer of self-deprecation marred it. It was almost as though Amelie was disappointed in herself. It was so strange.

The girl shook her head. "He won't find her."

THE SUBLIME

Gia stepped forward, and her shadow dropped down about a foot. An intense sapphire light flooded the space above her.

"That's it," Devon murmured. "The light I saw."

She sounded so amazed, and the light was so ethereal, my fear dissolved instantly. Devon moved dreamily forward, and I couldn't help but follow, any lingering dread pushed aside by a swell of curiosity. I joined her moving toward Gia's silhouette, squeezed in beside her. The passage ended abruptly with a short drop-off into an enormous cavern the size of a football field. Ahead of us, a stretch of sand extended toward a large body of water. Dark cliffs rose on the far side of the lake, encircling the end to our left. To the right, the shore stretched out about fifty feet and disappeared behind a wall of rock. The patch of land we stood on was littered with the occasional boulder, and the sand was soft and white.

The lake was glowing.

My gaze traveled upward, to an impossible sky of sparkling stars. My anxiety disappeared completely, washed away by a rush of wonder.

It took a moment for it to register that I was looking at

the rock ceiling of the cavern. It was covered in pinpricks of brilliant blue light, and they were reflecting off the water, creating a blue glow and casting glimmering shadows on the rock cliffs.

We walked forward, trancelike, and stopped at the edge of the lake in a line, staring up at the star-splash.

"Magic," I whispered, transfixed.

"Glowworms," Devon whispered back. "Their bio-luminescence is a trap. Insects head toward the light and get caught in their silk."

"Yuck," Gia murmured, though she didn't sound disturbed.

I had the fleeting thought that Devon knew a weird amount about predatory insects. But then my eye was drawn toward the water, to small ripples shimmering with light, making their way toward shore.

Strangely, the sight didn't unnerve me. I had no reason to believe the ripples were natural, that a breeze down here was likely, but a palpable calm had enveloped me, evaporating any sense of alarm.

An eerily beautiful tone rang out across the water, startling me. Gia was singing: one, brief note, that resonated long after she closed her mouth. Sonorous beauty, filling the space. The hair stood up on my arms, and my chest felt heavy; there was something so pure about the sound. I looked over at Devon. She was staring at the water, lost in her thoughts. And then I turned toward Gia, whose face was practically incandescent with wonder.

There was a part of me that had hoped for something

spectacular, though I knew it was just as likely the Sublime would be a large, muddy pond. But here it was: aptly named and as ethereal as anything I could've imagined.

"Amazing," Gia breathed.

"Yeah," I agreed. It was like some giant mirror reflecting the universe, chock-full of mystery and wonder.

Devon bent and trailed her fingers in the water, sending ripples away from the shore. "It's warm," she remarked.

"Really?" Gia crouched next to her and did the same.

I stood, mesmerized by the image of the two of them, clustered together at the edge of this serene body of water, moving their hands lithely, their expressions dreamlike.

It was so beautiful, I could barely remember what I'd been worried about moments before. Vaguely, I was aware that I'd been scared, panicked even, in the tunnel. That I was starting to distrust Devon. Now it was as though none of it had happened.

A strange emotion came over me. It suddenly felt important that Devon know . . .

"I'm sorry," I said.

She looked up at me.

"About before. The knife. I'm sorry about that. I overreacted."

She studied me a minute. Then she stood and reached into her pocket. "Here," she said, handing me the knife. "You keep it."

"Oh, I don't need—"

"You should have it."

I squinted at her.

"It's better with you." She smiled that weird smile. "Last one standing needs the knife."

She was kidding, but a twinge of unease surfaced as I accepted it. "Okay."

Gia rummaged in her pack and pulled out a small digital camera. She moved a few strides away to take pictures of the lake. She examined the screen, frowning. "It's blurry. You can't get a good sense of the size."

Devon tried it with her almost-dead phone. "You're right, it sucks."

"Should we get higher?" I asked. "Maybe put something in the shot for perspective?"

Gia's eyes lit up. "Let's take a selfie!" She crowded us close, me in the middle, and extended her arm like we were three friends on vacation somewhere.

Gia checked the photo, then looked over at me. "Thanks," she said. "For suggesting this." She was no longer the sullen, determined girl who had led us through the tunnels. There was an openness, a vulnerability, about her that felt contagious. "This is magical."

"Right?" I looked at the shimmering water again. And maybe . . . maybe it was? The lore could be true. This could be real. Maybe when we got back to Denver, Sasha would be fine. Maybe everything would be fine now.

I sent a little private plea to the Sublime.

Then Gia said, "Well, all that bullshit about the witch makes sense now."

I blinked. "What?"

"Of course locals would want to keep this secret by making

up some story." She said it like it was obvious. "It'd be tour groups down here all summer long, if people knew." She gestured at the luminescent water. "The lore wasn't created to keep people away for *their* protection; it was for the *lake's*."

A pit opened up in my stomach as her words sank in. It made sense. Of course it did. And if there was nothing to the lore, at all, then there was little chance my plea was going to be answered. And suddenly, that thought made me want to panic.

I'd come on this trip; I'd honored Sasha's wish; that alone should've meant something. But it wasn't enough. It wasn't even close.

"Seriously, Am. I'm really sorry about what I said."

I looked at Sasha. "Are you sorry because you're sorry, or because I don't want to go to that stupid cave with you anymore?"

"Forget about the cave. I thought it would be good for us, but . . . I mean . . ." She sighed. "I didn't mean for it to come out that way. I want you to know that people who are worth being friends with will like you for you, you know?"

If I hadn't planned on bailing on her already, her condescending tone would've clinched it. "So basically you think I'm an attention seeker and a liar."

"But that's just it," she protested. "That's not *who you are."*

I stared at her, my jaw working.

"Look, I get it, okay? Your friends started to ignore you when you weren't sick anymore."

I sucked in a breath, and the memory jumped ahead to . . .

"I'm not really feeling Dissent tonight." I gestured at the door. *"You go."*

"I don't want to go without you. I'm sorry, okay? I didn't mean—"

"Get. Out."

"Hiding a lake is a nice thought," Devon's voice broke in. "Far nicer than girls disappearing, facing their darkest fears down here. But I don't know."

"This again?" Gia sighed loudly.

Devon considered her with an amused expression. "I think you just *want* to believe the lore isn't real."

"You know how crazy you sound, when you talk like it is, right?"

I winced inwardly. Was it a good idea to throw that word around?

"Crazier than Amelie?"

"Excuse me?"

"Um, *you're* the one with the messed-up fear response?" Gia said. "So yeah."

Now Devon looked like she was amused *and* done with all this. She crossed her arms. "Tell us about the dog," she said.

"What?"

"The dog you saw."

"Why?"

"Why not?"

"Because. I mean, what does it matter?"

"What did it look like?"

"I told you: It was dark."

Devon raised an eyebrow, then looked at me. "And you have no idea what scared you, either." Something about the way she was looking at me—like she knew I was lying and found it kind of funny—made my skin crawl. "The thing is," she said. "I think you might need to admit what scared you in order to get what you want from the Sublime. It's telling you something about yourself."

"What are you even talking about?" Gia waved a hand. "Look, if you want to believe this lake has magical powers, you go ahead." She busied herself, tucking her camera back in her bag and standing up. "I'm going to look around for H." She said it brightly, like she was no longer irritated at the fact H may have been playing a trick on us.

I was completely unnerved now. What did Devon mean? What did she . . . know?

"Maybe you should look around for a way out," Devon said.

I cleared my throat, grateful for the new direction in conversation. "There has to be one. There's lots of this cavern we haven't checked?"

"Oh." Gia's cheery expression faltered. "Right. We can't go back the way we came in. Not sure how I forgot that little detail."

We looked around. There were no obvious entrances into the place aside from the one we'd used.

"Well, we should check down shore," Devon said. "Maybe there's a tunnel we can't see." She took a few steps away.

"I'll come in a minute," Gia said, sitting back down and pulling her knees up. "I need a second."

"Are you okay?" I asked, genuinely concerned but also not in a huge rush to join Devon, solo, on a journey into the dark.

"I'm fine," Gia said tersely. "It's hot in here." It wasn't, particularly. Gia leaned her head forward onto her knees.

I looked at Devon, gesturing at Gia, who was now sucking air, muttering softly to herself. "I'll just . . ."

"Sit tight. I'll be right back. Probably."

I watched Devon disappear, unease winding through me. It was like she was trying to freak us out. I looked at the ceiling of the cave again, and my thoughts doubled back to what she'd said about the glowworms, how they lured their prey. That could describe the Sublime itself: a place that lured the curious with its mysticism, its unearthly promise. Were we insects, about to be trapped by threads we couldn't see? And whose threads?

I pulled my gaze from the direction Devon had disappeared in and sat, scooting closer to Gia than she probably appreciated.

Eventually she pulled her head up again. Whatever the moment had been before, it had passed.

"I'm sure we'll find the way out," I ventured. "I mean, H went somewhere, right?"

"I don't care where H went," Gia said.

But she'd been talking about finding her a second ago. "Would you really leave without her?" It wasn't H I was worried about; it was me. I was getting a bad vibe from

Devon, and the thought of being on my own down here was panic inducing.

Gia sighed loudly and stared out at the water. She shook her head no. "My mom raised me better than that."

I stared at her poker-straight posture. I hoped that included not abandoning me, too.

"We'd better go check things out," Gia said, preparing to get up.

"Gia, wait."

"What?"

I hesitated. Maybe I was imagining things. Then, did it hurt to encourage Gia to realize that Devon was . . . different? It would make the similarities in her and me—the idea that we should stick together—more obvious. I threw a look down shore to make sure Devon had disappeared. "Does Devon seem . . . off? To you?"

"What do you mean?"

"I don't know," I said. "She has weird reactions. Or, like, no reactions. She seems kind of dead inside?"

Gia considered this. "You mean when she's not being totally condescending?"

"Yeah," I agreed, though I hadn't been thinking that. I ran my hands through the sand, sifted a handful. It was soft, and white as bone. "Don't you remember, at Dissent, how she was always so . . . out of it?" Out of it wasn't the way to describe her, but calm seemed too complimentary an adjective.

"I don't remember anyone from Dissent," Gia said dismissively. Then she seemed to regret the comment. "I mean, I remember Sasha, of course."

That wasn't true. She remembered what *happened* to Sasha, not Sasha herself.

I looked at my hand, distracted. It was covered in the dust of the sand; it looked bloodless, sick. Just like . . .

Sasha, so still in that hospital bed. Skin so pale, hands limp at her sides. Tubes and wires and machines and that steady, goddamn hum. A soft compressing sound: oxygen, rushing toward her, down into her lungs. Oxygen: wanted or unwanted? It didn't matter; she had no choice.

Why should I take responsibility for something I didn't choose?

I could tell Gia was looking at me differently now. She was remembering that good thing I was doing.

For Sasha.

Sasha, who'd had this immutable well of energy before ending up immobile in that hospital bed. Sasha, who could imagine the most bizarre things out of the ordinary, before she could no longer communicate her thoughts.

Gia reached forward and gripped my wrist. "I'm glad it's so spectacular here. I'm glad it was worth it." She squeezed. "I'm sure she'd appreciate it."

Except now all I could think about was that thing I'd seen in the tunnel. That sound, that smell. I knew why it was familiar.

That sound was how Sasha used to describe the nighttime noise in her old room in Wyoming. Their ancient house had rats in the walls, and she used to be so terrified of the sound of their scrabbling claws she would pinch herself.

And that smell . . . that smell was from her hospital room.

My aunt used this cloying dry shampoo on her hair. It, combined with that sick smell that seemed ever present in her room . . . that was it. My heart pounded.

"But *why* did she want this?" I hadn't meant to say it aloud. Or sound that unhinged. But now I couldn't stop. "She didn't even like Dissent! Dissent was *my* idea. She went because I wanted to. She was there *because* of me."

Gia's eyebrows rose. She let go of my hand gently. "Amelie," she began, "it's not your—"

"She was starting to actively hate Dissent, and then suddenly she chooses a goddamn spelunking expedition? In a cave with a deadly lore?"

"Hey, calm down," Gia said brusquely.

It brought me up short. I didn't want to look crazy. "Sorry." But that question flipped around in my mind: Why was Sasha barely tolerating Dissent by the end, when she was clearly okay with taking risks like this? "I just . . . don't get it."

Gia softened. "It's okay. You're emotional because you're finally here." Her brow creased. "But maybe she . . . believed the legend?" For once, she didn't say it like this was a stupid idea. "Maybe there was something she wanted?"

Right. But . . . "Her life was perfect."

Gia's lips twisted. "From your perspective."

Again, I considered the idea that she'd been homesick for her old life, that the change in her had been a result of her being overwhelmed. But when I thought about it, it didn't make sense. She'd fit in at her new school no problem; the kids there were the privileged-but-leftie-raised types who were motivated but kind, the sort who celebrated difference—small-town upbringings were probably described as "authentic" or some equally overly charitable adjective. And Sasha was smart, so she had no trouble with her grades, with fitting in. She had, actually, thrived.

Just not around me.

I pressed my lips together and looked at my hands. "She's been at Saint Joe's for three months. Coma."

Gia was silent.

"And I've been thinking about this lore." I closed my eyes briefly. "I mean, if there was a chance that it *was* real . . ."

"Oh." It left her mouth, a soft exclamation. "Oh," she said again.

"There's still time. Her brain function is there." I could feel Gia's eyes on my face. "So, I mean . . ."

"I get it," she said, sounding completely sincere. My chest tightened. "And I'd do the same thing. I'd hope for the same." She reached for my arm again. "And now we'll totally find our way out of here."

"What same thing?" We jumped. Devon had appeared out of nowhere.

"Jesus!" Gia said. "What . . ." She took a second. "What did you find out?"

"Dead end that way," Devon reported. "The cliffs are pretty steep, and I don't see any passageways." She peered at us and asked again, "What same thing?"

We looked at each other. I could tell Gia was reflecting on my earlier comments.

"We were talking about . . ." Gia hedged. "Why Amelie came."

"What she needs to change?"

"Well . . ." Gia hesitated. "We were talking about her cousin." She looked at me, unsure how to proceed.

"She's still in a coma," I clarified, a little reluctantly.

"Oh," Devon said. "Right. So you hope she wakes up. You hope the Sublime will help with that." She said it so matter-of-factly.

"Uh, I guess."

"Well, who's to say it won't?"

"Exactly," Gia said. She'd dropped her skepticism completely—to make me feel better, obviously.

Devon looked at the lake. "My brother was in an accident and had to stay in a hospital when I was young."

Gia and I exchanged a look. Was this Devon's way of . . . bonding? Stating some tangentially related fact out of the blue? She was getting more and more awkward down here.

"Burn unit. Years ago."

Besides, I thought she'd said she was the one in the hospital? Was I remembering that wrong?

"Uh." Gia looked at a loss. "That's awful?"

"Yeah," Devon said, but she sounded unsure. "He was okay, but he's still scared of things that can burn you."

"Right," Gia said, shooting me a look. "That makes sense."

I squirmed, uncomfortable.

Devon looked at me. "What was Sasha afraid of?"

Why was she asking that? I looked at Gia for help, but she just spread her hands slightly, like she didn't know, either. "Uh, old homes. Like, abandoned houses and stuff."

"That challenge would've messed her up, then," Devon stated.

My pulse accelerated. "I guess."

Devon tilted her head and smiled, without humor.

"Devon," Gia said. "Amelie might not want to talk about it?"

"Right." Devon nodded. "Of course she doesn't."

But something about the way she said it . . . she wasn't commiserating. I opened my mouth—not to ask, but to put an end to the conversation—but was interrupted by a rock clattering behind us.

Gia and I scrambled up as Devon turned. The reflection off the surface of the lake cast the shore in a blue glow and made the crevices out of sight pitch black . . . where something was shuffling.

It appeared. Something—someone—feet from us, hidden in the shadows. I panicked—fumbling with the knife in my hand, failing to pull it open—and the figure suddenly sprang to life. It lurched out of the darkness with a primal scream, launching past me and Devon, directly at Gia.

Gia turned, shielding herself from the impact, and went down like a sack of rocks. I turned to see her lashing out with her elbows, kicking awkwardly. She was facedown, and the figure was on top of her, hands around her neck. That figure . . . I could see her now. In the glow of the lake, her face was gaunt. She was bare-armed and covered in a chalky substance that looked like dust. Her eyes were wild, unseeing.

H's forearms strained as she pressed Gia's face into the sand, smothering her.

DEVON MOVED TOWARD THEM BEFORE I COULD REACT, BUT Gia recovered quicker. She twisted her body and bucked, sending H up and off her. She scrambled, tried to move away, but H flailed as she pitched, catching hold of her wrist, holding Gia fast and jerking herself to standing. She clung to Gia, eyes wild, drawing back her free hand to land a punch.

Gia moved so quickly, I barely had time to process. She snapped her wrist to break H's hold, grabbed her arm, twisted it, and shoved H to her knees, incapacitating her. "Stop!" she screamed.

There was a moment of shocked pause. Then the frantic look in H's eyes dimmed, and recognition took its place. "Omigod," H managed. "Gia."

H looked, in a word, terrible. Her eyes were hollow, and dust coated her hair and skin, giving her a specter-like appearance—like something that had crawled out of a crypt.

"I thought it was here," she managed. "I thought you were—" She burst into tears.

Gia released H's arm, and H went limp, crumpling to the sand. She curled into a ball, pulling her knees to her chest.

Gia stood over her, chest heaving from the scuffle, then looked at our wide-eyed stares. "I had to," she said.

"Yeah," Devon agreed, an undercurrent of wonder in her usual, detached tone.

"We . . . we n-need to leave," H said between sobs. "We aren't safe." She cradled the arm Gia had twisted. "I'm sorry," H blubbered. "I'm so sorry. But it's down here." Her voice hitched and dropped to a whisper. "It was hunting me."

The hair rose on my arms. Was she talking about the dog Gia had seen? Or was she talking about what *I'd* seen?

"I didn't mean to hurt you, Gia. I—"

"You didn't," Gia said curtly. "You're not exactly UFC material."

"I was just sure you were . . . I was sure . . ." H started crying again.

Gia, looking guilty now, gestured at the coat around Devon's waist. Devon untied it and handed it over, and Gia knelt down. "Come on," she said firmly. She helped H to sit up and draped her coat around her shoulders. "It's going to be oka—" Her words cut off abruptly. She leaned forward over H, then looked back at Devon and me in alarm.

"What?"

"Look at this." Gia was pulling aside H's hair, pointing at her neck. We ventured close.

Tiny marks peppered her skin. Gia stretched the neck of H's cropped tee aside, revealing that they continued down her collarbone and onto her shoulder. And now I could see through the dust on her arms that they were cuts—little striations, fresh wounds that were too small to be bleeding freely.

"What happened to you?" Gia demanded.

H wiped one hand across her face and looked up at us.

She searched our faces, her eyes wide. "The Skinflayer," she whispered. "It's down here."

There was a dead silence.

"Water," Gia instructed, her voice tight. "She needs water."

I fumbled with my bag and pulled my water bottle out, offering it to Gia, who gave it to H. H choked back a sob, then drank so greedily I wanted to take it back. She wiped a shaky hand across her mouth.

"Stop crying now," Gia warned. "Or I swear to god we will leave you here."

H handed the water back and turtled again, forehead on her forearms, with a moan.

Gia stood for a few moments staring at her, perplexed. Then she straightened up and gestured with her head in a "let's talk" way. We huddled together about ten feet away and kept our voices to a whisper.

"Well, this is great," Gia muttered.

"What made those marks on her skin?" I asked.

"She told us," Devon replied. "The Skinflayer."

"Could you be serious for a second?" Gia snapped, even though nothing in Devon's tone indicated she was being sarcastic. On the contrary, there was a strange satisfaction there that made my skin crawl. Almost like Devon was . . . happy H was freaked out?

"She's obviously lost it," Gia said. "And now we have to find our way out of here with a person who's having a psychotic break."

H was rocking now, pulling at the shoulders of her jacket.

"But what made those marks?" I asked again, trying to ignore Devon.

"She fell—maybe even down the same chute we did—and got scraped."

"Maybe," Devon said. "Or maybe we should consider the idea that there *is* something down here? She saw something."

"Or she got scared and imagined it."

"So, you imagined the dog?" Devon asked Gia.

Gia frowned. "Playing along with this isn't going to help H." She hadn't exactly answered Devon's question.

"Well, I think we should be ready for the possibility that there is something down here," Devon replied.

"What, like arming ourselves again?" Gia asked.

"Except that you almost stabbed me last time?" I pointed out. Any warm feeling I'd had toward Devon from before, when we'd arrived at the Sublime, was long gone.

"Please, Amelie." Gia pinched the bridge of her nose. "One crisis at a time?"

I flushed. Wait. Did Devon smirk?

"If we arm ourselves," Gia said. "It'll look like we believe her."

"Right. And then she'll stop freaking out," Devon said.

"Or she'll freak out worse."

"Not sure that's possible."

I had to say it: "Okay, but I don't love the idea of two people with . . ." I gestured vaguely at my head. "*Mental stuff* going on, carrying weapons."

"Oh Jesus, Amelie," Gia said, though I could tell she'd been thinking it, too.

But Devon looked amused, not offended. "Well, you two obviously stable individuals could carry them?"

"What is that supposed to—"

"Stop." Gia held up her hand. "I am not giving in to H's hysteria, the overactive imagination of a horror freak."

"*Something* scared her half to death," Devon countered.

"*She* did," Gia snapped. "She tried to scare us and ended up scaring herself." Gia was unsettled but headed for her comfort zone: the offensive. "And you know what? I'm going to un-scare her."

"What does that even—"

"H!" Gia wheeled and strode back to her. She planted herself directly in front of her, hands on her hips. H shrank back a few inches. "You need to get it together. You're scared because it's dark and weird down here. But there is nothing hunting you. You want to know how I know?"

H peered up at her. Devon and I ventured a few steps closer.

"Because you snuck away to try to freak us out, and you got so into it you scared yourself."

Confusion marred H's fear. She looked like a rabbit cornered by a fox.

"But the only thing we need to do right now is find a way out of here. So here's what you're going to do: You're going to pull yourself together."

H blinked through her tears.

"Hey," I said. "Gia—"

"And you're going to tell us everything you know about this place. And then you're going to help us get out, or so

180

help me god, I will make you the star of this little horror fantasy."

"Gia—"

"Worry about your own problems, Amelie," Gia snapped in my direction.

My own problems? "Excuse me?"

"Devon stabbing you?"

"D-Devon stabbed Amelie?" H stammered.

"I missed," Devon corrected blandly.

"It's not funny," I said. I frowned at Gia. "And you didn't see."

"Right. I was busy trying to get us un-lost. Which, remind me—whose fault was that?"

"You're the one who rushed ahead!"

"You're the one who insisted we go back! But you know what? All of this bullshit ends here." She stabbed a finger at H. "You need to explain."

H looked at us, as if for help.

But I wasn't in the mood. "Where did you go?" I demanded, redirecting my anger. "After we turned off our lights?"

"I don't remember."

"Come *on*," Gia said.

"I . . . I was with you, and then . . ." H trailed off. "I don't know."

"We were shouting your name!"

H touched the back of her head with one hand and winced.

Devon stepped up, tilted H's head forward with one hand and peered at her dust-coated black hair. "Looks like you hit your head," she said. "Did you fall down a chute?"

"I don't remember."

"Why did you take your jacket off?" I asked H.

H's face twisted, like she was remembering something awful. Her voice dropped to a whisper. "It grabbed me by the sleeve."

A vein of fear shot through me.

H ran trembling hands down her legs. "I peeled out of my jacket and ran."

And we, also, had run from something. We'd run blindly, terror propelling us faster . . . I turned my head away from H's haunted face to the lake. It had calmed me a moment ago.

"The Skinflayer grabbed you?" Devon clarified.

"Yeah."

The lake rippled, sending long shadows toward the blue-hued shore.

"What is it?" Devon asked.

H's voice dropped again. "A monster."

I sucked in a breath, looked at the other two.

"It has too-long arms and needle-thin claws and this giant, sucking mouth. It doesn't have eyes; it hunts you by smell."

"How do you know it?" Devon persisted. "Is it from some Korean fable or something?"

H shook her head. "It's from my nightmares."

Devon raised an eyebrow, but Gia was having none of it. "Let me guess," she said to H. "The Skinflayer is the witch's house pet? Is his name Henrik, too?"

"What?" H looked genuinely confused.

Gia's face hardened. She stepped close and knelt in front

of H. "You need to be straight with us: Did you bring us here to play out some kind of weird-ass real-life horror movie?"

H's brow creased with confusion. "Is that what you guys think?"

I looked down. Gia had run with it, but I'd suggested it initially. "It was a theory. Weird shit was happening."

"And you disappeared into thin air," Gia said.

"I'd never heard of this place until Amelie told us about it. I didn't bring you here."

Gia crossed her arms.

"I'm not lying!" H was getting upset again.

"No one's saying that," I said quickly. "We're just trying to understand."

"Where did you see this thing?" Devon asked.

"One time I was in a cavern with a bunch of those dripping rock formations and then, just a minute ago."

"A minute ago when you attacked me?" Gia looked at her skeptically. "Do I look like it, or something?"

"Well, I didn't exactly *see* it," H admitted. She rushed on, seeing the look on Gia's face. "I didn't need to! I know its sound. I know what it smells like, even. It was the Skinflayer."

My scalp prickled. I knew what she meant. What I'd heard, smelled . . . I hadn't needed to see it to recognize it.

Gia sighed. "Isn't it possible you got super scared and had a visceral reaction to the dark?"

H chewed her bottom lip. She released the death grip she had on her knees. "I could . . . feel it."

"*Something* did that to her neck," Devon pointed out unhelpfully.

Gia shot her a look. "The fall did." She turned back to H. "I'm not saying you couldn't feel it. That's the visceral part. But it's possible you were really scared, right?"

"I . . . guess."

"It's totally possible," Gia said. "You went too far with the 'increasing your adrenaline levels' thing."

H stretched out her legs and trailed her hands in the sand beside her. "I mean, I *was* trying to scare myself down here."

"Right," Gia said. "But the good news is that you're not lost anymore. We're here. Right?"

"Right."

"Well, we're here, but the lost bit is debatable," Devon said mildly.

Unhelpful wasn't the word. Devon was outright sabotaging Gia's attempt to de-escalate the situation. I should've been reassuring H, too, but I was caught in a weird headspace. I'd thought I'd seen something, too, and it had felt so real. But I also didn't want it to be.

Face your darkest fears: yourself.

I thought about my silent plea to the Sublime moments ago. What did it mean that H had seen her nightmare and I'd seen . . .

I swallowed hard.

H sat back. "I'm glad you guys are here," she said. "I . . . did not think that through." Before anyone could ask what she meant, her eyes sharpened on something behind us. She sat up. "Hey, is this the Sublime?" Was she just noticing the lake now? "It's . . . beautiful." She got to her feet and ventured forward, pausing at the shore.

We watched as she crouched and trailed her hands in the water. She glanced our way, her face full of wonder. "Did you guys see this?"

"Did we see the giant glowing lake five feet away?" Devon asked. "Uh, yeah."

Gia turned to us, her eyebrows sky high. I didn't know what to think. It was an abrupt shift, but the lake had had that effect on all of us. Hadn't I been in a bit of panic right before we found it?

We watched H turn back to the water. Her shoulders heaved with a sigh—she was visibly calmer.

"Well, one crisis averted," Gia muttered.

"What now?" I asked.

"Uh, find a way out of here?" Gia said peevishly. "Obviously."

"I know," I said. "I meant—"

"Give her a minute?" Devon jerked her head toward H. "I think she needs it."

Gia rubbed a hand across her brow. "So do I." She grabbed her pack and thumped back down to the sand. Devon and I sat, too. H was now staring, rapt, at the glow-worm ceiling.

Devon pulled a bag of Skittles from one of her larger pockets. "Picnic time?" she asked, in that weird, detached tone.

"I guess," Gia said grudgingly.

"I have a granola bar and an apple," I offered her, rooting through my bag.

"I have stuff." Gia waved off my peace offering and pulled out her pack. She did have stuff, a whole cache of energy bars and prepackaged trail mix. Enough to feed all of us . . . not that she was going to.

But she surprised me by breaking an energy bar in half. "H?" She offered her a chunk.

H looked over. There was a clarity in her expression that was absent before. She actually seemed unbelievably normal, given her state moments ago. "Thanks."

Gia waved it off. "I have tons. I've been rationing my supplies, just in case of . . . well, something like this, I guess."

Rationing her supplies. Like a flashlight. I flushed, embarrassed that I'd assumed she was being selfish, had been looking out for herself.

Devon held out the now-opened bag of candy, and H took that, too, then offered it to Gia. I was surprised to see Gia take a handful before H passed it back.

"Everyone needs sugar." Devon held out the bag to me. I hesitated. "You don't like Skittles?"

I did; I was just weirded out by Devon. But I didn't want to add any tension, now that we were finally chill, so I took some.

We sat, looking out over the lake and its starry ceiling.

Placid water, yawn of dark space above; I tried to imagine we were friends camping out in the wilderness. I'd never been, but this must be what it was like, if you added in forest sounds and insects. And everything else normal.

"Better?" Gia asked H when she'd had some water.

H nodded. "Thanks." She darted a look between us. "Thanks for coming to look for me."

"Amelie insisted," Gia said. "She was not taking no for an answer."

H looked at me gratefully. A swell of emotion hit, kind of like when we'd first arrived. Suddenly I wanted them to know. I wanted to be honest. "I bailed on Sasha the night of her accident." I said. "I wasn't going to make that mistake again."

They were quiet. I hoped it was reverence, not disgust, that they were feeling.

Then H's shoulders slumped. "I'm so sorry. I feel like a total asshole now."

"It's okay—"

"No. It's not." She ducked, like she was preparing for a blow. "I . . . got lost on purpose."

There was a beat. The water in the background shimmered, dancing pinpricks of light toward us.

"You said you couldn't remember how you got lost," Gia said slowly.

"I can't, but I remember *wanting* to get lost." H squeezed her eyes shut. She opened them. "When I saw that second tunnel in the bat cave, I remember thinking I was going to wait until you were distracted, then go back and take it."

Gia closed her eyes briefly, looking vindicated but annoyed. "I knew it."

"I planned to mark my way with a Sharpie so I could find my way out, but then I . . . I don't know what happened."

"You therapy'd yourself real good?" Devon said.

"No," H said. "That's the asshole part." She looked at us.

"That adrenaline-level thing . . . I made it up. I'm not trying to get rid of my parasomnia; I'm trying to make it worse."

We stared at her.

"Why in the hell would you try to do that?" Gia asked, finally.

H chewed her lip.

"*H.*"

H looked miserable. "A few years ago, I started having nightmares. And I realized how fascinated my parents were with it all." Her parents, who were psychiatrists. "So I found ways to . . . keep them going."

Gia looked horrified. "You're scaring yourself to get your parents' attention?"

"It's not that, exactly. My family is exceptional. And I've always been unexceptional." She swallowed. "Once you've watched every horror on earth you start to need better scares. Like, real-life ones."

Real-life ones like the ones at Dissent. It explained why she'd been so into this place. It was perfect nightmare fodder.

"I was pretty sure getting lost in a cave would do it." She darted a look at us. "I mean, I researched medication that causes nightmares? But they're hard to get your hands on, and then, I didn't want my parents finding out, and . . ." She chewed on her lip again. "It needed to be organic."

Wow. It was so embarrassing. It was . . . I looked away, uncomfortable.

There was a long silence.

"That's not fair, you know," Gia said. "Who says you're unexceptional? Who decides *that*?"

H looked at her, puzzled. "Um, the same standards that decide you're perfect?"

"I'm not perfect—"

"Yes, you are. You have everything, like my sister." H shook her head. "But I've never had anything. Now I do."

My feeling of discomfort deepened. It mattered that much to her to get her parents' attention that she was willing to endure nightmares? Maybe I'd felt weird when my parents joined that church, stopped fussing over me, but it wasn't like I'd *wanted* them tracking my every move, either.

H dipped her head. "I didn't mean to fuck up this trip."

Gia cleared her throat. "It's not fucked up," she said charitably.

"It's actually getting better and better," Devon remarked.

I cut a glance at her. Devon couldn't be referencing the heart-to-heart turn this had taken. She didn't care about stuff like that.

"I don't expect you to understand," H said. "I just wanted you to know."

A weird look crossed Gia's face. "I do understand," she said. "And for the record, 'being perfect' isn't everything you think it is."

"Yeah, I know: pressures and stuff. But a full ride to Duke on a soccer scholarship is a pretty good consolation prize?"

"First of all, it's not a full ride," Gia said. "And my mom's worked double shifts for the past three years to pay for the rest. I can't let my grades slip a fucking inch, and I have to practice every spare goddamn minute."

"You don't want to go?"

"Of course I want to go! It's basically a dream opportunity."

"So why would you be down here, risking a broken neck?" Devon asked in her weird, forward way. But it was a good question. One I'd been wondering this whole time.

Gia's brow creased. "I told you. I need to challenge myself."

Devon tilted her head.

"I like to know I can stay in control." Gia played with the sand between her feet.

Was that why *she'd* been at Dissent?

Devon said, "That's not how panic attacks work."

Gia pulled her head up. "I don't have panic attacks."

Devon squinted at her.

"Sometimes I feel like I can't catch a breath, is all," Gia said.

"But you're sure it's not asthma," I said. I thought about her putting her head between her knees. She'd done it only a moment ago.

"It's not asthma."

"But how do you know?" Before we knew how to handle my asthma, we had to understand what triggered it. Sometimes it was an irritant I didn't know was present.

"Because I get all hot and my heart races for no reason."

"Oh," H said. "Anxiety."

"No," Gia said. "It's a balance thing. I . . . feel like things are going to fly apart."

"A panic attack," Devon said again.

"They're pretty common," H agreed. "Especially for someone with a lot of pressure on them."

"They're not panic attacks!" Gia snapped. "I have more control than that!"

H's brow wrinkled in consternation. "They aren't a moral failing." She peered closely at Gia. "Were they starting to interfere with your sports or something?"

Gia blinked furiously. She looked away. "I can't not take that scholarship."

We were quiet. I bent my head, thinking. Gia was proving to herself she could gain control of her panic attacks. It explained her weird determination, pressing on even though she was clearly not enjoying any of this.

And H was down here trying to remain a parasomniac. I had no idea how scientific her method was, but she was definitely scaring herself effectively.

I looked at Devon, who claimed to have no fear. She'd said she was testing that. Hadn't she? Why the weird interest in Sasha, what Sasha had been scared of?

"Can we talk about something else?" Gia said. "Like, as an example, getting out of here?"

"Sure." Devon pointed across the lake. "Are you all seeing that?"

We followed her hand. Below the most brilliant part of the cavern roof, halfway up the rock wall, there was a dark spot.

"That black space?" Gia asked, squinting.

"Yeah," Devon said. "It looks like a tunnel."

I peered harder. It was hard to know if it was even a hole from this distance.

"How would we get there?" H asked.

"Swim?"

"It has to be ten feet up," Gia pointed out. "Maybe more."

"Maybe there's a way to climb up to it," Devon said.

"Maybe," Gia nodded. "Those cliffs look pretty sheer, though."

"There might be a path we can't see," H said, chewing her index nail.

"We should go check it out," Devon said. She was contemplating the dark spot on the far rocks again.

"I don't swim well," I said.

"Don't swim well or don't swim at all?" H asked.

"I never had the chance to learn. My lungs."

H and Gia made sympathetic noises, looking at me with concern.

"You'd be amazed at what you can do when your life depends on it," Devon remarked.

I glanced at her. What did she mean by that?

"Our lives don't depend on it," Gia said.

"Not yet," Devon agreed. She lay back in the sand and stretched out, like the thought didn't bother her. "Anyone else tired?"

My skin prickled. Our conversation from before: Devon admitting she'd been responsible for the really dangerous challenges at Dissent. Talking about the lore like she was sure it was real. Like we should've been honest about what we'd seen.

Like she knew?

"I am," H said. She leaned back, resting on her elbows. "Can we check it out in a little bit?"

Gia blinked slowly. "Yeah," she said. "We should rest a second."

I was also suddenly bone tired. Like, wanted-to-sink-into-the-sand exhausted. The cavern was comfortably—strangely—warm. My eyelids fell shut as I sat there. I could feel the others around me quieting.

And in that stillness, I suddenly remembered Devon answering Gia when she'd asked about Devon's hope for this trip:

I want to know what I'm capable of.

At the time I'd assumed she was talking about being able to experience fear, but what if that wasn't it? What if she meant the lengths she'd go to to . . .

The end of that sentence drifted out of my grasp.

"Someone should stay up, right?" I managed, my voice sounding far away. It wasn't a good idea for everyone to fall asleep.

"Yeah." Whoever said that sounded super drowsy.

That scene from *The Wizard of Oz* rose in my mind: Dorothy and her friends falling asleep in the field of poppies.

The witch had done that.

I didn't want to, but I couldn't help it; I curled onto my side in the sand.

Another thought drifted by: It was Devon who'd said she

was tired first—and then we all were. It was like she'd told us to be. Like she gave us the idea? No, that was stupid.

But she had given us Skittles.

The thought dissolved into the dark warmth of my mind, and any desire to care about that—or anything—melted away as sleep rushed in. For me, for all of us.

And we were left to the mercy of the Sublime.

WEDNESDAY, JULY 26, 2:45 P.M.

THE CB WAS CRACKLING LOUDLY. "C451, COME IN." VARGAS tore her attention from the girl, disoriented, irritated at the interruption. "C451."

Draker left his position and jogged back to the patrol car.

Vargas kept her attention on Amelie, trying to parse through this new information. She couldn't remember seeing these "striations" on H's skin. Then, it had been such a mess when they'd arrived, and the paramedics were intent on getting the two to the hospital—she might've missed it. "Devon drugged you?" she clarified.

"It seemed that way," the girl replied.

"You say she was acting weird." Amelie had also, more than once, mentioned Devon's strange interest in Sasha.

"Yeah."

"You thought she was dangerous?"

"Yes. And I tried to convince the other two of that, after."

"After."

"After we went into the lake."

A chill touched Vargas's arms.

Amelie's gaze flicked to the patrol car. "Should I wait for the other deputy or keep going?"

"You went into the lake?"

"We had to."

"Because of the lore? Because you wanted it to . . ." Vargas hedged. "Change something?"

"Oh, no. I mean, yes. I wanted that. But . . ." The girl paused. "Well, Gia wasn't on the trip because she thought the lake could cure her panic attacks."

"She thought *she* could, if she put herself in enough dangerous situations," Vargas clarified.

The girl nodded. "And H . . . well, for all of her talk, I don't think she ever believed in the lore, either. She was like Gia: taking control of her life in a very specific way."

"With her parents."

"Yeah."

"And Devon?"

"Devon's harder to explain," Amelie said. "But she definitely believed the lore. She and I were the same, that way."

That way, but very different, by Amelie's account.

"So why did you go into the lake?" And was this what had happened to Devon?

Amelie's eyes were suddenly guarded. "I need to tell you about the dream I had, first. When we fell asleep onshore."

The car door slammed. Vargas glanced back to find Draker looking at the ground, one hand gripping the back of his neck. It was his thinking stance. He was making no move to head their way. He obviously had information he wasn't sure what to do with.

"Can you hold that thought?" Vargas asked Amelie. "I'll be right back." She hurried to the car. "Hey."

Draker raised his head, took a moment to focus. "That was Cheyenne. I'm not sure how or if this fits."

"Okay."

"The Desmarais accident wasn't the first time Devon Kirneh was questioned by police."

"Oh?"

"Her name comes up from an incident eight years ago. Her brother, who she was alone with at the time, suffered burns from a space heater on the lower half of his body."

Vargas paused. Amelie said Devon had alluded to this; she'd talked about her brother staying in the hospital burn unit. "Okay . . ."

"The mother suspected her daughter had something to do with it. She insisted on a psych eval. The girl was recommended for a stay in Denver Children's."

"Diagnosis?"

"Those records aren't available. But based on the police intake and what Cheyenne searched up, she mentioned . . ." He looked at his chicken scratch. "Alexithymia?"

Vargas squinted. "Never heard of it. A mental disorder?"

"More a personality trait? Characteristics are lack of empathy, lack of ability to understand others' emotions."

Vargas thought about this. It could certainly explain Devon escalating the dares at Dissent with such apathy about the danger, other peoples' safety. Maybe it explained the strange behavior Amelie was recounting.

Or maybe Devon was just an atypical teen girl. Regardless, a personality trait or nonfunctioning amygdala wasn't an indicator of criminality. Drawing conclusions based on atypical behavior wasn't scientific, could be coded in all sorts of prejudice. It was something she had to explain to Draker practically daily.

"You think Devon posed a threat to these girls?" Vargas asked. "Because I'm not convinced this tells us very much."

"I think the important piece is her mother's reaction. Whether or not she was criminally responsible for her brother's accident, her mother thought she could be." He tapped his pen on his notebook. "And perception is important. Amelie, here, has indicated, more than once, that she was starting to distrust Devon."

That was true. And when you were scared, in a situation you had no control over, your perception could get pretty distorted. She *was* unspooling, a bit, by her own account.

"And listen to this." He pulled out his phone. "Soustracs texted. The Rodriguez girl said that Amelie went after Devon." He flicked open his messages and read: "Quote: 'She would've killed her.'"

Vargas raised her eyebrows. "You didn't want to lead with that?"

"I was thinking through this burn accident stuff, trying to figure motive."

"And what was the context?"

"No context. The girls are talking in half sentences, nonsense most of the time. The Kim girl is still on about a monster, so, I mean . . . it's hearsay, at best?" Draker tucked his phone away. "But I'm going to head up the trail, do a prelim search of the area."

"You don't want to wait for the search?"

"I already filled them in with what we know."

Vargas glanced at her watch.

"I'll be quick." He moved to the back of the car to open the trunk, prep for a search. "Then we'll take her in." He waved Vargas off, indicating she should deal with their detainee.

Vargas needed to read the girl her rights. Of course she did. Amelie had led those girls into the cave knowing the dangers with the rain—dangers she'd deliberately not told them about. She was accused of stabbing one of the girls, attacking Devon. Devon was missing. They'd been gone five days. She was omitting information, clearly.

Reading the girl her rights would put a halt to story hour, but maybe that wasn't such a bad thing. The more she listened, the more she felt herself drawn in by the girl's earnestness, to the degree she couldn't help but wonder about this place. Whatever had happened down there . . . well, intense was an understatement. And now she wasn't sure it was a good idea for Draker to head into these woods alone. She couldn't shake the feeling there was something about them. Something preternatural.

"Vargas?"

She blinked, raked her wisps back, and tucked them into her bun.

Get it together.

"On it." What was definitely true: The girl was struggling with telling the story. There was palpable guilt there. And none of this made sense. She strode back to her, her face friendly but noncommittal. "Amelie." Her voice stayed measured. "We've learned some things that change your jeopardy. Do you know what that means?"

The girl regarded her for a moment. "It means it looks like I did something criminal?"

Vargas nodded. "At this point, I have to stop you and read you your rights."

The girl blinked. "Oh."

Vargas started in and finished by reiterating: "You shouldn't say anything more without a guardian present."

"Like my parents?"

"Right."

"They're off the grid," she said, and looked at her hands. "I gave you their number, but I knew you wouldn't be able to reach them."

"We got hold of them. They were headed home."

Amelie's brow furrowed. "Why would they leave before it was over? They've been talking about that stupid retreat for weeks."

"It *was* over," Vargas replied. And at the confused look on Amelie's face, it finally dawned on her . . . "Today is Wednesday, Amelie."

The girl's frown deepened. "No," she said.

Vargas pulled out her phone, flashed the screen at the girl. Her delicate face registered astonishment. Vargas clocked the shift in the girl carefully: Her incredulity seemed genuine. And now as Amelie processed this, her expression was shifting again . . . from amazement to some sort of realization? Vargas couldn't guess what.

"We'll take you to them shortly," Vargas said. "But first, we're going to do a quick search for Devon."

A beam of sun dappling through the leaves overhead caught Amelie across the eyes. Her brow knit again. "You think I'm responsible."

"You don't have to keep talking."

The girl's eyes went back to Draker, who had obviously rethought his preparedness for the search. He was now rummaging in the trunk of the cruiser. He grabbed a can of bear spray and added it to his belt.

"You think I did something to her."

"Like I said," Vargas replied calmly. "We're here to help."

Draker slammed the trunk and headed their way. He passed by them, ignoring Amelie, and paused at the faded trailhead sign.

Amelie looked between the two of them. "The other girls are talking," she realized. "They're okay?"

She did it. Amelie did it.

"Like I said," Vargas repeated. "You can save it for the station."

Amelie shook her head. "No, I can't. I said I'd tell it straightaway. I promised . . ." Then her eyes slid sideways, as though she was remembering something. "Wasp," she said, so quietly Vargas wasn't sure she'd heard her properly. She looked up, a strange expression crossing her delicate features. It wasn't resignation exactly. More like . . . relief.

She turned to Draker. "It's straight up to the Elk's Peak sign. Take a good look at the sign there." And something about her tone . . . "From there you'll head north to the ravine. Look for the witch's charm."

Draker turned, and Vargas could practically see the gears turning in his mind, scanning through the directions he had, weighing the chances she was actually trying to help. He looked at Vargas. "I'll find her."

The girl's eyes had a new brightness. She shook her head. "I don't think so."

"Why?" Vargas pressed without thinking. "Did she drown?"

"No." The girl smiled ruefully. "Devon survived the lake. She's indestructible. Couldn't kill her if you wanted to." She locked eyes with Draker. "Believe me."

Amelie would've killed her.

Draker muttered an expletive under his breath, threw a look at Vargas, then skirted the sign and hurried off up the path. His soft footfall on the wooded track dwindled and went quiet.

And Vargas was left with the girl in the silent parking lot.

Couldn't kill her if you wanted to. Vargas realized with a start that she had repeated the girl's words under her breath.

The girl turned back around and fixed Vargas with that earnest look again. "Do you want to know how I know that?"

IMMERSED

"Breathe, Amelie." My mom was pressing an oxygen mask to *my face.*

School nurse, cocking her head. "Are you here again?"

"Wow, Amelie." Sasha, eight years old, sitting on my bedspread. "You almost died?"

Inhaler pressed into my hand.

"Are you all right? Are you comfortable? Can I get you anything?"

My dad, wheeling the oxygen tank from my room where it had sat, unused, for half a year.

Sitting on my bed, listening to my parents argue in the living room downstairs.

Dissenters, a crowd of them, moving around before us. Swirling, colliding, morphing one into the next. The kaleidoscope shifted, revealed Sasha standing there.

"You aren't special anymore."

My voice. "Get. Out."

Sasha, hooked up to tubes and a breathing machine—no steady, thrumming sound; a skittering. Scritchscritchscritch.

So pale, so still in that hospital bed. Eyes locked on mine. Tubes and wires and bloody teeth, bared.

I sat up. The sand beneath me was damp, heavy. Fog had rolled in from somewhere and was now pressing in close, cloaking the shore.

Where was everyone?

To my right, lying on the sand, was the end of a rope— Gia's rope. I grabbed hold, feeling resistance—it was tied to something I couldn't see.

I got to my feet, grasping the rope, following it, hand over hand, into the mist. A large shape came into view, sharpened as I got close: a boulder.

H was crouched beside it, the rope wrapped around her waist. She was caught like a spider in a web—the other end of the rope disappeared into the fog again.

She darted a look up at me, putting a finger to her lips. "It's hunting," she said. "It'll be here any minute." Her voice dropped to a whisper. "They'll feed me to it."

"Why don't you run?" I asked.

She looked down at the rope. "I can't."

She was right. I continued, hand over hand.

Now the rope was taut, pointing down down down into the sand.

"Amelie." The voice came from my feet. Gia, buried to her waist, her baby-blue Adidas jacket bunched and wrinkled around her torso, her hair disheveled. "I think I'm stuck." The rope was looped around one of her wrists, which she held aloft. "They're . . ." She blinked. "They're going to shoot him. My uncle said he's not right, in the head."

A low growl came from somewhere in the fog.

"Amelie." Her terrified eyes found mine. "Are they going to shoot me, too?"

I reached for the rope and stepped over her, pulling my way into the fog.

The mist furled and wound around me. I pressed through until I was standing on the edge of the blue-hued lake.

Devon was calf-deep in the water, holding the other end of the rope. "Where are the others?" she asked.

"I didn't help them," I said.

"Of course you didn't," Devon replied. "That's not why you came."

"I want to let go of the rope," I said.

"You can't." She looked around. "This is a nightmare."

"It isn't my fault," I said.

She tilted her head. "What isn't?"

"Any of it. This. The accident."

"Is that what you're afraid of?"

The rope between us became taut. It burned my hands, but I couldn't drop it. "I don't know."

Devon shook her head. "I don't know, either. I think . . . I think maybe it's my fault."

"What?"

"All of it. This. The accident." Devon pointed with her free hand at the lake. "We have to go in there, now."

My mind woke before the rest of me, an alert pinging in silently. Around me, everything was quiet—no sound. My eyelids were stuck shut as if with cement, but there it was all the same: A hardwired instinct, the sense that . . .

Something is near.

I could picture the four of us, strewn on the sand, limbs splayed and tucked, bags and coats here and there. The other three were fast asleep, completely unaware.

Something was creeping around among us.

The sand near my head depressed with the weight of a footfall. I clawed my way out of immobility, forcing my eyes to open—

And saw sand stretching toward the star-spattered lake, a large rock sitting on the shore. No, not a rock. A figure crouched at the water. Back toward me, curve of spine visible through a thin shirt, hair a tangle. A wasted frame, pale and unnatural looking. One bruised hand dropped to the side, and long fingers trailed in the water. It was impossible. She couldn't be down here. She couldn't be moving; her neck was, visibly, broken.

My breath seized. I struggled to a sitting position, wide awake now.

"Amelie?" The voice snapped my head to the left. Devon was looming over me. "Are you seeing this?"

My heart stuttered. I looked back for the figure, but she was gone.

"You saw her?" My voice was a rasp, as though I were in a dream and couldn't force it loud enough to be heard. I pushed to my feet. But now I noticed there was no shore, either. We were, very suddenly, at the edge of the lake.

"Who?" H sat up.

Gia, lying to my right as I remembered, squirmed. "I just

had the weirdest dream," she said groggily. She stretched one foot out as she woke, inadvertently putting her foot into the water. She woke up with a start. "The hell?"

The hell was right. Who had moved us closer to the lake?

Devon stepped past H to the edge of the water, gazing at the far side.

"I was dreaming, too," H said. "You were all there."

And I'd been dreaming a moment ago. I shook my head, trying to focus, but as I woke fully, our situation dawned: The lake was larger, the sandy shore smaller. Adrenaline shot through me. "Is the lake rising?"

"Yeah," Devon said. "And fast."

"Rising?" H asked, now fully awake and sitting up.

"How long were we asleep?" Gia asked.

We scanned our surroundings.

"Maybe we're not remembering properly," H suggested, a twinge of desperation in her voice.

"That corner of the shore had a large, jagged rock on the end." Devon pointed. "It's not there anymore."

She was right.

"So . . . ," H said.

"So we need to move," Gia finished.

"Which way?"

To our left the shore had completely disappeared under water. To our right it remained a white sliver, stretching toward the jumble of rocks, but definitely diminished in size.

"The tunnel on the far side," Devon said, pointing. The dark spot was much lower now, or, rather, the water was much higher. Reachable. Maybe.

"We don't even know if it *is* a tunnel," Gia pointed out. "It might be a cave, a dead end. I'm going to check down shore."

"I checked," Devon said flatly. "It's sheer rock walls. And we should get over there before it's underwater, too."

"What about the way we came in?" I asked.

We turned to look at the passage. That part of the beach was obviously lower than the one we'd perched on; the lake had seeped in toward the passage, enclosing us in a crescent of water. There was a large puddle in front of the entrance. I thought about the Eye, pictured us trying to squeeze through while water was climbing.

"Too dangerous," Devon said. "When it rains, the cave becomes unstable, practically ephemeral."

"What—"

"Our best bet is that tunnel over there."

Her comment resonated in a weird way, but I was preoccupied with the idea of crossing the lake. How could she be sure it was a tunnel? I tried to keep the quiver from my voice. "I don't know if I can make it."

Gia pulled her backpack on. "I'll check down shore— maybe there's a way to scale along the walls."

"There's not," Devon said.

"I'll decide if there's not," Gia said, adjusting her headlamp. She headed off.

"Do it fast," H urged. The water was now reaching our toes.

I watched Gia become a penny-sized dot of light as she moved farther along the shore toward the far end, where the cliffs rose to the ceiling. She disappeared behind a column of rocks.

"Nice of her to think about your lungs?" Devon said, sounding amused.

A chill touched my neck.

All at once I wanted to call Gia back. I craned my head, staring in the dark shadows down shore, but there was no movement. Her light had disappeared. Panic crept from my gut up into my chest. It wasn't a good idea to split up.

My dream lingered, ghosting around the outside of my memory. There'd been something about Devon, telling me she was responsible for . . . what? Something wasn't right.

Everything I'd experienced as we searched for the lake— that falling sensation, the breathlessness, that abject terror as something skittered around me—the more I thought about it, the more I was sure it was something Sasha had gone through the night of her accident.

The farther we descended in this cave, the stronger my fear got.

"Wake up, wake up," H was muttering. She'd started to pace in a small line back and forth, darting glances toward the only other way out of the space—the way we'd arrived.

"Yo, H," Devon said. "You're wide awake."

H appeared not to hear her, but my thoughts stalled there. I'd been thinking something about Devon, right before I'd fallen asleep. Something about *why* I'd fallen asleep.

I looked at her. It was like she was waiting for a friend to return from ordering fro-yo. And her calm was nearly as spooky as everything else. So calm, she could fall asleep on the shore. And then we all had.

No. Before that, the Skittles.

"What?" Devon asked.

"Uh, nothing." I turned away, trying to catch hold of my thoughts and knit them together into a coherent picture. I remembered that I'd been wondering if Devon had drugged us. I took a breath, trying to get my pulse to slow. She hadn't, of course. To what end?

But . . . I couldn't shake the feeling that something was wrong.

"Amelie," she said. "What are you thinking?"

I gestured feebly at the lake. "That this isn't the time to learn the front crawl?"

"Are you scared?"

"Of drowning, yeah."

She tilted her head like she was considering this. Clinically. Methodically.

My heart raced. *Had* she drugged us? Maybe she got off on seeing people panicked, afraid. Maybe that's what this trip was for her. It didn't explain our current predicament, of course, but that, too, was needling me in an urgent way. Her explanation of the danger: the cave getting unstable.

Had I told her that?

No. I hadn't told them anything about the dangers of it raining. She and H had postulated theories about flooding, but that wasn't what was bothering me. It was the wording. Unstable.

Henrik had said something like that.

My throat tightened. No. *Ephemeral.* Henrik had used that descriptor, but not on his website . . .

Suddenly a loud blast split the air, freezing us in place. It was sharp, violent, with an echo that reverberated around the cavern.

H turned wide eyes on us. "Was that a—"

"Gunshot?" Devon scanned the dark. "Sure sounded like it."

A gunshot? There was someone with a . . . gun down here? I spun around to face the shadows, moving closer to the other two. In the distance, there was a slow, sliding sound . . . like something heavy was moving down a smooth surface.

"Where's Gia?" H asked.

Yes, where was Gia?

"Gia!" H shouted.

Had she seen that dog again and had to defend herself? No. She wouldn't have a gun in her backpack . . . would she?

H opened her mouth to call again, but the rushed sound of footfalls interrupted her. Gia burst from the shadows, headlight bobbing.

"Gia!"

I threw a hand against the glare. "What was that?"

"We have to go!" She slid to a stop beside us and pulled off her backpack, eyes wild.

"What—"

"We'll have to swim!" It was a panicked command. She

rummaged in the side pocket, retrieved her car keys, and threw the pack to the ground.

"What the hell?"

That soft, sliding sound was growing in volume. I turned away, disoriented but distracted by how loud it was getting . . . and noticed the cliffs behind us were coming apart. Chunks of rock were sliding down, one over the other, rushing in a whoosh and clattering to the sand. The entire wall was crumbling, faster and faster . . .

"Uh" was all I could muster. I couldn't get my tongue to work. It didn't matter; Devon and H had turned to witness the wall disintegrating. The slide was building on itself, rushing debris toward the lake, toward us.

"We're going to get buried," Devon remarked.

"Come on!" Gia splashed into the water to her knees, zipping her keys into her pants pocket, and jerked forward.

"But what—" I was trying to think through my panic. So Gia *didn't* have a gun? Had that sound been the cave falling away?

Devon stripped off her jacket and set it on the sand. "See ya, big green."

H splashed in ahead of us. The panic in her voice had escalated into a squeak. "Gia, wait!"

I couldn't move. My feet were stuck in the bone-white sand.

Devon turned to me as she waded in. She tilted her head and, incongruently, grinned. "Ephemeral was an understatement."

Ice shot through my veins.

"Amelie, come on!" H screamed.

A loud rending sound tore through the cacophony of the rock slide, jolting me from my reverie. I looked back to see a huge chunk of the ceiling dislodge and plummet down.

I yanked my messenger bag off over my head and threw it to the ground, tucking my flashlight—which I hoped was waterproof—into the waist of my jeans. Then I splashed in after them.

The lake bottom dropped away, and I was suddenly trying to keep my head above water. Now that I was floating, my clothes felt four thousand times heavier. I thrashed, trying to dog-paddle, and caught a mouthful of water instead. Fuck. No one to save me here. I gathered my resolve, took a breath, and dropped under the water. For a moment the shock rendered me motionless. Then my foot found the bottom, and I pushed up and with all my force, using the momentum to break the surface and begin paddling forward.

I realized then that it was nothing like an ordinary lake or swimming pool. There was a buoyancy to the water that made floating effortless; my clothes were awkward, but not actually heavy. Water sluiced around me as I moved forward, closing the gap toward the girls. When I was more than half-way across, and surely safe, I looked back.

Beyond the concentrated light of the glowworms overhead, the shore was in dark shadows, but it sounded as though the crumbling wall was finally relenting, slowing its rock shower to a trickle. The beach we'd been standing on was a black mass, probably buried.

I aimed for the others, heart in my throat, my thoughts

spinning. On the cliffs opposite me, that dark mouth beckoned—it was now, clearly, a passageway. Gia was nearly to it, but as I reached Devon and H, I saw Gia stop swimming. She was treading water.

Waiting for us? I craned my neck over the splashing as I paddled, trying to see if there was something preventing her from swimming a direct line to the tunnel. She turned back toward us then, her eyes wide with fear. It looked as though she was struggling. And then, quickly and quietly, she disappeared under the surface.

H let out a cry.

We stopped swimming.

"Gia!" My voice was hoarse.

The water was silent, undisturbed where Gia had disappeared, and the only sound was our labored breathing. H's was escalating to a wheeze. Devon swam forward, searching the water.

Gia didn't surface. A flush of hot fear washed over me. Did she have a panic attack? Had something . . . grabbed her? I steeled myself and paddled toward the spot she'd disappeared, peering for her below the surface. Nothing.

Devon took a huge gulp of air, raised herself in preparation, and sank out of sight. The pocket of air she created broke the surface and ringed out toward H, who looked at me with alarm. For several long moments there was nothing but the sound of her panicked wheezing.

Then the water burst with movement as Devon surfaced, gasping for air.

"Did you see her?" I called.

Devon shook her head, trying to brush her hair from her eyes, and began to move sideways, to a small shelf alongside the cliff wall—away from the tunnel entrance. "There's something down there," she managed. "Come on!"

"But the tunnel—"

"It's right near the tunnel!"

H's eyes were wild. "What is it?"

"I don't know!" Devon called. "Just come this way!"

H began paddling madly toward her, away from the cavern entrance. I hesitated. The tunnel was nearly within reach, and the shelf Devon was urging us toward looked barely big enough to hold us.

There's something down there.

I changed direction and began making my way toward the cliff walls. Devon had clambered up on the shelf and was beckoning to us. The water suddenly felt heavy, though, as if it had turned viscous, like syrup. I struggled toward her, could see H doing the same.

The water began to churn around us, and H hesitated, scanning below the surface in fright.

"Come on!" Devon urged.

I paused—what was she looking at?—and felt an impossibly strong force from beneath grab at my ankles, my calves. I pulled upward with all my might, trying to stay on the surface, and there was a split second where I saw a terrified look in H's eyes, saw her struggling the same . . .

She disappeared below the surface.

I had a split second to take a breath. Then I was dragged under, too.

Black. Nothing but black and that insistent pull. Down and down.

Pressure, in my ears, in my head. Disorienting and suffocating.

Open your eyes.

A stream of bubbles rushed past, chased by a second, larger stream. Clouds of murkiness and then . . .

Blue-light infusion around me, that tugging feeling, persistent, unbreakable.

I floundered, threw my hands out to pitch forward and peer down. Nothing; no deadly tentacle or set of jaws around my leg, yet I was captive. I strained upward with all my might but continued traveling to the bottom of the lake.

And then I heard a sound, an impossible, rasping sound, under the water.

Scritchscritchscritch.

My lungs needed oxygen, but fighting the pull was impossible. I was at the bottom now—dark sand so close I could stretch my tiptoes to stand.

And then, all at once, the force let go.

I was free, drifting in the iridescent blue.

Go now.

But wait. There was someone here. Blurry, obscured by the murky depths. Gia? H? I pushed toward the figure.

Long, stringy hair. Back to me.

Scritchscritchscritch. Louder and louder.

ScritchscritchSCRITCH.

A cacophony of new sound enveloped me: laughter, crunch of tires on gravel, wind rushing, water lapping. A tug from inside now: my lungs, straining. Begging for air. I pushed forward, reaching a hand to turn her . . .

Her head snapped around to look at me. Impossibly fast. Impossibly angled, it had swiveled backward on her body. One eye was gone, and her skin was sallow and loose, melting from her face like candle wax. Skin mottled, fingers blackened; a rotting, animated corpse, reaching for me. She opened her mouth to scream, and a black, dusty cloud poured forth, enveloping me.

I clawed away, trying to push for the surface, but she had me now, her limbs tangling with my limbs in the darkness. I writhed and fought. The water cleared, and I pushed away from black glossy hair that swirled to reveal ivory skin.

H. Her eyes were wide, her mouth open, coughing giant bubbles of air.

That pull came again, and we were bashed together once more, roiled about, upside down. Then she was gone, and I slammed into something sharp and solid, was pulled along a rough surface—I could feel rock rushing past and that tugging feeling in my lungs becoming a desperate jerk. I needed air . . .

Suddenly I was rocketed forward and up. I burst through

the surface of the water with a ragged gasp, emerging into warm pitch black.

I coughed, splashing, treading water. With effort, I stilled, trying to listen. Other than my panting, it was silent around me. Muggy.

My flashlight. I fumbled for it in my waistband as I clumsily treaded water. I clicked it on and held it above the surface to scan my surroundings.

The light revealed rock walls on all sides of me, maybe ten feet away at most, and a small low shelf to my right. Rock above me here, too. I was in a small cavern with a low ceiling. I paddled toward the ledge, banged my shins into something hard before I reached it. I fished around with a hand and found a submerged outcropping of rock, a kind of stair to the ledge. Before I could climb onto it, the water beside me erupted as something burst through the surface.

I swung my light around and found a wild-eyed H, who took a staggered breath and exhaled it in a loud cry. She started to thrash.

"It's me!" I called, trying to catch hold of her arm. "It's Amelie!"

She stopped struggling for half a second, then began splashing toward me in a panic. "Get me out! I need to get out!" She pushed past me. Her feet found purchase on the submerged shelf, and she scrabbled ashore, crawling up and away from the edge.

I followed. The ledge wasn't much, but it was out of the water. We scrambled back and huddled together, soaking wet and breathing hard, staring at the inky black. I shone my flashlight around the little cavern, trying to shut the horror of what had been under the lake from my mind.

We were trapped in this little cave, and the water was still rising.

The way out was obviously under one of these walls, but there was a strong undercurrent to the water—how would we swim against it? We'd been pushed under rock that separated the larger lake from this tiny atrium, but there could be dozens of chambers like this around the lake. I had no idea how long I'd been underwater.

Or what had dragged us down.

Sasha.

My chest tightened.

No. Of course not.

H whimpered loudly, and I shone my light at her, which caused her to jerk her head away from the glare, exposing her neck. I sucked in a breath. There were more striations on her skin—marring her entire neck now. She tugged at her shirt, revealing that the marks continued down her other shoulder. These were deeper than the others; they were bleeding.

"It hurts," she whispered. She was shivering violently, and her eyes were distant.

I stared at the blood, the scratches, feeling my breath coming in tiny, painful sips. And then my flashlight died, encasing us in darkness.

Panicked, I banged at it with my palm.

Nothing—we were engulfed in the black. H moaned, then started to cry.

I tried to suck in a deeper breath, but the dark was like a

sickly warm blanket pressing in from all sides, stealing what little oxygen remained in this tiny atrium. That sensation of my chest being squeezed by an invisible vise was back, worse than before, and I had the irrational thought that if I could just see, I could break free. Desperately I banged my light on the ground. It flickered once. Twice.

"It's here." I could feel H rocking beside me, blowing out her breath in a sound that was between a moan and a singsong.

Bang.

The light winked back on. Air rushed into my lungs, and I exhaled loudly with relief. Then the water near us stirred softly, and H let out an earsplitting scream, pushing back into the rock wall like she was going to bust through it, as I swung my light toward the water. Nothing.

"It's here," H whispered.

It wasn't. *She* was.

No.

There was nothing here, nothing *down there*. We'd been caught in a kind of current and panicked. First Gia, then H and me. And Devon? Devon. That moment before we'd run into the water, I'd realized something about her. Something about—

"What was that?" H asked in a panic, grabbing for my flashlight and jerking my arm to shine the light at the water. The water was still. "It's here, oh my god, I know it's here!"

I forced myself to breathe, clinging to the last of my composure. I dug in the pocket of my jeans and produced the knife Devon had given me. "Here," I said. "Take this."

She stared at it like it was a foreign object. I opened it up and offered it to her, handle first. She frowned. "Where did you get my knife?"

My light blinked out again. Total darkness.

H whimpered. I banged at the flashlight—it had worked last time—but now, nothing.

A soft splash nearby. I felt H freeze beside me as water lapped at the rock.

A deep inhalation. There was something in the water. It had surfaced beyond the ledge.

H started to make tiny strangled sounds, like she couldn't breathe. I squeezed back farther and hit my flashlight again. Or maybe light would attract it?

Whatever it was sounded close now. It sounded like it had found purchase on the rock shelf and was slithering ashore, not two feet from us.

I had to see. If we were going to die in this tiny cavern, I needed to know how. I banged my flashlight hard on the ground as the thing labored onto the rock and crawled toward us. H pushed against me, darting forward with a sudden scream.

A different cry rang out, one of pain and surprise, and my flashlight blazed on, revealing H holding Devon's knife in a trembling hand.

At her feet, Gia. She was collapsed on the rock shelf, dark hair splayed over her face, hand gripping her leg, gushing blood.

H DROPPED THE KNIFE. IT CLATTERED TO THE ROCK SHELF.

"Oh my god," she said, covering her mouth with a trembling hand.

"Gia!" I fell to my knees and scrambled toward her, grabbing the knife where it lay. My relief at seeing her was smothered by new alarm as all of the blood registered. Gripping her thigh, Gia pulled her head up, and her hair fell away from her face. She was staring at us like she'd never seen us before. Her skin was ashen.

She looked at me, at the knife.

"Why?" she asked, her voice hoarse.

"It was an a-accident," I stammered. I quickly folded the knife and pocketed it, then thrust my flashlight at H. "Here." I tried to pull Gia into a sitting position. She complied, dazed, pushing herself up and moving away from the water to lean back against the wall. She had one hand clamped to her leg, but as she sat back, her grip relaxed. The blood bubbled, frothing between her fingers. My stomach turned. I pulled my hoodie off and pressed it to her thigh.

"It's going to be okay." I pushed hard on the wound, wondering if I should make a tourniquet or what. I'd never taken first aid.

H sat abruptly and started to moan, flashlight clasped between her knees. It lit the low ceiling, casting us in shadows.

Gia looked ghastly. Her eyes were absent. Shock. She was going into shock.

"Gia! Hey!" I said sharply. What should you do with a person going into shock? Give them a task? "You need to press hard, here." I took her hands and put them on top of my hoodie. "We need to stop the bleeding."

She nodded, her face pale.

I pressed down on her hands. "It's okay. It'll stop." I was trying to convince myself. Because what if it didn't? "It's not that bad. It's really not."

Incredibly, my assurances were working: She sat up a bit and looked at her leg. "I . . . I couldn't stay on the surface," she said in a confused tone.

"It was the Skinflayer," H whispered from the corner. "I told you it was down here, but you didn't believe me."

"H—"

"Devon saw it! In the water, she saw it."

No. My earlier thoughts were flooding in now. About how we'd all fallen asleep after Devon had given us candy. And there was something else . . .

"She said something was blocking the tunnel. That's what grabbed us!" H insisted.

Gia shifted and winced. "Nothing grabbed me. I just couldn't stay on the surface. It was like some weird undertow."

Undertow. Yes, that's what I'd thought. And it hadn't grabbed us until Devon had gotten us to change course. A chill ghosted over my skin as the dots started connecting again.

"Little help?" Gia interrupted my thoughts, her hands full with the makeshift bandage. She was pressing down like she was determined to stop the bleeding in record time. Her headlamp was hanging around her neck, and I pulled it gently up, positioning it on her forehead again. The Gia I knew was resurrecting. I clicked the switch, and it sputtered on, lighting up the small space further. But not by much.

"My batteries are dying," Gia said. "We can't stay here."

"I'm not going back in there," H said adamantly.

"H. The water is rising."

H's eyes filled with tears again. "But . . ." Her breath hitched. "I don't want to see it. Please."

I expected Gia to lay into her, tell her it was in her head and that she didn't have a choice. Instead, she looked away, uncomfortable.

H noticed. "What happened on the shore? With that gunshot?"

Gia squished her eyes shut.

"What happened?" H demanded.

Gia's face cracked, and her upper lip quivered. "I saw it again."

"The dog?"

She nodded. "Kibby."

"What?"

"Kibby. My old German shepherd." She opened her eyes. "When I went to look for another route to the tunnel, he was there."

"Your . . . dog is here?" I clarified.

Gia shook her head, her eyes desperate. "Kibby died ten years ago."

Ten years ago.

I cleared my throat. "So there was a dog that looked like him?"

"No," Gia said, her voice rising. "It was him. He was dead, but he was alive—"

"Gia—"

"It was him! He had the same collar with his gold tags on it. And he . . ." Her face distorted with terror. "He was rabid. Just like when he died."

H swore under her breath.

I stared at Gia.

"You asked, okay? You wanted to know? So now you know." Her bottom lip trembled as she turned her attention back to her leg, pressing with hands that now seemed fragile.

"This is what happened to those girls. This is why they didn't come back," H said. Her voice rose. "We need to get out of here." She glanced around the cavern wildly, but her gaze froze on Gia's leg. "The Skinflayer smells blood," she whispered.

"Shut up!" Gia hissed.

"It'll smell you! You'll lead it straight to us!"

"Just—" Gia took a staggered breath. "Shut—" She stopped dead and went stark white. Her head dropped back, and she started to gasp like a fish that suddenly found itself onshore.

"Gia!"

"Help," she rasped.

I looked helplessly at H, who was frozen, staring at Gia wide-eyed. In the light Gia's pallor shifted—becoming a grayish blue. "What do we do?"

H snapped out of her panic spiral. She thrust the flashlight at me and scrambled toward Gia, grabbing her behind the neck. "Gia. Breathe. You're okay. You're fine."

Gia's eyes locked on H's.

"You're okay," H said. She put her forehead to Gia's. "You're here. I'm here."

Gia's wheezes slowed gradually.

"You're fine."

Gia swallowed, regaining calm. "I'm fine," she repeated with some effort, between breaths. She whispered it again and again, until she was breathing normally.

H let go of her and pulled back. "Okay?"

Gia nodded. She let her head drop back against the rock.

Gia's panic attack had jarred H from her terror for the moment. But I was cycling back on H's words: *This is what happened to those girls.*

A deep dread was seeping into my core. *Face yourself— your darkest fears.* My dream resurfaced, cycling through my mind.

"It isn't my fault," I said.

Devon tilted her head. "What isn't?"

"Any of it. This. The accident."

"Is that what you're afraid of?"

I squished my eyes tight shut.

Devon had said reconciling that would give us what we

wanted from the Sublime. But what else had she said? Something I needed to remember . . .

When it rains, the cave becomes unstable, practically ephemeral.

Henrik had told me the exact same thing.

My eyes flew open as I connected those two facts.

"Hey!" The voice was muffled, resonating from somewhere outside the little antechamber we were in. "Gia! Amelie! H!" Devon. H's eyes met mine.

I watched H suck in a breath to call back.

"Don't!" I hissed.

Her eyes dimmed with confusion. Gia stared at me but, thankfully, seemed to no longer possess the energy to shout.

"Stay quiet! Please!" I whispered to them urgently.

"But why—"

"Just trust me!"

"H? Gia . . ." The voice dwindled into nothing.

"It was Devon," H whimpered. "She could've helped us."

But I remembered now. I remembered what I'd realized as we'd plunged into the lake. "She's not going to help us."

"Why would you say that?" Gia's voice had returned.

"Remember she said she was trying to see what she was capable of down here?" I stood. Yes, it was all coming clear now. It was so obvious. "We don't need to be afraid of these . . . things we're seeing."

"What do you mean?"

And I finally gave voice to what I'd been piecing together, what, in retrospect, I'd suspected ever since her butterfly and ants story: "We need to be afraid of Devon."

GIA SAT UP STRAIGHTER, LOOKING MORE PRESENT THAN SHE had since she'd surfaced. "Explain."

"Devon catfished me," I said. "She's Henrik." The pieces were knit together in my mind now. "She's probably already been here to chart the tunnels."

"Chart the tunnels?" Gia frowned. "Amelie—"

"She found the path to the cave no problem because she knew it was there! She stole H's knife, tried to stab me— maybe not to hurt me, maybe just to scare me, which is what she's been doing all along. She's been drugging us—"

"*What?*" Gia said.

"The candy. It's making us see things! It made us fall asleep on the shore and have weird dreams."

"Wait—"

"It's why H is seeing this Skinflayer, why you're seeing Kibby. She knew it was dangerous down here in the rain—she brought us *because* it was going to be dangerous!"

"Slow down! None of this makes sense."

"Yes it does! She pretended to see H's monster in the lake. She knew about the undertow and lured us to a place she knew we'd get rolled under. She hung back; she was obviously taking a different path to get to that entrance. She knew."

"You're telling us she's been here before?" H asked. "She knows the lake?"

"Yes!"

"She couldn't have known we'd have to swim it!" Gia argued.

"Unless that tunnel was the only way out. Then we would've had to swim anyway. It was more urgent with the rising waters. She didn't suddenly spot that tunnel; she knew it was there!"

They both looked utterly confused.

"I'm telling you: She's orchestrated everything."

"But how could she orchestrate everything we've . . . seen?" H asked.

"By drugging us and then getting in our heads!" I said. "First the Jolly Ranchers. Then she got you to talk about your worst nightmare on the way in, then made some comment about the caves being its perfect habitat."

"But—"

"She kept asking you about the dog," I said to Gia. "And if we were drugged—"

"But I didn't take a Jolly at the cave entrance," Gia protested. "And I saw Kibby after that."

The same thing had happened to me, sort of, but . . . "You *thought* you did. So she kept asking, and then, after the Skittles, you were sure you did."

They stared at me, trying to process. It was a lot of information, but it was so clear, so *obvious* now.

Gia shook her head. "I don't know. This is some serious mad scientist shit. It feels impossible."

"It makes more sense that your dead dog is down here?"

"But I don't get it," H said. "Why would she do all of this?"

"Because she's a psychopath!" The air in the little chamber was warming up with our breath. Our carbon dioxide. Talking as much as we were wasn't helping our oxygen situation. "She's set all of this up to toy with us."

"This sounds a bit like your theory of H's hidden cameras," Gia said.

"My what?"

Gia ignored her. "It's a reach, Amelie. Devon is a psycho who lured us down here for her own amusement?"

"She said herself that her amygdala is messed up. She obviously likes messing with people, putting them in dangerous situations. You know what she was doing at Dissent. I'm telling you: She's Henrik."

Silence fell, but they seemed unconvinced.

"What's the alternative?" I asked, exasperated.

"I don't know! Maybe . . . maybe there's some weird poisonous gas down here that is making us freak out?" Gia waved her hands around.

"Like the plant spores in that godawful horror *The Happening*?" H asked. "Unlikely."

"Super unlikely," I agreed vehemently. Something dark stirred in my chest, and my next thought burst out, my voice thick with emotion: "Honestly? She probably had something to do with Sasha's accident."

Indecision flickered across Gia's face. "But they cleared everyone who was there."

"So? The cops might've missed something. You heard her—talking about how scared Sasha would've been that night? It was like she knew something."

"This is so crazy." Gia pressed her hands to her temples and closed her eyes. "I need to think."

I appealed to H. "That story she told about the ants and the butterfly? It's like that—she's making us devour ourselves. She practically *told* us she was going to do it."

"Why would she tell us a story that hints at what she's about to do?" H asked.

"That's what psychopaths do!" They weren't convinced yet. I needed to hit the Sasha note again. "And if my cousin—"

"Wait." Gia's eyes flew open. "You said she *knew* that the rains made the cave dangerous."

"Yeah."

"How does that prove that she's Henrik?"

I stumbled for an explanation. "H-he used the same word she did: ephemeral."

"Meaning, Henrik told *you* the cave would be unstable if it rained." Gia pushed herself more upright. She was regaining her composure. Her strength.

A flush coursed through my body.

"You *knew* it was dangerous down here," she stated. "And you didn't tell us."

"I . . ." I swallowed hard. "I didn't remember."

H looked at me, horrified. "We talked about it. *Devon* brought it up!"

"The fact that Devon brought it up is just more evidence she's a psycho!" I protested.

"But *you* said nothing!" Gia said.

"I obviously didn't think it was a real possibility!"

"Well your inability to identify real possibilities means we are now about to die in an underwater cavern!" Gia snapped.

"Look, I'm sorry about that," I said. "But the important part is that Devon's the reason we're down here, and Devon's the reason we're scared out of our minds."

I looked at them plaintively. They *had* to see this for what it was.

"I mean, that would actually be good," H ventured, finally. "Far easier than meeting up with the Skinflayer." Her brow knit. "Although maybe we should consider what to do if we do. You know, just in case."

"Enough!" Gia cut H off. "None of this is helping us get out of here."

I drew a breath. The air around us definitely felt thinner. It was making me feel dizzy. "We don't have much time," I said.

"Agreed." Gia looked at the end of the shelf we were on and shone her headlight up. At the top of the rock there was a strange shadow. "Is that a hole?" She pointed.

"I can check it out," I offered quickly. I needed them on my side; I needed to be the one to go.

Gia pulled her headlamp off and passed it to me.

I gave my flashlight to H. "Shine this on the wall?" Then I adjusted the headlamp length, secured it on my head, took a breath, and moved close to the wall. There were a few little cracks and crevices that could be used as handholds, and the climb wasn't too high. I started up. It was tricky, but not impossible, and would be easier for someone taller and stronger. I was at the top, about twelve feet up, in a matter of seconds, and was rewarded with the discovery that the shadow was indeed a hole. I peered through. My headlight lit up another chamber with a small dark pool of water, a little shore, and a tunnel entrance about twenty feet farther along.

"This is a way out!" I called over my shoulder in excitement.

"Really?" H's voice rose in hope.

The space to crawl through was small and the drop was sheer, but maybe if we held on to hands and lowered the first two people down, those two could catch the last? Or . . . wait, did Gia still have the rope attached to her belt? She did. I descended clumsily. "We can make it," I said.

Gia got to her knees but cried out when she put pressure on her wounded leg to stand. "I can't climb," she said, sucking in a breath. "There's no way."

"Well, we need to figure something out," H said, pointing at the water, which was now lapping gently over the edge of our shelf. It had risen in the short time we'd been arguing. The cavern was feeling unreasonably warm; oxygen was waning, despite the small opening at the top of that wall.

"Wait until the water rises to where Gia can swim through the passage?" I suggested.

"Wait until the other side of the wall is also flooded, you

mean?" Gia said. "That's a spectacularly bad idea. We need to go now."

H nodded reluctantly.

We looked at one another, one solution hanging awkwardly between us.

"You need to leave me here," Gia said.

THE WATER LAPPED GENTLY AT THE LEDGE.

"No," H said emphatically. "If we were in a horror movie, we'd lose all points with the audience—ditching a wounded friend? We'd be sealing our own doom."

Gia's grave expression wavered. "Um, we're not in a horror movie."

"Aren't we?"

"We'll figure something else out," I said, trying to sound confident. H referencing horror movies was a good sign and Gia was back to her practical self, but I knew, deep down, that I'd lost their confidence. I needed to regain it somehow.

I closed my eyes, picturing the adjacent cavern in my mind. There was a pool of water over there, just like this one. Maybe it was a puddle, or maybe it was being fed by this one. If so, the most likely scenario was that this shelf of rock we were sitting on intersected it. Which meant . . .

I turned around. "The water on that side of the wall is probably the same water as this." I pointed at the pool in our cavern. "Which means there's probably a way to get under this wall to the other side."

"How far is it?" Gia asked.

"The wall isn't very thick at the top," I said. "Maybe a

foot?" But who knew how thick it widened to underwater, or where the passage might be?

"We can use my rope," Gia said. "If you're wrong, at least we'll be able to find our way back here."

H let out a moan. "I don't like this."

"There's nothing in the water," I said.

"It's pretty much our only option," Gia said.

"I'll go first," I said. "You keep the flashlight and hang on to the end of the rope. I'll call to you when I'm on the far side. You can help Gia into the water."

"But what if it isn't that simple?" H asked. "I mean, can you hold your breath that long? Your lungs—"

"I'm going to get us out of here," I assured her.

Gia was already undoing the rope. H reluctantly took it from her and unwound it. It looked to be about fifteen feet long. Long enough, hopefully.

I wrapped one end around my wrist, and H followed me, holding the other end, as I crawled to the far edge of the shelf and prepared to lower myself into the water. All I needed to do was duck below the rock and find a passage, push to the far side. My heart was beating triple time as I sat, dangling my legs, then pushed off and dropped in.

I treaded water for a quick second, took a deep breath, then bobbed under the surface, keeping my hands in front of my face, pushing myself as quickly as I could down the rock shelf and feeling for its underside. I found it straight-away—it was only about two feet below the surface—but before I could push farther to get below it, a force grabbed me and pulled me violently sideways. I turtled, covering my head with my hands, and had the presence of mind to grip the rope tightly as I was thrust upward and against the underside of hard rock.

Panic shot through me. It had been so calm on the surface in the cavern, I hadn't banked on the undertow still being here. I scraped along the rock, bashing against it. All at once the rope struck me as idiotically useless. H wouldn't even know I was in trouble until it went completely taut, and then what was she going to do? She'd never be able to pull me back against the drag. I held my breath and squeezed my eyes tight.

The rope was only about fifteen feet long, so it had to be all over soon, didn't it?

But no, it didn't. The initial tug might've ripped the end from H's grip. The undercurrent might have pulled me in a different direction. It was possible that the water here went on for miles beneath the rock without a break, that I would be traveling this underground current long after I'd run out of oxygen, long after my corpse had swollen twice its size and turned blue—

Scritchscritchscritch.

Rodents in the walls, creatures rustling behind peeling wallpaper.

Gnawing, scrabbling, biting.

What was Sasha afraid of?

My chest constricted violently, like I'd slammed backward on something and lost my air, and I fought the urge to gasp, knowing even in my panic that I would only swallow water. Then, all at once, I burst through the surface.

I flailed, disoriented, but quickly realized I'd made it into the adjacent chamber. There was the small sandy shore, and beyond that the tunnel entrance. Where someone was standing.

I squinted, rubbed the water out of my eyes with one hand.

Neck at that terrible angle . . . My breath seized. I blinked hard.

"*Amelie!*" Gia's voice was muffled.

A slight breeze puffed over my skin, like the tunnel had let out a breath, and she disappeared. Fuck. *Fuck.*

"*Amelie!*"

"Yes!" I croaked. "I made it!" I could feel the rope jerk as someone dropped into the water on the far side, and I grabbed hold tight. My small frame was tugged backward a bit as she began her underwater journey.

H surfaced a second later.

"Oh!" she said. She wasn't even breathing hard. "That wasn't so bad."

"Gia was supposed to be next." I darted a look over my shoulder at the tunnel entrance.

"She insisted I go. She didn't believe I would." H peered at me. "What's wrong?"

"N-nothing. My eyes played tricks on me when I surfaced. I thought I saw . . ."

"What?"

Sasha. I squished my eyes tight. "Devon." I opened them. H was peering at me. "But I didn't." That expression on H's face: She knew I was lying. I looked past her, raised my voice. "Gia, come on!"

H turned, distracted for the moment. "Hold on tight to the rope!"

"And the flashlight!" I added. The headlamp was barely casting a glimmer now.

The water lapped gently at the rock wall.

"Gia?"

Nothing.

"Gia!"

Her voice came back, echoey and haunted. "*I'll slow you down.*"

"What?"

"*I'm too slow. My leg.*"

"What? You're fine. Come on."

"*It's really bad.*" Even muffled, her voice was tight, high. Oh shit. Was she crying?

"We'll get it fixed!" I called. "We need you over here to do that."

"*No! I'm useless now!*" she screamed.

H and I looked at each other. There was no way either of us could negotiate that current and get back to her. I squinted up at the wall of rock that I'd climbed on the other side. It was definitely sheer, like I'd thought. We were going to have to talk her over.

But before H or I could even try, a terrible moaning sound echoed through the small space above us. Gia? Or—

It came again. A low cry, infantile. A child was crying, on the far side of the wall.

"Gia?" H whispered.

Her voice rasped out, choked with panic. *"He's here! Oh god, he's here!"*

"Gia!" H yelled.

A violent tug on the rope yanked me forward, and I bashed my face into the back of H's head. We were pulled forward the remaining foot, pressed against the wall. Something was tugging from the far side.

"They're going to shoot him!" Gia's voice came, hysterical, terrified. *"They'll shoot me, too! They're coming! I can't—"*

"Gia!" H screamed. "Wrap the rope around your wrist! Do it now!" She grabbed hold of the portion of the rope she'd dropped and said to me, "We're going to pull her through." She put her feet against the wall, and I realized she was going to use it as leverage.

"But—"

"She can't do it by herself!"

I obeyed, tightening my grip, planting my feet the same. I was worried we'd rip the rope from her grasp. And then what?

A growl emanated from the other side of the wall, primal and guttural. *"They're here! They're—"*

"Grab the rope tight!" H screamed again. The rope went taut. "Now!"

We pushed ourselves off the wall, yanking just as the sound of a gunshot exploded beyond the wall. It reverberated out through the small space at the top as we splashed down and the rope went slack.

Crumbling rock echoed within the antechamber, followed by a sickly silence.

I looked at H in horror.

Then movement erupted near us as Gia burst through the surface, sputtering. She was clutching the flashlight in one hand, illuminating her panicked eyes.

"Gia!"

H and I splashed toward her, grasping for her arms. I took the flashlight, and together we paddled the short distance to the shallow end. Coughing and wheezing, Gia crawled ashore.

We followed, watching as she collapsed to the rock floor, then pulled herself to a sitting position, wrapping her arms around her one good leg and putting her head to her knee.

"Are you okay?"

Gia didn't respond.

I set the flashlight on the ground and coiled the rope with shaking fingers, and then set it beside her. I was shivering uncontrollably, and my chest was still squeezed tight.

H took off her jacket and started to wring it out. "Kibby?" she asked Gia quietly.

Gia looked away.

"She had a panic attack," I said. And I'd panicked, too, under the water, which was why I saw Sasha when I surfaced.

They must face themselves, their darkest fears.

Stop. We needed to get out of here before Devon found us and . . . well, I didn't want to find out what she'd do when she did.

"Then what was that gunshot sound?" H demanded.

"The cavern caved in. Like before." I rubbed my chest, feeling out of breath. "Is the air thin here? It feels thin."

H didn't respond, so I pushed myself to standing. I needed to stay focused, keep them focused. We couldn't let our imaginations interfere with getting out of here. "We need to keep moving." I contemplated the tunnel, which, I could see now, forked immediately. "I feel like this," I said, pointing to the one on the left, "heads back toward the direction of the lake?" And Devon. "So I think we should go right."

"Amelie," H said. "Slow down. Gia needs—"

"I'm fine," Gia said. She had pulled my hoodie off and was tying her own around her leg, replacing the bandage. She held mine out to me. "We need to go."

"Wait," H said. "Just wait a goddamn second. We're not going to talk about what just happened?"

"We did: panic attack." I wrung out my hoodie and tied it around my waist.

"A panic attack that triggered a cave-in? Twice? I don't know if you've noticed that mine, also, have had effects that are pretty freaking corporeal?" She pulled her head to the side and tilted her chin. It looked like she'd been attacked by a thornbush.

Something flashed in Gia's eyes. She got clumsily to her feet and started to tie the coil of rope to her belt. "We're wasting time—"

"The characters who die in horror movies are always the ones who don't take time to figure out what's happening!" H

snapped. "They run pell-mell from one danger to the next."
She crossed her arms over her chest. "It's, like, the most cli-
chéd thing ever."

"For the last time—"

"Stupid choices are stupid," H said. "And I'm not moving
until we talk about why we're seeing what we're seeing." She
looked at Gia. "You said, 'They're going to shoot him.'"

Gia's jaw worked.

H waited, unmoved.

Gia's eyes flashed again, but it looked like she was trying
to cling to her anger. She failed, her expression melting into
resignation. "Fine," she said. "Fine." She took a breath. "We
got Kibby when I was four. We lived in a shitty neighborhood
back then, and my mom was putting herself through nursing
school, so we were home alone a lot, so she got him as security.
I loved him so much . . ." Pause. Pain flickered across her
face. "One day, he got out of the yard. Lost for a week. We
were so worried. But then one day he returned, and I was so
happy to see him. But he'd"—she swallowed—"contracted
rabies. I didn't know; I realized, too late, he was different. He
attacked me, and my uncle who was visiting got the shotgun
from the safe and shot him." She blinked furiously. "I'd never
heard of rabies, and no one explained it to me. My uncle just
said, 'He wasn't right in the head; can't have something like
that around.' It wasn't until I was a teenager that I realized
what actually happened."

There was a pause.

H bit her lip, like she was thinking. "You also said, 'They'll
shoot me, too.' Why?"

Are they going to shoot me, too?

"I mean, I don't know—I was freaked out?"

My unease was blossoming.

"Under the Sublime," H said. "My parents were there."

"Your parents?"

"They were there to feed me to the Skinflayer. Part of their research. It's what happens in my nightmare."

They'll feed me to it.

How could I have dreamed this? How could I possibly know that's what they were afraid of?

"Jesus," Gia said.

H's mouth pulled into a half smile that trembled at one corner. "And the crazy thing is, in my nightmare, I think I deserve it?" Her eyes were suddenly red. "I think . . . I think that's what I'm most scared of. That I deserve it."

I think maybe it's my fault. Devon, in my dream. *All of it. This. The accident.*

Gia's brow knit. "Admitting what you're scared of," she murmured.

She was repeating what Devon had said. She'd said it was the only way to get what we needed from the Sublime.

Gia looked at us. "What if—"

"What are we doing?" I broke in. "This isn't helping us get out of here."

"It might be the only way we get out of here," H countered. "The lore says something about facing yourself, your darkest fears, right? So if that's—"

"Devon brought us here to mess with us!" I practically shouted. "Devon is Henrik!"

H tilted her head. "And you're *sure* she's Henrik because . . ."

"Because she knew about the rain!"

"*You* knew about the rain," Gia said. She shifted her weight. "Maybe *you're* Henrik."

"What?" I stared at her. "Why would I bring you all here?"

"Why would Devon?"

"Because—" Oh. She meant *I* was the psychopath. Anger and desperation sparked in me. "If I was crazy, I would've left you back in that cavern."

"Maybe you don't know you're crazy," H said. "We're just, like, collateral damage."

"Devon—"

"Devon could've guessed by the way the shore was flooding that the caves would become unstable," Gia said. "The bigger question is: You knew, so why didn't you tell us?"

"I didn't remember—"

"Bullshit!" Gia snapped.

"You didn't have to come!" I shot back. "You had a choice. I gave you the option to turn around."

"With respect," H said. "'Turn around if you're scared' and 'turn around if you don't want to drown to death' are fairly different options."

"I didn't think drowning was a real possibility! Obviously!"

"That's because you were only thinking about yourself," Gia said.

"Um, you were so determined to reach your stupid goal that you led us past the point of no return."

"Oh Jesus, Amelie. First H was messing with us, now Devon is, and the only reason we're here is because *I* made the wrong choice? You constantly accuse others—"

"I do not—"

"Because *you* won't take responsibility." Her eyes flashed with disdain. "Doesn't it get exhausting, looking for someone to blame?"

The words hit me like a physical blow. My mouth opened. Closed. I didn't do that, did I? I grasped at what I knew to be true: "I'm not Henrik," I said. "And if you haven't noticed, we're doing exactly what Devon wants: devouring ourselves."

Gia uncrossed her arms, uncertainty flickering on her face.

"But why did Devon *need* to be Henrik?" H pressed. "That's what I don't get. Why trick you?"

I barked a humorless laugh. "Which of you would've followed *Devon* into the middle of nowhere?"

They exchanged a glance.

"Good point," Gia conceded.

H was studying me. "What are you seeing? What did Devon 'put' in your head?"

"Why do you need to know?"

Gia spoke up. "Maybe you need to reconcile whatever you're scared of—"

"We are not using the psycho's psycho theory to make sense of this!"

"Make sense of what?" H crossed her arms. "Just tell us and I'll drop it."

She and Gia waited.

I shifted under their scrutiny. "Devon keeps talking about Sasha. So I . . . saw her."

"What scares you about Sasha?" H asked.

"Nothing! I think . . ." I sucked in a breath, feeling that vise grip my chest again. "I think I'm afraid if she dies, it'll be my fault." It was true. But it wasn't quite right . . .

"How?" H and Gia were waiting.

"I was supposed to be with her, that night," I said. "I bailed because we had an argument." But we hadn't had the argument that night. We'd argued after the night of the freezer challenge. So why had I pretended I'd go to the farmhouse? Why had I driven her out there, then left her alone?

H frowned. "So?"

I stared at her.

"What, were you her babysitter?"

"N-n-no." I looked at Gia. "But I left her, even though I knew she'd be scared. I knew she'd be so scared, at that challenge." And I'd left her because I was angry. I was angry because . . .

People can see through that, Amelie.

"But how could you know that would happen?" Gia asked.

I gestured at the door. "You go."

"I don't want to go without you. I'm sorry, okay? I didn't mean—"

"Get. Out."

"Amelie?" Gia was waiting.

Doesn't it get exhausting, looking for someone to blame?

My name came again. "*Amelie?*" Not Gia's. A distant voice.

We stared at one another, frozen.

Devon. "*Amelie!*" It came again. "*Over here!*"

"VARGAS!" THE VOICE WAS DISTANT, MUTED BY THE DENSE woods.

Vargas startled and looked away from the girl's haunted expression, scanning the trees.

"Draker?" she called.

Nothing.

She looked at the girl. "Did you hear that?"

"What?"

Vargas squinted at the rows and rows of tall evergreens. Had she imagined it? Her skin crawled. The woods were silent. The parking lot was silent. Everything was too damn silent—

BZZZZGGGHHH.

Vargas jumped, adrenaline knifing through her. The sound had come from behind her . . . and was the CB radio, of course. She collected herself quickly, but the girl had noticed.

"There's something about this place, right?" Amelie peered at her. "I felt it, too, when we arrived."

"Stay right there."

Vargas hurried to the cruiser, checking her watch. It had been twenty minutes already since Draker had left. It had felt like two. She plunked onto the passenger seat and grabbed the radio, pulling the door partially closed.

"Vargas here."

A burst of static.

"Hey, it's Vero." Deputy Veronica Soustracs, calling from the hospital. "No match . . ." More static.

Damn it. What was wrong with the CB?

Vargas pulled out her cell phone and held it up. Two bars. She left the car, holding the phone up high. Closer to the highway she got three and quickly dialed Soustracs. "Make it quick," she said. "Bad signal."

"Right. So, there was no match on that hoodie. It's not Rodriguez's blood."

Vargas paused.

"The what?"

"Hoodie? Came in the ambulance. Draker asked me to match the blood against the girl with the stab wound?"

Vargas turned around. Amelie's hoodie. She'd been wearing one after all, and the paramedics had taken it. Maybe it went in the ambulance by accident, maybe Draker had "accidentally" sent it. Either way, one of his phone calls to Soustracs had involved the directive to test it against Gia's blood. It would've been simple enough, even at the backwater lab in Rifle.

So had she lied about tying it around Gia's leg? Maybe not. Her time in the water could've washed that blood away. It didn't mean she hadn't stabbed her, but she said she'd been wearing the hoodie when they arrived back here, which meant the blood on her arms wasn't Gia's, either.

"Anything else from those girls?"

"They've obviously had a shock. They're—"

Soustracs's voice came in stutters and spurts. Vargas

cursed and held up her phone. Two bars now, even though she hadn't moved an inch.

"—a witch."

"Pardon?" Vargas put a hand to her free ear. Maybe she'd said *which*.

"—hysterical. They say—" It dropped again.

Vargas gritted her teeth, and not just at the crappy signal and broken conversation. "I'm losing you. Did they say anything more about the fourth girl?"

"Yeah. I said they say Amelie was the last one to see her." More breakup.

"Last one to see her when?" Vargas asked.

"In the cave?"

Devon was definitely still in the cave. Lost or incapacitated. Or dead.

"Anyway, I have to—" A robotic whine broke up the call.

"—to you later."

Vargas realized Soustracs was signing off. "Wait. Can you check something else? Hello?"

"I'm here." Clear as day, suddenly.

"There were DNA samples taken by Denver PD at an accident scene three months ago. Victim was Sasha Desmarais. Cheyenne was looking into it. Can you call her? See if we can test the blood on the hoodie against the DNA of a Devon Kirneh? Female."

"How do you spell that?"

"One second." Vargas hurried back to the cruiser and grabbed Draker's pad of paper from the passenger seat. She retraced her steps to where she had service.

"You there?"

"Go ahead."

Vargas read out the name and finished the call, unsure if Soustracs had heard her properly. It wouldn't matter. There weren't going to be samples from two Devons. Plus, the process would take days. They'd have to enter the hoodie into evidence, transport it across jurisdictions, convince the DA to release evidence from a possibly unrelated case.

But it would match.

Quite suddenly Vargas had no doubt of that.

She looked down at the name she had just spelled out, something twigging.

Kirneh.

She spelled it backward, one letter after the other: *Henrik.*

Amelie was watching her from afar.

She said she'd been trying to convince the other two that Devon was Henrik. Vargas frowned down at the paper. But would Devon be that obvious in her catfishing? Would anyone?

Vargas ground her teeth, trying to sort out the possible from the probable. Probable: Amelie had decided Devon was a threat to them and either left her there or incapacitated her so they could leave. It was the premise Draker was operating on. But maybe it was deeper than that. What was also possible: She'd decided Devon had had something to do with Sasha's accident and enacted revenge. Also possible: She thought that all along. In other words, Amelie had lured Devon here with some kind of vigilante-justice intention.

She was telling the story as though the probable were true,

that she'd realized, in the cave, that Devon was Henrik. But this trip could have been much more premeditated. Amelie could have left the email instructions on purpose, hoping whoever found it would put two and two together. It was something that corroborated her story without *her* producing evidence. It was a classic liar's inception.

But it was a fairly sophisticated red herring in a story from a girl who had, initially, struggled with how to tell it.

Vargas massaged her jaw. They needed to be recording this at the station. She pocketed her near-useless phone along with the pad of paper and pulled her walkie-talkie out. She switched it on as she made her way back to the girl.

"Draker? Come in."

Nothing.

"Draker, come in."

The walkie-talkie hissed softly.

Goddamn it.

She stepped past the girl toward the trailhead, reflexively touching the cuffs on her belt, which was ridiculous. The girl weighed all of ninety pounds. Whatever had happened in the cave, she was no threat to Vargas. Vargas scanned the trees.

"I hope he's okay," Amelie said. Perfectly sincere.

Vargas took a beat, reflecting. In the beginning, she'd seemed so earnest, so hopeful that Vargas would listen and understand, but she had also been unsure—catching herself and retracting, rephrasing. That caginess had disappeared. Now she was focused, aiming at something deliberately, though what that something could be, Vargas had no idea.

One thing seemed certain: There were enough contradictions

in the story she was spinning that it was clear she would trap herself, and they needed it on record when she did.

"You shouldn't say anything more until your parents are present." Vargas touched her walkie-talkie again, pressed the call button. *No response.*

"My parents can't help," the girl said. She bit her lip. "They're part of the problem."

Vargas turned to regard her.

"It's not like H's situation," Amelie said. "But it's like Sasha said: I was used to being the center of their attention, of everyone's attention. When I wasn't, I . . . found something else." The girl's hands balled into fists. "I was so angry with Sasha for saying that."

Vargas stared at her, perplexed. The girl's thoughts were clear enough, but piecing together the connections between them was like grabbing smoke.

"It wasn't even about the people at Dissent; it was the fact that *she* could see through me. It was humiliating." The girl's voice got small. "She asked me to be honest with her. And instead . . ." Her lips twisted, like she was trying not to let tears come.

Instead, she'd let her cousin go to the challenge alone, where she'd been in an accident. An accident Amelie had started to believe was Devon's fault.

"It showed me the truth about that night, you know."

"It?"

"The Sublime." There. Vargas suddenly pinpointed what had bothered her about the way the girl had said it before: There was a reverence in her tone. Like she was grateful.

She couldn't help herself: "Amelie," she said. "Is Devon Kirneh alive?"

The girl's eyes flicked to her bloodstained arms, back to Vargas. "I don't know," she said.

Vargas's skin crawled. She could put the girl in the back of the car. Maybe then she could go looking for Draker. No. It would be hot in the back seat, unnecessarily cruel. And nothing about heading into the woods after Draker felt like a good idea.

"But there was nothing I could do," Amelie said.

Vargas stared at the girl.

She pulled her knees close. "And I'll tell you why not, if you want to hear it."

UNRAVELING

WE PAUSED, LOOKING AT THE TWO TUNNELS.

"Did she say *it's* over here?" Gia said. "Like, the way out?"

But how was she finding her way down here without a light?

"Where is she?" H looked between the two tunnels. "Where is that coming from?"

"*I can hear your voices!*" Devon's voice echoed around us.

"There?" Gia said, pointing to the tunnel on our left. She moved toward it, like this was a good thing.

I obviously hadn't convinced them. But Devon had to be behind all of this. She'd wanted us to be scared, believe in the lore. And maybe I'd wanted to, at first, but . . . I was seeing a dead Sasha down here.

It's telling you something about yourself.

No. Devon was behind this. She was Henrik; I could feel it.

Gia opened her mouth to call back.

"Don't!" I hissed. "We shouldn't yell. It could cause a cave-in." I had no idea if that was true.

Gia looked uncertain. "Is that a thing?" she asked H.

"I don't know," H admitted. "In the miniseries adapted from Stephen King's *The Outsider* it did."

"Any real-life reference we could use?" Gia asked peevishly.

I seized the opportunity, reiterating: "Voices are dangerous. It's the resonance. Come on." I pointed at the other tunnel. "This is the way."

"Are you sure?" H asked.

"*Over here!*" Devon's voice echoed around us. This time it was farther away and sounded like it could've been coming from anywhere. But initially it had come from the tunnel on the left.

"Yes," I said. "And we should hurry." I moved farther in and looked back expectantly.

Gia relented, hobbling toward the tunnel I'd chosen, and H, obviously unwilling to be left alone again, joined. "I'm going to be slow," Gia reminded us.

"So you lead," I said. We went. Gia's light was nothing but a weak glow. And the tunnel we'd chosen was progressively getting narrower, to the point where I was starting to worry it was a dead end. But Devon couldn't know that, could she?

A prickle crawled through my hair.

Who could guess what Devon knew?

I fixed my eyes on Gia, limping ahead determinedly. Did I really think Devon had something to do with Sasha's accident? It was much more likely that she'd been scared. So scared she . . . I stumbled, a tiny knot of dread forming in my stomach.

"*Amelie.*" It was quiet, like a breath letting go.

I froze. "Did you hear that?"

"What?" H whispered, stopping behind me. Gia turned around.

Silence.

"It's the dark," Gia said. "It changes things." In the shadows, her face looked gaunt. We'd been down here too long. We needed sunlight. Fresh air. This carbon-dioxide-laden tomb was going to claim us.

Stop it.

"Can you go a little faster?" I asked Gia.

She hunched her shoulders determinedly and picked up her pace.

Gia's wan light illuminated the narrow tunnel before her. My flashlight, also obviously low on batteries, lit up her limping form from behind. The bandage on her leg was practically black with blood, glistening. That wasn't good. We needed to get out. We needed—

"Amelie!"

I froze. That had echoed from somewhere . . . in front of us?

"What now?"

"You didn't hear that?"

"No."

Behind? I pushed at Gia, moving her forward. But at the next curve the tunnel forked again.

Gia turned, looking unsure.

"Just keep moving," I said.

"Which way?"

The two paths facing us were equally uninviting: dark, damp, ripe with a strange odor that was earthy and metallic and putrid all at once.

"Amelie!" Or was that coming from above us?

"What's wrong?" H noticed me glancing around.

Why couldn't they hear it?

Gia's headlamp chose that moment to die completely. "Fuck."

"It's okay," I said, shoving away a swell of panic. "We still have my light." But for how much longer? I pointed at the tunnel on our right. "This way." We headed off, Gia breathing loudly as she struggled to keep up with me. Too loudly. We were all out of breath. Ragged gasps of air, shuffling steps—that sound was us, right?

Suddenly it felt as though the tunnel was ascending. Thank god. We were headed back to the surface. The passage was widening, too. Curving and widening.

But we hit another fork.

I shone my light around the space. It looked identical to the very first fork we'd taken.

"Why are we running?" Gia panted.

"Are we going in a circle?" H asked in alarm.

"No," I said, though I honestly didn't know. In the weak beam, everything looked the same. Dark, glistening walls, like fibrous tributaries, aortas. Maybe we'd gone the wrong way. Maybe we were now in the belly of the beast and headed for its heart—

"*Amelie!*"

It sounded like the voice was everywhere, all around us.

"*Over here!*"

I chose the tunnel on the left, rushing forward like I had any idea where it would lead.

"Amelie, slow down!"

I meant to set a reasonable pace. I meant to make sure they didn't fall behind. But dread was coursing through me—a sense that something had been waiting for me down here, all along—and it was so strong all I wanted was to get far, far away.

The weak beam of my flashlight glanced off another wall. The tunnel was branching again. It was like a damn maze, and none of us were keeping track of the choices we were making. We needed a system. Some way of marking—

"Amelie."

The voice was close. I snapped my head to look over my shoulder, past the other two. There was a dark figure standing in the tunnel. The shadow was off-kilter, head tilted.

I spun and bolted down the nearest tunnel. The presence stayed with me, a hot breath on the back of my neck. And it was gaining ground.

I pushed faster, but the cave floor was suddenly thicker, sucking at my tennis shoes, trying to hold me in place. I glanced down, saw that I was running on something that resembled wet cement—a thick, slippery mud. I'd entered a puddle of it.

Something splashed in behind me, and I pulled my legs up and forward with all of my might, leapt for the far side, where the flashlight showed smooth, flat rock.

"Amelie!" Gia cried.

I reached solid ground and turned. She was struggling toward me, reaching out a hand with a frightened look in her eyes. Behind her, a few feet back, H had stopped and was struggling in place. The mud I'd skipped over, pulled my shoes from, was up to her knees. She was tugging at one of her legs with both hands, making a whimpering sound.

I grabbed for Gia and jerked her violently toward me. She pitched forward, freeing her remaining foot as she fell. She took me down, letting out a primal scream of pain as we landed.

"Help!"

I scrambled for purchase, untangling myself from Gia, and got to my knees. Gia pulled herself upright, panting.

I shone the light back at H. The mud was at her thighs now, and she was panicking, trying to buck her body forward.

"Don't move!" Gia screamed at her. "You'll sink!"

H froze. There was a terrible moment of stasis: Gia and me staring into H's terrified face. Her eyes pleaded with us: *Help me.*

Gia's voice was a determined growl. "Stay calm. Just stay there." She crawled back to the edge of the mud and reached out a hand. H grasped it gratefully. "Small movements," Gia instructed. "Just small."

H nodded, her gaze locked onto Gia's for direction, reassurance, and wiggled her legs back and forth gently. "There's something . . . under . . . the mud," she whimpered.

"Just keep coming," Gia commanded.

H shut her eyes, her face twisted as though she was feeling something repulsive. There was a sucking sound, and H's legs let go, pitching her forward. She landed on the surface of the mud, her torso and elbows smacking wetly.

Gia's voice rang out, clear and calm. "It's okay! I've got you. Just wiggle." She reached out her other hand and grasped H's.

H wiggled and Gia pulled backward, dragging her and a huge sluice of mud toward us slowly, slowly. H finally was on solid ground, coated in mud and gasping for breath.

Gia lay back, looking pale.

I ran my light over the two of them and watched as H writhed. "There's something under me," she said hoarsely. She pulled her knees up and got to all fours to look. Then she let out a cry and scrambled up.

A jumble of angular shapes lay on the rock. Even coated in mud, it was clear they were—

"Bones," I whispered.

Gia struggled up in alarm and pushed herself away. I looked at the girls, then across the mud, into the dark cavern. And saw Sasha, standing deadly still in the oily blackness.

"Come on." My voice was hoarse. I took a step back. "We have to—" My light flickered. The figure shifted, moved out of the shadows.

Devon's voice rang out again, this time close and plain as day, her deep timbre unmistakable:

"There you are."

SHE PEERED AT US. "WOW. ALL THREE OF YOU SURVIVED?"

I squinted at her, my head fuzzy, my terror dissipating. Not Sasha. Devon. A surge of new alarm crashed in.

Gia pointed at the square object in Devon's hand. "Your . . . phone still works?" she asked faintly. It was an odd question in the circumstances, but Gia looked how I felt: dazed.

Devon waved it. "Waterproof." She looked at H, soggy and caked with that white mud from toe to midriff, then down at the puddle. She shone her light at the side, revealing a thin shelf alongside one wall. Through my jumbled thoughts it occurred to me that if I hadn't been running blindly, we could've avoided the mud.

She started along the shelf toward us. "What happened to you?" She pointed at Gia's blood-soaked jacket-bandage.

Gia shifted closer to H and me.

"That's going to be a pain in the ass," Devon remarked. We shuffled backward, retreating farther into the tunnel. She reached our side of the puddle. "It's going to take some—"

"Stay there," I managed.

She paused. "What?"

"Just stay there."

There was a beat. She cocked her head. I spread my arms and stepped back, shuffling the other two behind me a few more steps.

"You need to explain what's going on," I said. Yes. That was what she needed to do.

She looked puzzled. "What's going on?"

"Yeah." I was having trouble keeping track of my thoughts. "I—I know you catfished me," I said with some effort. "I know you're Henrik."

She crossed her arms over her chest and widened her stance. "Huh," she said.

Huh. She was admitting it, wasn't she? My head was fuzzy. I was so sure Sasha had been behind me. That she was down here. But I was equally sure of this. Wasn't I?

"You're messing with us," I said. "And congratulations, because it worked."

Her eyes sharpened, like she was digesting this information. We were frozen in this weird tableau: the three of us huddled like prey, with Devon blocking the path like some demonic creature from the deep, except a demon who looked like she was contemplating which show to stream online.

"Just get us out of here!" Gia blurted.

"I was trying to show you the way." Devon gestured ahead of us to where the tunnel split, yet again. "The right leads back to the lake," she said. "And the water's still rising. So we should go left."

"Why would we believe that?" I demanded.

"Why wouldn't you?"

"Because you're a psychopath?"

Devon stilled. There was the slow *drip drip drip* of water from somewhere, echoing through the tunnels. "Well, I guess it says something that we've been stuck in this subterranean hellscape for hours, and . . . I don't mind, so much."

I felt the girls shift behind me. My head started to throb with a dull pain, and my chest was tight. I needed more air.

"I've been wondering," Devon continued. "Maybe my mom was right. Maybe I'm—"

"Devon," H whispered, like she was pleading with her to stop talking.

"—crazy." Her tone was reflective.

"Don't hurt us." I tried to think over the pounding in my ears. Which way was the real way out? The opposite tunnel, because she was clearly lying about the exit, or the other tunnel, because she was using some reverse psychology bullshit?

Devon frowned. "I won't."

Gia shifted on her good leg, trying to steady herself.

"You *said* it was your fault," I said. "In my dream." Hardly a compelling argument, but everything was muddled, and I was grasping, thinking aloud. "You said this, the accident, was your fault."

"I did?" Devon didn't say it like she was confused or skeptical, she said it like . . . she was realizing something.

I couldn't be sure the other two knew the danger we were in, but even if they did, what could we do? Gia was vulnerable, and Devon knew it. H wasn't going to do anything. I looked too frail to be a threat.

Which is why it had to be something drastic, and it had to be me. Through the haze of my thoughts, I suddenly knew that without doubt.

The mud was only a few feet away, so it was a risk. If I'd hesitated, I would've lost my nerve. I snapped my flashlight off, threw it to the ground, leaving only Devon's face illuminated by her phone. Then I put my head down and charged.

Like I'd hoped, she was caught off guard.

I knocked her off-balance easily, hurtling into her, slamming her toward the rock wall behind. I'd aimed low, around her waist, and I snagged her shirt in my fists as I barreled ahead. Her phone flew out of her hand, and there was a dull splash as the light winked out, plunging us into darkness. We hit the wall, and I heard her head crack against it, waited for her to go limp.

She was stronger than I'd bargained on. Instead of crumpling, she used the wall for leverage, pushing against it, bouncing off, and throwing me backward. I fell but had the presence of mind to use the momentum to my advantage, twisting my body to the side and pulling her with me so that she fell beneath.

It was a strange sensation, wrestling with the unseen: visceral and primal. Soggy cloth, muscles jerking beneath my grip, sharp intake of breath, sweet shampoo scent mixed with sweat. In the pitch dark she was a nightmare entity, all limbs and teeth, and I fought back like something possessed. I scrambled to straddle her body, knocking her flailing hands aside.

The sound of our struggle was muted but obvious, and

Gia's cry punctuated the din, echoing in the cavern. It was one of confusion, alarm—because without light, what was happening? What could she or H do?

No, I was on my own.

I clenched a fist and drew it back, planning to aim in the direction of Devon's face. But when I pictured that—her face—I hesitated a split second.

And lost my chance.

One of her hands, searching the air above her like a tentacle, caught my wrist in an iron grip. She bucked her body and yanked my arm to the side, and I toppled, throwing out my hands to catch myself. In a heartbeat she was on top of me, and my chin was pressed into the rock. I writhed and scrabbled, but she had a knee in my back, pinning me like an insect. Instinctually I turtled, pulling my hands beneath me.

And remembered the knife in my pocket . . .

I bucked, displacing her weight for an instant—long enough to pull a knee up and snake a hand out. I fumbled the knife from my pocket as she leaned her weight onto me again. I writhed, getting my hands to my chest and pulling the blade open. There was a brief moment of pause where all I felt was the painful crush of her body on mine. Then she moved again, like she was feeling for something on me to grab onto, and I lashed out.

She let out a howl and her weight released.

"Amelie?!" H's voice. A scrabbling sound to my right.

I twisted onto my side, preparing to scramble away, but Devon recovered, grabbing my shoulders and yanking me all the way around. She threw me flat on my back, faceup, cracking my head against the ground. A burst of pain behind my eyes, disorienting, dizzying. She moved again, pinning my arms at the elbows with her knees and jamming a forearm into my throat. Something wet gushed onto my neck and pooled in my collarbones. The smell of iron filled my nostrils. A strange humming started in my head as I gasped for air. I felt the knife fall out of my hand. I could see nothing, but the sensation of a new darkness rushed into my head, closing off other sensations, scent, touch . . . I heard a distant voice: "Stop!"

The pressure on my windpipe let up.

"Stop!" The voice came more clearly. It was H, screaming. A bright light flashed. "Please stop!"

Devon was above me, her head turned, squinting into the beam. She looked back down, met my eyes. Then she hauled herself off me and retreated into the shadows.

I curled into the fetal position, coughing, catching my breath.

"Are you okay?" H stood halfway between me and Gia, holding my flashlight in a trembling hand.

I squinted into the glare and put a hand to my neck. My fingers came away sticky and dark. Dazed, I pulled at the bottom of my T-shirt and looked down. I was wearing a crimson bib: Blood was all over the neck and shoulders of my T-shirt. I gasped, feeling for the wound, but couldn't find one.

I stood unsteadily, grabbing the knife from where it had fallen beside me, and retreated to the safety of H and the light.

Gia hobbled close to me, and H backed up, forming a kind

of defense around me. I realized H still had the light trained on the far wall. My breath caught. I'd imagined Devon fleeing, retreating into the darkness, but there she was, standing against the wall, grasping the inside of her elbow. There was blood everywhere—all over her forearms and the front of her shirt. Blood was seeping between her fingers where she held her arm.

"You're right," Devon said dully. "It's probably my fault." She nodded, staring at the ground as though she was thinking hard. She gripped the wound tighter, then looked up. "That's why I'm here."

A SPURT OF BLOOD.

Devon looked at her arm, clamped her fingers tighter, and winced. "Wow, Amelie, you're a wildcat when you want to be." We watched her clumsily unbutton her plaid shirt with one hand and struggle out of it. She had to let go of the wound a couple of times to wrap the shirt around her elbow. By the time she was done, blood was everywhere. She glanced at the mud. "Damn, I liked that phone," she said. A large bubble lay on the surface, its only trace.

I held the knife shakily in front of me.

She looked at it. "You can put that down."

I gripped it tighter.

She shrugged, forgetting her bandage for a minute, and winced at the movement. But there was a strange resignation to her all at once.

"What the hell is going on?" Gia demanded.

"Why did you bring us here?" I added hoarsely.

Devon drew herself up, wincing once again. "Did I bring you here?"

"You just said you did," I said. "You catfished me and brought us here, and now you're going to . . ." What was she going to do?

Devon looked amused. "You're scared. Understandable. You've been seeing things."

"Because you're *making* us!"

"Oh?"

"Like the butterfly and the ants," H said, repeating my explanation, though she didn't sound convinced. It had all made so much sense before, but now I was having trouble remembering how.

Devon blinked. "That's a chemical reaction," she said slowly.

Chemical. My earlier thought pinged in. "Exactly. Like whatever was in the candy you gave us!"

A genuine laugh burst from her. "That *would* be crazy." She shook her head no. Then she paused. "But maybe I am. You all seem to have these vivid emotions: ups and downs. I've never had that, I don't think. I don't feel fear, when I should. In the hospital they had a name for it."

Hospital. Her stay at Denver Children's, when she was young.

"But is there something wrong with me, or am I just . . ." Devon waved her good hand. "Not what people want?"

We stared at her. Her analytical tone, her demeanor . . . it's what had unnerved me all this time. Detached, like she didn't care what we thought of her. Like whatever we thought wouldn't change anything.

The slow dripping sound from before was increasing. It sounded like there was a tiny cloud shedding raindrops, somewhere off in the tunnel.

"I started to put myself in extreme situations to see how I'd react. Turns out, I don't." Devon pushed off the wall.

273

I shied back and ran into Gia, who gasped loudly. She grabbed for the wall with one hand, her leg with the other. Her bandage had slipped, and her wound was weeping again.

"Omigod." H bent to help her tug it back in place.

Devon stepped forward. "She needs to—"

"Just stay there!" I shouted.

Devon stopped and looked at me quizzically. Gia and H managed to get her jacket around her thigh again. Gia pressed at it, looking pale.

"She needs a better bandage," Devon said. "Take my knife and—"

"It's not your knife." Yes, that was one of the pieces to this puzzle. "You stole it out of H's pack."

"Uh, no. The blade has my initials engraved on it."

I turned it on its side, held it to the light. *DK.*

"Oh," H said quietly, behind me. "It, uh, looked a lot like the one I packed."

Fuck. But . . .

A deep rumble echoed around us.

"Did you hear that?" H jerked the flashlight, searching the space.

"Did we hear the soggy cave collapsing?" Devon said. "Yeah."

"Shit," Gia muttered.

But there. *That* was the piece that proved all of this. "Only Henrik knew the caves would be unstable in the rain— '*practically ephemeral*'?"

Devon squinted at me. "Only Henrik and *you*, you mean?"

I faltered.

Doesn't it get exhausting, looking for someone to blame?

"We should go," H urged. "It's not safe."

But it wasn't safe with Devon, either. Was it?

"I might need help," Gia said, and H moved in close.

Devon gestured with her good arm. "I can show you—"

"No!" I shouted at her. "You need to tell us what the fuck is going on!" H and Gia flinched. But the pieces were falling back into place. All the things Devon had said, done . . . "How did you get out of the lake?" I demanded. "You said something was blocking the tunnel."

"It disappeared."

"You knew there was an undercurrent there!"

"It wasn't an undercurrent," she said. "It was this large cloudy spot and some . . . thing inside." Black cloud. Somehow dusty, under the water. Impossible. "And a . . . sound." *Scritchscritchscritch.* "And a figure . . ."

"The Skinflayer," H murmured. "The Skinflayer was in that—"

"Can't you see what she's doing?" I rounded on her. "She's using something we've already told her—"

"But there *was* a cloud," Gia said.

"Devon's Henrik!" I insisted. "She's the butterfly, and we're the ants!"

"We're *all* the butterfly and the ants," Devon countered. "Metaphorically speaking." She tilted her head. "But if the lore is true—"

"You're behind all of this!" I insisted, my voice high and hysterical-sounding.

"Amelie, calm down," H said. She peered at Devon. "Were you responsible for Sasha's accident?"

"She already said she was!"

"No, *you* said that," H snapped. She turned back to Devon. "You need to tell us, yes or no."

Devon looked at me, and my insides swooped. She shook her head no. "I was talking about my brother's accident," she said. "My mom thought I did that to him."

H shifted. "Did you?"

"I don't know. I don't remember." Her expression was strangely blank. "But if I did because there's something wrong with me, then maybe the Sublime can change that. Me."

Another rumble.

My thoughts were going a mile a minute. She was here to change herself? But if she hadn't brought us here to toy with us, then the lore was real. Like I'd wanted. Except I didn't want it like this.

It's not my fault.

What isn't?

Any of it. This. The accident.

Devon's gaze rested on my face. "But maybe you understand that. Wanting to be something different."

Our headlights lit up the gravel road in a long tunnel of light.

"You're sure you're okay to drive?" Sasha asked again.

"Of course."

The forest was dwindling into the dark behind us, the last of the Dissenters were dispersing to their vehicles.

I threw the cold compress I'd been pressing to my neck

into the back seat. I'd done the freezer challenge like everyone else but had collapsed afterward because of a blinding headache. Some girls had dashed around, finding something they could soak for a compress.

Sasha had been quiet since I'd emerged. Now she was side-eyeing me.

"What?" I asked her.

She shook her head. "Nothing."

The tunnel outside the glow of the flashlight was suddenly smaller, closing in on us, darkness creeping ever closer. That smell was back, packed into my nostrils. Cherry rot, sliding down my throat.

"You've been weird recently," I said. By weird I meant no fun. It was like she was distracted or impatient or something. Whatever it was, it was getting old. "What's up?"

"Nothing," she said. "I mean, I'm not trying to be weird."

"I thought you were okay with Dissent." She'd never loved it, but she used to make fun of the fact that she didn't. "Are you getting freaked out?"

"It's not that." She twirled a piece of her long brown hair in her fingers—a nervous habit. "I was just wondering . . ."

"What?"

"Well, we don't know any of those people, right? You don't go to school with any of them?"

"Right." The fresh start had been part of the allure of Dissent. I didn't need Sasha knowing my social status at school.

"So how does everyone at Dissent know about your health issues from years ago?"

"Kind of obvious, isn't it?"

"Not . . . always." There was a tone there I didn't like. I shrugged. "It must've come up sometime."

She was still looking at me. That weird, guarded look. "What?"

"Why do you go to Dissent?" This question again. She'd asked me it when she was trying to convince me about that trip to the Sublime.

"I told you: I like it."

"You like getting a, what did you call it, CO-two headache?"

"Well, no, but that's what happens to me in a locked freezer. It's just part of the game."

"And at the reservoir when that guy had to rescue you?"

"That was a pretty crazy leg cramp," I admitted. "But, again, oxygen issue. I just don't absorb it like normal people."

"But I thought you were better."

"Um, ever hear of residual complications?"

She was quiet a moment. "Be honest with me?" Her voice softened. "What are you afraid of?"

My skin prickled at the serious tone in her voice, so I made a face at her, trying to lighten the mood. "Uh, peeling wallpaper," I said sarcastically, recalling her fear I regularly made fun of. "Creatures behind the walls."

Something flickered in her eyes. Resentment? "I don't mean those kinds of fears," she said. "I mean: Are you that afraid that people won't like you . . . for you?"

My smile vanished. "What?"

"Like, do you think you have to have some issue for people to be interested?"

Blood rushed through my head. *"Why would you say something like that? Of course not."*

"Well, everything is always so dramatic."

"Things are dramatic because I have residual complications—"

"I get it, okay?" Sasha cut me off, irritated. *"You had all kinds of special attention when you were young. But you don't have that anymore—"*

"That's not—"

"And you want it. You want to be special." Sasha's irritated frown dissolved into a gentle trepidation—like she was telling me a hard truth—which was so much worse. *"So you do these attention-seeking things."*

"Stop." I forced the word around the fetid taste in my throat. My breath was coming fast, too fast.

Devon frowned. "Amelie—"

"Stop!" I shouted.

My voice echoed into the space. But then, as it faded, a reply: a clunking sound, emanating from the tunnel on the left.

H swung her light toward the sound. "What was *that*?"

It came again, but now it sounded like a . . . shuffling. The slow approach of something with dragging, shambling steps. A fruity, acrid stench preceded it. A terrible, hollow feeling came over me.

I glanced wildly at the others—would they leave me here?—but the sound stopped; the smell disappeared. And things shifted again.

The sound came again, now a rumble, echoing out from

the tunnel. The cave was moving. A bit of shale rained down, a waterfall of dust in the flashlight beam, and a musty, earthy aroma enveloped us. A stabbing pain appeared behind my eye.

"Shit," Gia muttered.

"Like I said?" Devon offered. "I know the way out."

I'd lost my conviction. I didn't know what to think anymore. Still, I tried one last time: "You guys—"

"Getting crushed to death is for B characters," H said flatly.

Gia nodded grimly. She looked at me expectantly.

Another rumble.

My eye pain was blossoming into a raging headache. I handed Devon the flashlight, then I undid and pulled my zip hoodie on. I was shivering.

"We're trusting you," Gia said.

"I'd take it as a compliment," Devon said. "But what choice do you have?"

DEVON IN THE LEAD, ME, THEN H AND GIA. MY HEAD WAS ON fire; it felt as though my mind was going to splinter inside my skull.

I tried to stay focused on what was directly around me: rock growing increasingly slick, water dripping in rivulets, twists and turns, the tunnel big enough for two side by side but no more. Earthy, dank aroma permeating everything. If I didn't think about that night with Sasha, I'd be fine.

Devon led like she'd memorized the damn thing. Several times the tunnel branched, but she moved ahead without hesitation. The jacket around Gia's leg was black with blood, and her face was ghost white. H was similarly pale, breath labored and determined.

Twice the cave let out that heart-stopping rumble of protest that made Devon pick up the pace, before she realized that we were leaving Gia behind. We made our way down the tunnel in a discomforting yo-yo pace, rushing ahead but then pausing, remembering Gia.

Finally, H dropped back completely and, ignoring Gia's protest, put her arm under Gia's arm and along her back. Our pace picked up. That was good.

And if I could just stay focused on the girls, the rock in

front of me, everything would be okay. I wouldn't need to think about who was responsible for what. I wouldn't need to think about that night.

But I wasn't feeling so good. And focusing on what was around me made everything heighten and sharpen, made it all more real, more suffocating. The dank rot, the black shadows gobbling up everything the light didn't touch. Unrelenting rock, slapping at the bottom of my tennis shoes. The dark, pressing in from everywhere. It was coating me, winding its way inside my mouth, down into my lungs, choking me. And now . . .

Now there was a sound accompanying us.

Underneath our steps and panicked breathing, that shuffling sound was back.

Labored, dragging steps. She was following. Slow, slower than our pace surely, but gaining somehow, closing the distance. And then . . .

A scrabbling. Like insects, rodents, nails on wood, grasping, losing purchase . . .

The others didn't seem to notice.

I swallowed bile, following the bobbing light Devon held as she forged ahead. But the sound was getting louder, and my breath was coming faster, and the dark was pressing in.

"I get it, okay? You had all kinds of special attention when you were young. And you don't have that anymore—"

I stumbled. She was following *me*, not them. Of course she was.

"And you want it." Sasha's irritated frown dissolved into a gentle trepidation—like she was telling me a hard

truth—which was so much worse. "So you do these attention-seeking things. You pretend some of the challenges at Dissent pose greater risks for you because you think it's impressive. But people will start to see through that. Some of them already do."

I stumbled. All the times I was sure people were impressed by me, were cheering me on. Had they been mocking me?

"And what you're doing isn't cool, Amelie." She looked sad now. "You manipulate people. You lie."

"I don't—"

"Just be honest, at least with me!"

That night, I'd dropped her at her house. Then I didn't talk to her all week. She'd called, tried to apologize via text. I left it all unanswered.

Until the following Saturday, when I texted and said I'd pick her up for the Dissent gathering. She'd been so relieved, so grateful everything was obviously okay between us—

A cry split my thoughts.

I pulled up, spun around to see Gia force H to jerk to a stop. She grasped, drunkenly, for the wall. She went down, pulling H with her.

"Gia!"

Devon swiveled, and the light bounced off the glistening walls of the cave and back toward us. Gia was collapsed in a heap, and H was untangling herself.

"I'm light-headed," Gia said, breathing hard. "I can't stand."

"Yes you can," H urged. She righted herself and tugged at Gia's arm. It was as though Gia was adhered to the ground for all it mattered; Gia had obviously been bearing most of her weight on her own.

"I. Can't."

"Gia," H begged, a sob in her voice.

Devon frowned. She handed me the flashlight, strode back to the two, and bent, a determined look on her face, to help Gia to her feet. She hooked her shoulder under Gia's arm, practically lifting her feet from the ground, and nodded at us. "Go."

I paused. Behind them, in the gloom of the tunnel, she was there.

Impossible to tell from this distance, but I knew.

No. I squeezed my eyes shut.

"Amelie."

They flew open. Nothing. Darkness. No one. I turned and moved on, but that terrible truth was lighting in my consciousness. Devon wasn't behind this. She wasn't the reason there was something hunting for me in this dark. It wasn't her fault.

It was mine.

We hit a stretch of open space—the tunnel widened and the ceiling soared high. We were in a cavern, but as we hurried across it, the situation became clear. It was a dead end. My heart stuttered.

"Ahead, to the right," Devon said. I shone the light. There was a rope ladder hanging against the rock face. We hurried toward it: a twenty-foot climb to a ledge that obviously led somewhere. The only way to go was up.

"Whoever can help Gia needs to go first," H said.

"I'm stronger with one arm than you are with both," Devon said. "No offense."

"Hurry?" I urged.

Devon was halfway up in seconds, and Gia started her climb. She was awkward, putting both feet on each rung and shifting her weight to her good leg, rather than one foot after the other, and that rope, looped on her belt, wasn't helping. It was getting caught on the wooden rungs, slowing her down.

She descended, landing with a wince. "I need to lose this," she gasped.

"Give it to me," I said hurriedly. I helped her free it and then urged her back up the ladder. Her arm muscles strained as she tried to transfer most of her weight to her upper body. Damn it. She was so slow.

And now the sound was closer.

Scritchscritchscritch.

A rumble sounded from somewhere deep in the cave.

Devon reached for Gia as she got near the top.

"Go!" I shoved H. She scrambled for the ladder as Devon pulled Gia up the last few feet. H started up but was almost more awkward than Gia had been. She was moving carelessly, losing her footing every other step.

"Focus, H!" Gia urged from above.

H gritted her teeth and climbed. I looked back. On the far side of the cavern, emerging from the dark recesses through which we'd fled, I was sure I could see a figure—

"Come on, Amelie!"

I turned, securing the coil of rope in the crook of my elbow and tucking the flashlight into my waistband, and started up the ladder. Above me, H was laboriously reaching the top. A few steps into my ascent, I realized the flashlight was an issue. It kept catching on the weird wooden rungs, slowing me. I stopped and pulled it from my waistband.

And felt a stillness come over the cavern.

That smell. Wafting out from the darkness. Musty, rotten, sweet; decay and flesh and hair and blood. A feeling of foreboding settled on my neck, crept into my hair.

I turned, fumbling with the flashlight, aiming its beam at the cavern entrance.

A pale hand emerged from behind the rock and wrapped around the edge, grasping at the wall with blackened nails, blue-white skin.

That searing pain inside my head intensified. I didn't want to see, didn't want to know, but I couldn't pull my gaze away.

A figure emerged from the shadows: pale, bruised arms, head hanging, stringy hair obscuring its face. It took a shuffling step into view: dirty jeans and crimson top. Sneakers caked in black mud. The head lolled up awkwardly, as though its neck was broken. The hair fell away. Unseeing eyes narrowed against the glare and, inexplicably, sought my gaze.

Her pupils were enormous, and her skin was puffy and riddled with blue veins. Her mouth opened:

Scritchscritchscritch.

Sasha.

The flashlight winked out, plunging us into darkness. I gasped and knocked it against the rock. It flickered and caught, and I swung it back to look.

She was halfway across the cavern now.

Not Sasha. Sasha's corpse. Sasha, if she had died that night and was now wandering a subterranean maze. Looking for me. Head at an impossible angle, hateful black eyes seeking mine.

Scrrrrriiiittttccchhhh.

Black again. I banged the flashlight a second time, forcing it back to life once more.

The place she'd been standing was empty.

I shone the light into the gloom, searching for movement. Some sign that I hadn't hallucinated—

And felt a tug on the ladder below me.

I snapped the light toward the ground. She was standing at the foot of the ladder, neck bent, staring up at me. She grinned. And reached a hand.

I recoiled, losing the spool of rope off my arm as I spun and fumbled with the ladder rungs. I didn't look to see where it landed. I scrambled up and away. My heart lodged in my throat so that I couldn't scream, couldn't breathe.

Can't. Breathe.

I was caught. Somehow I'd had the presence of mind not to drop the flashlight with the rope, but it was in the way again, caught on a rung. I could feel her behind me, grasping.

"Amelie!" Above, H was offering her hand. I dislodged the flashlight and stretched, passing it to her so I had both hands free. She quickly transferred it to her other hand and reached for me again.

Fingers closed around my calf.

I screamed and tore free, grasping at H's hand, letting her pull me as I scrambled up the ladder. The fingernails, scrabbling

287

at my heels, disappeared. But as I got to the top, I knew it wasn't enough. I needed to be sure she couldn't . . . I grasped at the rope ladder, following it to its end to see how it was anchored, and found two metal spikes on either side of the last rung—the top of the ladder was hung over these, easy to dislodge.

"Amelie, what are you . . ."

I grabbed the sides and pulled it up and over the spikes, unhooking it, then turned and shoved it all over the side. The rope ladder dropped down into the cavern below with a soft thudding sound. I waited, crouched on all fours like frightened prey, trying to listen for my predator over the sound of my pounding heart, my ragged breathing.

Nothing.

She was gone. For now.

I turned to look at the others. They were staring at me like I'd lost my mind.

"What in the hell?" Gia demanded. "Did you just . . ."

H shone the light over the edge. "Yeah," she confirmed. "I hope you know where we're going, Devon. There's no way to retrace."

"We don't need to retrace, but we could've used Gia's rope," Devon said.

"Great," Gia said.

"I *had* to," I insisted. "It was . . ." I trailed off. H and Gia looked annoyed, confused.

Devon was studying me. "She's not down there," she said, jerking her head toward the drop. *She.* How would she know—

"There's nothing there," H said.

"Except the ladder and my rope," Gia groused.

A rumble resonated from below; a kind of rending sound from the cavern we'd just climbed from. A crash of something heavy followed.

"There's nothing we can do about it now," Devon said. "Let's keep moving."

My breath was coming in shallow sips. It felt as though a knife were carving across the front of my brain, a vise squeezing the air from my chest. It was how I used to describe my body reacting to the challenges at Dissent. Except this time it was real.

I stumbled along behind the others, trying to fight down my terror.

It wasn't real.

It obviously wasn't real. None of the others had seen what I had been seeing.

Except Devon.

No.

She hadn't seen Sasha. She just *knew* . . .

But I couldn't think about it. Thinking called her to me, and if I saw her again, I wasn't sure I'd make it out of here. I stumbled along behind H, hugging my arms across my damp T-shirt and focusing on trying to breathe.

Ahead, a blue light pierced the black. Static, but glowing. Familiar.

H slowed. "Are we back at the lake?" There was a tinge of panic in her voice.

"No," Devon said. "But . . ."

The tunnel emptied onto a wide ledge. Above, the ceiling was lit with a starburst of sapphire, a cluster of the same glowworms that had occupied the ceiling of the Sublime. Below, our path fell into oblivion.

"We're going to have to get creative," Devon finished. She left Gia to stand precariously and took the flashlight from H.

There was a deep crevice before us. It couldn't be what we'd heard collapsing; it looked as though it had been here a long time. Across the gap, slightly below our perch, the route continued on the other side.

Devon shone the flashlight along the length of the fissure. To our left was a rock wall where it began. The crevice itself was one long, twenty-foot length that widened and split into three separate crevices to our right, stretching into the dark. The floor of the fissure was beyond the flashlight's reach.

Even at its narrowest, the crevice was too wide to leap over—at least ten feet.

"*This* is the Crow's Foot," Devon said. "The shape? I'm pretty sure this is where we were headed after the bat cave." She kicked a rock forward and off the ledge. There were at least two full seconds before we heard it clattering below.

I looked into the abyss. From here, it was bottomless. A terrible depth.

Gia hobbled back a step and sank to the ground, sucking in a breath. She put her head in her hands. "Dizzy," she murmured.

"How are we getting across?" H's voice was tight. She had both hands pressed to her neck, a pained expression on her face.

"I have one idea." Devon focused the weak beam above us on something I hadn't noticed: a thin line of rope that stretched from the wall behind and above us to the far side, where it was attached to a hook, embedded high up on a chunk of boulder. There was a second coil of ancient-looking rope below it. "But now we'll need that rope."

"Well, great. I was looking for a moment to show off my tightrope skills," H said. "Seriously, though."

"Look." Devon shone the light to the left, where the top of the Crow's Foot met the rock wall. She ventured closer, illuminating a series of craggy steps leading from our side to the other. "Stairs, sort of."

These "stairs" were tiny—toeholds, practically. We were going to have to pancake ourselves to the wall and spider across, and there was no way Gia could do it. It would be difficult for Devon, too, with that wound.

Nausea swept me.

"If we can get that rope, we can make a sort of sling to bring Gia across."

"What?" Gia's head snapped up in alarm.

"We'll use your jackets."

"What if it doesn't hold me?"

"It doesn't need to for long. The issue is making it slide along that rope," Devon said. "But if we attach that other rope and pull it from the far side—"

A muffled boom echoed through the cavern.

"This isn't going to work," Gia said, her breath accelerating.

"Yes it will," Devon said. "I'm going to get you out of here. All of you." Again, that strange expression flashed in her eyes. Worry? "We just need the rope."

H took a deep breath and nodded. "I'll go get it," she said.

I should go. I was the one who'd dropped Gia's rope. I was the one who'd wounded Devon, who'd run from her instead of getting her help. The caves were more unstable by the second, and I'd wasted precious time. But that pain in my head was increasing, making me want to take tiny sips of air and . . .

"Are you sure?" Devon asked.

"It has to be me." H shrugged out of her jacket and handed it to Devon. "Amelie's lungs aren't adjusting anymore."

I wanted to correct her. I needed to correct her. But I couldn't—physically couldn't. And then she was already at the edge and stretching a foot to the first step, grasping at the hand-hold. And just like that she was on the wall, starting across.

What are you afraid of?

I blinked, watching H move, grasping at the finger holes, pulling herself along, feeling for the steps.

You aren't special anymore.

H stopped. "Can you hear that?" She looked back at us. Her eyes suddenly had a strange sheen to them. She let go with one hand, gesturing at the abyss. "Down there?"

"H," Devon said calmly. "You need both hands."

"I know." She repositioned her hands, but her gaze drifted back, over her shoulder.

There was a rumble deep in the tunnel behind us, punctuated by an echo of falling rock.

"Just keep going," Devon urged. "Don't look down."

H moved laterally another foot. She was moving in the right direction, but she seemed unable to go with any urgency. She stopped again and looked behind her.

"Her skin," Gia whispered.

I squinted. In the blue glow, H's arms and hands looked black. Now I could see they were covered in thin cuts, weeping inky blood.

She was searching the abyss, her eyes shiny and liquid.

"Keep going!" Gia hissed, startling her.

Her next grasp for a handhold was hasty, imprecise. Her fingers slipped, smearing the rocks with dark blood, and she pitched dangerously to the side.

"H!"

She clung tight with her left hand and pulled herself steady once more.

"You're okay!" Devon said. "You're almost there."

The ledge was maybe three feet away—almost leaping distance. But her hands were slick now, and she was struggling. It didn't help that she was preoccupied with whatever she could hear down in the crevice. Something kept drawing her attention that way.

We held our breath as she contorted her body to look. And then she repositioned her grip so she could turn away from the wall.

"H," Devon said nervously.

She gathered herself. Oh god. Was she going to . . . jump?

We watched helplessly as she took a deep breath, her eyes fixed on the crevice. Gia let out a cry as H pushed off from the rock, springing into the air.

She landed on the far side unsteadily and took a knee.

We let out a collective exhale.

"Jesus," Devon looked at us. "She had me worried."

"Can you grab the rope?" Gia called.

H had turned back but was kneeling, staring down into the crevice. Her shirt was wet with blood, and her eyes were fixed on something only she could see. "It's coming," she said. She looked up at us, eyes unseeing and face terrified, and rose to her feet. "I have to—" And then she spun and bolted, disappearing down the tunnel on the far side.

Leaving us alone.

"H!" Devon hollered.

"H!"

Nothing.

"Did she just bail?" Gia demanded. "Again? Are you kidding me right now?"

"H!" Devon called a third time.

Nothing.

I stared at the crevice. That strange, squeezing sensation around my chest was back. I put my hands on my knees, trying to take a breath.

You manipulate people. You lie.

"I can do it," Devon said. "I told you, I'm stronger than you with one arm—"

"No." I pulled myself upright with effort. "I'm going."

"Your lungs—"

"My lungs haven't been a problem since I was eight," I said. "I was faking it at Dissent. For attention. I was faking it here, too." I wasn't faking it now, but that was beside the point.

My confession didn't seem to surprise Devon. She paused, and a kind of relief registered on her face. She stepped aside. It was strange: The relief seemed to have nothing to do with the fact that I could help her get the rope. It seemed larger than that, as though my revelation had cemented something in her mind. Something she found reassuring.

I moved into position. Being this close to the abyss sent an icy shock through the bottom of my feet up and into my throat.

"I'll light your path," Devon said, gesturing with my flashlight. It wasn't totally necessary—the cavern was awash in blue—but it couldn't hurt.

I took a shallow breath, gathered my resolve, and stretched a foot to the first step, flattening myself against the rock wall like a starfish. My fingers scrabbled for holds as I shifted my weight to my right leg, brought my left in close, and found another toehold.

"Don't look down," Gia said faintly.

Immediately I glanced at my feet to make sure I was placing them correctly. The dark beneath was absolute, dizzying, and I missed my next handhold, my body pitching to the side.

"I said don't!" Gia cried.

With effort I tightened my core and pulled myself stable again. I blew out what little air was in my lungs, pressing my cheek to the rock. The other side was no more than eight feet away. Practically leaping distance.

I closed my eyes and continued, reaching, feeling for the next crag in the rock to rest my foot, grasp with my hand. Moving like that was easier. It was dark. Nothing but black.

The black of my laptop screen.

> **AsphyxiA: got a suggestion for you.**
> **Dissent: shoot**

Hard rock bit into my fingertips.

"Are you okay?" Devon.

"Amelie?" Gia.

I reached with my foot again, brought it down—

> **AsphyxiA: abandoned farmhouse on 40th, by the factory.**

—and the rock under my foot crumbled.

"Amelie!"

I recoiled, gripping desperately with my fingers. Someone was shouting, but the voice was muted. Other voices joined, making it a fuzzy din. Panic swept through my chest and into my head in a dizzying swell. I couldn't breathe. Couldn't breathe—

A rumble pierced the white noise in my head.

You manipulate people.

And the rock under my left foot crumbled, too, dissolved

into nothing. Hot fear knifed through me, and I threw my body to the side, aiming for the ledge.

"Amelie!"

But I was falling.

Falling through the dark.

Down, down, down.

An impossibly long way down.

THE BLACK DISAPPEARED AS THE FREEZER CHEST SWUNG OPEN. *Light from the bonfire poured in. "Fucking amazing." A guy helped me out. "If I had bad lungs, I would've freaked."*

I hit with a bone-jarring crunch and rolled to the side. Sasha's voice echoed in my head.

"You want to be special." Her irritated frown dissolved into a gentle trepidation—like she was telling me a hard truth—which was so much worse. "So you do these attention-seeking things. You pretend some of the challenges at Dissent pose greater risks for you because you think it makes you more impressive. But people will start to see through that. Some of them already do."

A rancid smell hit my nose. I pulled my head to the side and retched.

"What you're doing isn't cool, Amelie. You manipulate people. You lie."

"I don't—"

"Just be honest, at least with me!"

Absolute dark. Inky nothing. I retched again. But now, a sheen, like night outside a window.

The window of my parents' car. Driving to the gathering at the abandoned house.

Darkened buildings came into view on our right. A graffitied, abandoned factory, stretch of unkempt field, and beyond that, a group of people gathering. Behind them, the house. Sasha hadn't noticed yet; she was still waiting for my reply.

"Seriously, Am. I'm really sorry about what I said."

I looked at her. "Are you sorry because you're sorry, or because I don't want to go to that stupid cave with you anymore?"

"Forget about the cave trip. I thought it would be good for us, but . . . I mean . . ." She sighed. "I didn't mean for it to come out that way. I just want you to be yourself. People who are worth being friends with will like you for you. We don't have to do . . ." She gestured ahead of us as I parked. "This."

If I hadn't planned on bailing on her already, her condescending tone would've clinched it. "So basically you think I'm an attention seeker and a liar."

"But that's just it," she protested. "That's not who you are."

I stared at her, my jaw working.

"Look, I get it, okay? Kids started to ignore you when you weren't sick anymore."

"And?"

"That must've been lonely. It makes sense that you'd lean back into that, play up these 'residual complications.' Just . . . I just want you to know that you don't have to do that, with me."

"You mean manipulate you?" I threw at her. "Right. Yeah, that wouldn't be cool."

"That was too far—"

"Look, we both know I don't fit into your new life. So why are we even trying?"

"What do you mean?"

"I mean that maybe it made sense when we were little kids, but we're not little kids anymore. You have your life and I have mine."

"Amelie," she said. *"Come on."*

"And you know what? I'm not really feeling Dissent tonight." I gestured at the door. *"You go."*

"I don't want to go without you. I'm sorry, okay? I didn't mean—"

"Get. Out."

The memory shattered.

The dark was back, absolute once more. Cold air, rotten smell.

I groped around, fumbling through the mud, until my fingers hit something hard, metal. I didn't remember having my flashlight with me when I fell . . .

I sucked in a ragged breath, a half sob, scrabbling to click the switch on. Its weak light was an intense relief. I scrambled to my knees and shone it around in an arc. I was in a small, square hole, no more than eight feet from wall to wall.

I craned my neck up, but there was nothing, no end to the hole that I could see. Dust motes danced in the light, which disappeared into black. How had I survived that fall?

"Devon!" I hollered. "Gia!"

My voice echoed above me. No reply.

"Devon!"

Again, nothing.

"Gia—" My voice caught on a sob.

I staggered to my feet, examining the wall. It was slick with sodden earth on all sides, but solid like hard clay—no way to dig a handhold to climb.

"Can anybody hear me?" My voice was like an animal's, building up to a hysterical howl. It echoed back at me a third time.

I sagged against the wall. A dark and terrifying vortex felt like it was opening up inside me. A nothingness.

I was alone. With what I'd done.

AsphyxiA: got a suggestion for you.
Dissent: shoot
AsphyxiA: abandoned farmhouse on 40th, by the factory. Lock us inside to search for the dice of death, hidden in the walls.

You manipulate people, Amelie.

I pressed my hand to my mouth, suppressing another sob.

Gia asked me how I could've known what would happen to Sasha that night. I knew because I'd suggested it. And I'd suggested it because I knew she'd be scared.

She was afraid of abandoned houses. I knew that.

Sasha used to pinch herself when she was scared. When she got desperate at night in her old house, listening to the things creep behind the walls, she'd try to pinch herself out of the nightmare.

I knew that, too. I used to tease her about it.

Scritchscritchscritch.

Behind the walls, skittering. Insects, rodents.

The sound of shifting in the dark.

I swung around, pulled the flashlight with me reluctantly. There was a figure standing there, beyond the edges of the light, but I knew, by now.

I pulled the light up with a trembling hand.

There, in the corner. Neck broken, skin a decaying pallor. Bruises all up and down her arms, her body twisted as though she'd been shoved into an underground plot, her limbs bent to fit the space. As though she'd died that night.

Sasha pulled her head up slightly, a jerky movement, and found my gaze. Stared straight into my soul with bloodshot, blackened eyes.

I closed mine in desperation. *I'm sorry.* Opened them.

I was in a long, dark hallway.

Foul smell. Dust, bird shit, mold. The hall stretched out, wavered like a fun-house mirror. One foot after the other. Find the dice of death. Room after room of rotting clapboard, peeling wallpaper. Laughter, echoing down the hall. The others are running, laughing, searching.

Wait.

Don't leave me.

Wait.

This door leads to another hallway. And I can hear them now: skittering, gnawing, clawing. Creatures. Rodents, insects, nasty little creatures behind the walls.

I need to get out.

This isn't the way. There is no way. The house doesn't

end. I'm on the stairs now—the cellar? The sound is so much louder. They're everywhere. *Scritchscritchscritch.*

Wake up. Wake up.

Pinch, pinch, pinching flesh, bruising skin.

But I don't wake, and now the stairs crumble beneath me—

And I'm screaming. Screaming and falling.

"Amelie!"

My scream cut off. I blinked. I was pressed into hard earth. I wasn't falling. I wasn't—

"Amelie!" Devon's voice was sharp, urgent.

Now Gia's: "Are you okay?"

I pulled my head to the side and sucked in a breath, feeling rough stone beneath my cheek.

I rolled over. A million blue stars burned overhead. I coughed, feeling my chest release, feeling cool air rush into my lungs. I'd made it across the crevice. I'd—

I glanced to the side. The stairs were gone. The toeholds, the handholds had crumbled into nothing. Not one remained. I'd destroyed the path.

I pulled my gaze back to the glowing ceiling, hot tears burning my temples.

What you're scared of is usually a reflection of what you fear in yourself. Devon had said that. I raised an arm, pinched myself hard, trying to break skin. Like Sasha's, when they'd found her.

You want to be special.

But what happens when you aren't?

You manipulate people.

I was humiliated when Sasha had called me out. I was devastated at the thought that people had been laughing behind my back. I wanted her to know what that felt like; I wanted her to absolutely freak out during a challenge. And I left her there so she wouldn't have anyone she could turn to for help.

Police on the doorstep, red and blue flashing against our house. Hospital hallway. Antiseptic. Cherry candy. Sasha, so small and pale in that hospital bed. *Whoosh.* Oxygen moving in and out. My mom's wide and frightened eyes, grateful it hadn't been me.

All the notes and cards and expressions of concern. DMs and emails from Sasha's classmates I'd never met.

So sorry to hear about Sasha. Are you okay? Can I get you anything?

The police investigated; they suspected there'd been a struggle.

I could have set down the sympathy cards and flowers, gone to them with my theory. It was just a theory, though, and deep down, I wanted them to find someone to blame.

They didn't. DNA cleared any suspects, and no one interrogated had any idea of who would've wanted to harm Sasha.

I told myself I'd never know what truly happened that night, so I boxed it away in a little corner of my mind, slammed the lid shut. That box was torn open now, and that singular truth was hot and bright in my mind: It was my fault.

I'd made a choice. Like coming here. Like bringing these girls here.

"Are you okay?" Devon called again.

Was I? I wasn't hurt, nothing was broken. But I was very far from okay.

I knew now why I'd been so desperate to believe Devon was behind this. Why I'd assumed that these girls were manipulating our situation—H with her "acting," Gia with her selfish MO, Devon with her hallucinogen-laced candy.

That ants and the butterfly story Devon had told . . . it was about me.

And I knew now why I'd carried that latent hope this trip could change things.

"Can you talk?"

Whatever Sasha had wanted to change, she'd never get the chance now. And whatever these girls wanted or needed . . . they might not ever get the chance for that, either.

People . . . will like you for you. Sasha had said that.

Except they didn't. They didn't even notice me.

But Sasha had. She was the one person who liked me for me. The one person who, when I looked back on it, didn't care when I was no longer cheating death, who'd tried to get me to be honest about it because it mattered to her that I was honest with myself.

And instead, I'd made the choice to hurt her.

Devon had said that our decisions were hardwired into us; we don't exactly make choices.

Another rumble.

But we needed to take responsibility.

How was I ever going to take responsibility for Sasha?

A loud crack split the air, drowning out my next thought, and I turtled instinctively, rolling away from the edge, afraid it was collapsing. The sound reverberated through the cavern, punctuated by the sound of falling rock, and I realized it was coming from the far side. I scrambled to my knees.

Gia was panicking, trying to pull herself up and away from the mouth of the tunnel, which had lost part of its roof. Several large chunks of rock were blocking the way, and now rivulets of water were raining down from above.

Gunshot. That's what the sound had been; I could tell by the look on Gia's face.

"Gia!" I called.

Water streamed down behind them, dislodging small bits of the tunnel roof. Another rumble came; this one shook the ground, causing Gia and Devon to grab onto each other for balance.

"Amelie!" Devon called. "Throw me the rope!"

"I—"

"We'll each use the sling, but you have to hurry!"

I wiped at my tears, pushed myself to standing. I grabbed the coil of rope and staggered to the edge, throwing a hand out for balance as the floor swooped with a tremor. It stopped, but it felt as though the cave was only gathering breath for another shock.

Hurry.

I gripped one end of the rope in my left hand, did a couple

of practice swings with the coil in my right, then pulled my arm back a final time and whipped it forward and up, letting go in one motion.

Please.

The rope unspooled in the air, up and up, arcing across the space like a ribbon. I lost it in the flashlight glare as Devon's shadow moved. The light danced to the side as she dropped her arm and darted forward, reaching.

I sucked in a breath, pictured her plummeting over the edge.

But the light stopped, jerked to the side, and now I could see Devon standing a foot from the edge, holding the end of the rope and, incongruently, grinning.

I didn't have time to feel relief: A loud, feral-sounding growl reverberated through the air.

Gia glanced back in terror. Devon looped the rope around the one that spanned the crevice and then bent to her task: tying the sleeves of H's and Gia's jackets together, her face a mask of pain with the movement. "We'll each use the sling," she said again. "Gia?"

When Gia turned back, her expression had changed: from abject horror to defiance. She pushed ahead of Devon. "There isn't time."

The tunnel entrance was raining mud and debris.

"Yes there is." Devon was tying the end of the rope I'd sent over to the circle of coats. "Here!" she urged.

But Gia was already to the edge and lowering herself to one knee, her wounded leg stretched out to the side. "It's only twelve feet, and my arms are fine." She gripped the rope that extended over the abyss in both hands and then inched out over the side.

My breath caught as she dropped, dangling from the tightrope.

Devon and I shared a look. Her expression was one I hadn't seen before—one I hadn't imagined I'd see. She'd said herself she wasn't capable of it, but I could see from here: Devon was afraid.

The muscles in Gia's arms strained as she began pulling herself along. By the look on her face, it was burning her palms painfully, but she kept coming. She gritted her teeth. And then she was over to my side, dangling over solid ground.

I scrambled to help her as she let herself drop. She sucked in a sharp breath when she hit, her bad leg buckling, taking us both down.

"Are you okay?" I gasped.

"There wasn't enough time, and Devon can't do that with one arm," she breathed, untangling herself from me. "Probably not even with two." She turned back. "Come on!"

A large chunk of the ceiling dislodged behind Devon and plummeted down, hitting a puddle of water and spraying it everywhere.

Devon pulled the sling over her head and fastened it around her butt. She took the end of the rope and tossed it high and in an arc so that it looped over the tightrope. Then she sent it back to us, no practice swing required. I could see that moving her wounded arm was painful.

I pulled the end of my rope to get rid of the slack, twisted myself in it once by wrapping it around my waist, and then passed the end back to Gia. She moved away from the edge and lowered herself painfully to the ground. "Okay."

Another crash of rock.

"Ready?" Devon asked us.

"We've got you," I said, and moved backward, pulling firmly on the rope to demonstrate. We had no choice but to believe that. Devon's eyes were fixed on me as she tucked the flashlight into her waistband and then gripped the sling with her good hand.

"I'm going now," she warned. And stepped off.

The force of her weight was instant, and even though I'd anticipated it and braced myself, it jerked me forward. I corrected quickly, but the movement sent her swaying.

Another rumble, followed by another chunk of the tunnel caving in on her side.

"Go!" Gia urged hoarsely, panic lacing her voice.

We pulled steadily backward, dragging Devon slowly toward us. Too slowly. Gia's little stunt had obviously taken its toll; I could hear her gasping for breath as she pushed herself backward along the ground. Devon was halfway to us, but I could see that that the sleeves of H's jacket that attached the sling to the rope were stretched taut as elastic bands. My heart sped.

Devon gripped the rope with both hands, her face a mask of pain. The shirt she was using as a bandage looked purple in the blue glow. She was three feet from us now. Almost in reach. I could get her . . .

"Hold up," I said to Gia. I pulled myself toward Devon,

hand over hand, which loosened the rope around my waist. If I just tugged her the last little bit . . .

A sharp, snapping sound split the air as the sleeves of H's jacket ripped and the sling broke, dropping Devon.

Gia's scream cut the air, seeming to freeze Devon's descent. No. She'd caught herself with her good hand. The sling was slack around her waist, hanging down around her knees, and the flashlight had dislodged and was teetering precariously. Her wounded arm dangled uselessly. I froze, no idea what to do next.

Devon tried to get a second hand on the rope but missed. She gasped, her grip slipping.

"Can you reach her?" Gia's voice was tight with fear.

I stretched out a hand. Devon's brow furrowed as she reached her wounded arm toward me. My fingers grazed hers. No. And it was a stupid idea anyway. I wasn't strong, and there was no way she wouldn't take us both down into the abyss.

"Uh," she said, her voice small.

"Can you swing toward us?" I asked.

She couldn't. Where would she get the momentum? She needed something to push against. My thoughts raced. Or pull toward.

"Gia, can you pass me the end of the rope?"

Gia sounded confused, but she didn't question it: "I can try."

Keeping Devon aloft was requiring both of us, and loosening our grip would make the rope go slack. Any movement might cause her to slip off the rope.

I heard Gia moving slowly behind me, sucking in her breath as she fought to keep tension on the rope that suspended Devon. She wriggled, pulling hand over hand toward me in an army crawl.

"Here."

I reached a hand back slowly, feeling my shoulder scream as I transferred all of my strength to one arm. I grabbed the end of the rope with my left hand.

"I'm going to pass this to you," I said to Devon. "You grab it and pull toward us." It was going to create a strange kind of circle: Devon gripping one end of the rope that passed over the tightrope above, around my waist, and into Gia's hands, and the end of it traveling back to Devon. But it would work, wouldn't it?

"Amelie—"

"It's okay." I cut Devon off. "I promise it's okay." I used my teeth to move a small length of the rope along my palm. Gia and I were both dangerously close to the edge.

I reached out, flicking the last few inches of rope toward her. She caught it, but flailed her legs as she reached, which in turn caused the sling to slip farther down her body and the flashlight to dislodge more. The sling caught on Devon's foot and hung there, dangling off the toe of her boot for a moment. Then it fell, and so did the flashlight, the wan light plummeting into the darkness and winking out.

"It's fine." I forced my voice to sound calm. "Just pull toward me."

Devon let out an audible gasp as she strained, feet dangling, face gaunt in the blue glow. She was within reach now, but my hands were occupied. I'd have to let go of something to grab her.

"You're going to have all of the weight," I warned Gia.

She nodded, her face ashen. She didn't look capable of holding a feather aloft, in that moment. And I was banking on Devon having some strength left to throw herself toward me, which wasn't certain.

But there was nothing else we could do.

"Okay," I said. "Now!" I let go of the stabilizing rope with my right hand and grabbed for Devon's shirt, planning to throw my weight backward once I had her.

I missed.

Gia gasped as she took on Devon's full weight. Hot fear shot through me as I swayed precariously out over the side.

It would've been okay, we could've tried again; in the end I managed to right myself, and Gia stayed strong. But Devon had obviously anticipated me succeeding and had relaxed her grip on the rope overhead. And now, as I regained my balance, her fingers slipped off completely.

I reacted without thinking: reaching out and grabbing for her as she fell. I should've gone with her, but the rope that was wrapped around my waist caught tight as I pitched forward, tethering me to Gia, who reacted lightning fast, throwing her weight backward, which halted our plummet. I had Devon by the T-shirt—the shoulder of it, which was stretching the neck wide—and the crook of her bandaged elbow with my other hand. It felt as though both of my shoulders were dislocating as she banged against the side of the rock face below.

I gasped in pain. My torso was out over the ledge—too

far to right myself, and I could hear Gia slipping along the ground behind me. Devon reached up her good hand and grabbed my wrist. I wouldn't be able to hold her for more than a few seconds.

"I'm losing my grip," Gia gasped.

Devon's hand slid incrementally.

"Let me go." Devon looked up at me. "Consequences."

WEDNESDAY, JULY 26, 3:23 P.M.

Vargas's phoned buzzed. She fumbled it from her shirt pocket, held it up. Three missed called from Soustracs. Attempts that had been dropped before Vargas had noticed they were trying to come through.

Amelie had paused her story, her gaze snapping to Vargas's phone. She seemed anxious about the interruption.

Vargas should call Vero back, but she didn't want the girl to stop talking now.

Another buzz. A text this time. It had finally pinged off a satellite, found its way to Vargas's phone:

> More about a monster from this H: "It was with us all along." ?? The Rodriguez girl says Amelie was the last one to see Devon alive, talked about there being "a lot of blood." Amelie came back to them "covered in it."

Vargas looked up, traced the girl's small frame. She'd been distracted listening to her story and had gotten used to the sight of the girl. The horror of her appearance had become invisible.

Now it was all Vargas could see: the dusting of chalky white, the dappling of slime, mud, gore, the patina of blood on her arms.

So much blood.

Covered in it.

Vargas's phone buzzed a second time:

The girls said Amelie blamed Devon for everything.
Quote: "She probably killed her."

"Amelie," Vargas said as calmly as she could manage. "What happened to Devon?"

ABSOLVE

GIA LET OUT A RAGGED SOB.

But then H was there, beside me, dropping to her knees. She reached down and grabbed Devon, one hand on the neck of her shirt, one hand on her wounded arm, and let out a primal scream of exertion as she launched herself backward. I snapped out of my shock and launched myself with her, pulling for all I was worth. Devon bucked and strained, and then, somehow, we were hauling her up and over the edge.

The pressure around my waist, the tearing feeling in my shoulders, all of it dissolved as the rope fell slack. H and I flopped back, breathless. Beside us, Devon lay still, holding the crook of her bloodied arm. Gia took several loud gulps of air. We stayed like that: dark shapes, wildly beating hearts slowing in increments, our uneven breath filling the cavern. Gradually we pulled ourselves to sitting, stared at one another in amazement.

"You came back," Gia said to H, equal parts grateful and surprised.

"Yeah," H said. She took a deep breath. "Well, I hid at first. But then I realized it didn't matter. I hid before, and it found me. And when I tried attacking it, I was wrong. But that's just it . . . I was just wrong. About all of it."

We stared at her.

"But more than that? Hiding is for B characters." She smiled suddenly. "Did you see that? I just came out of nowhere in the eleventh hour. Like *bam*!"

"It was amazing," Devon said.

"Definitely an A character move," Gia agreed.

H grinned.

A rumbling sound came from the far side of the abyss.

Devon said, "We need to keep moving."

Another low rumble echoed toward us, accompanied by the sound of something sliding. Closer this time.

The others got up. H patted herself as though she was feeling for broken bones. The cuts on her arms and hands were healing fast: They were pink scratches, no longer bleeding. The ones on her neck had disappeared.

"It's going to be dark," Gia said, staring ahead into the tunnel.

"Yeah, but," H said. She pulled her penlight from a side zip in her pants and held it up. "I remembered it when I was hiding. It's waterproof, too!" It clicked on with a faint glimmer.

I swallowed, pushed to standing. Looked back at the abyss.

"Amelie," Devon said, and the urgency in her tone drew my attention. "Come on." She looked anxious.

H reached a hand to me. "We need to hold on to one another." When I didn't move, she stepped forward and took my hand, tucking it inside her elbow and then facing Gia. Gia took the penlight and turned, and H grasped the back of her shirt, and I felt Devon's hand clamp down on my shoulder.

We headed away from the soft blue glow, into the dark recesses of the tunnel.

THE GIRL PAUSED AGAIN.

Vargas frowned.

She raised her eyebrows, particulate spatter moving up into her pixie hairline. "Not what you expected?"

Vargas glanced at the text again, but her phone had gone dark.

"I have to tell it all," Amelie said. "All of it."

ATONE

GIA LED, A TINY PINPRICK OF LIGHT GUIDING US. IT DANCED along before her, illuminating the briefest glimpse of the path. We were one shadowy figure with many limbs, spidering along in the dark.

Rough, slick granite against my left palm, the clammy inside of H's elbow in my right hand. The erratic sound of our breathing pulsed around us, and a metallic, earthy scent permeated everything. But no rot. No decay. And I could breathe again—my chest no longer felt tight.

Gia was nearly invisible ahead, one hand on the cave wall and her free arm jerking to propel her forward. I could hear her laboring, could see the penlight dip and feel H hitch forward when Gia stumbled. Devon's hand was heavy on my shoulder.

Fifteen steps, fifty steps, five hundred—who knew.

We should've been nearing the place we'd deliberately turned out our lights to see what absolute dark would be like, but I couldn't be sure. That moment felt like a lifetime ago. How long had we been down here? Hours, days, weeks. I didn't even know how many minutes had passed since we'd left the abyss.

The sound of our footsteps was a desperate shuffle. Panting, sweaty, dusty, bloody. The cave was making its worrisome groans and noises of distant collapse, and it was more sodden with every step. Rivers of water were running in small streams down the cave walls beside us, between our feet. How much water had potentially accumulated in other chambers of the rock here? What were our chances, truly?

The thought should've panicked me.

But I couldn't feel the ache in my muscles that were long tired of wandering, couldn't access the part of me that had been desperate to escape. A strange numbness had taken hold.

I was thinking about that abyss. About Sasha.

A part of me had always known what I'd done. It had taken coming here to admit it to myself, like Devon said. But what were the chances that coming here had actually changed anything?

I could go home, confess what I did. But without proof that's what truly happened, I wouldn't be blamed. It would remain an "accident." There would be no consequences, for me.

Only for Sasha.

The thought sent a wave of nausea through my fugue state.

Around us, the cave walls fell away.

"You guys," Gia said. "I think this is that bat cave."

"Is it?" H said.

The penlight beam was weak—it didn't quite reach into the recesses of the ceiling, so it was impossible to see for sure.

"It doesn't smell like it did," H observed.

But maybe we'd just gotten used to the smell down here. We were walking through something that was slick, though it might've been mud.

"It is," Gia said determinedly. "Let's go."

We were almost across to the tunnel when Devon dropped her hand from my shoulder.

"Gia," I called, trying to alert her as I turned back.

The penlight danced a thin line over Devon. She was standing, looking back the way we'd come, bare bloodied arm pressed against her side. At her feet was the sodden mess of the shirt she'd been using as a bandage.

"Devon," I said.

Her head swung back around. Her eyes were unfocused, like she was listening to something.

"Hey," I said, pointing at the bandage.

"It won't stay on," she said absently. "Too soggy."

That wasn't good. Her shirt already had a bloom of blood on it from pressing her elbow onto it.

"Keep going." She waved us on with her good hand.

I frowned, pulled from my fogginess. Something wasn't right. "Hold on to me," I said.

She looked back.

"Devon."

She reached out her good hand, and I turned, waiting for her to grasp the back of my shirt before I continued.

We left the chamber and entered a narrow tunnel. Gia stumbled again and gasped, grabbing onto the sides of the walls, which were now pressing in from both sides. "I'm okay!" she reassured us, though she didn't look okay.

The passage got narrower.

"Where's that really tight spot?" H wondered aloud.

"Isn't this it?"

But hadn't we turned sideways and pressed ourselves through? It was hard to remember. Just like it might've been the bat cave behind us, but maybe not. It was like everything had shifted or, like Henrik had said, the caves had become "ephemeral." Beautiful surfaces, terrible depths.

Or maybe, conversely, it was our perception.

Shifting, re-forming.

I felt Devon's grip loosen on my shirt. She was slowing, dragging.

"Devon," I said. "Come on." But her hand got heavier, her steps more reluctant. She was turning back, as though beckoned by an inaudible call. And I remembered the moment at the ladder.

She's not down there. Devon had said. How had she known?

The cave groaned, and the moist smell of dirt intensified.

No. I inhaled deeply. The air was taking on a new quality: No longer the dank smell of rock and ancient earth, this scent was something akin to . . . rain.

Rain.

"Do you smell that?" H's voice was unreasonably loud in the dark.

We paused.

"Yeah." Devon's voice. "I hate that smell."

A burst of relieved laughter came from Gia.

We pressed forward, fingers groping, feet sweeping along

the rough ground. That smell of fresh rain was like a beacon. And now . . . now it seemed noticeably lighter in the cave— the black had softened to a kind of gray, such that I could almost make out the shapes of H and Gia. Like we were heading toward a source of light. We were ascending.

"I feel like we're close," Gia gasped, laboring forward.

Devon had fallen behind, but she caught up to us at the incline. Her face was porcelain white as she hauled herself forward, her T-shirt dark and wet with her blood.

At the top the tunnel narrowed further. There was no doubt in my mind now; we were in the aorta that led to the first chamber. We were almost at the exit.

Gia stopped abruptly.

We craned our necks to see.

Dead end. A heap of rock and mud blocked the passage from floor to ceiling.

"Omigod," H said. "Omigod."

We stared at the rubble.

"Huh," Devon said. She looked back the way we'd come.

H grabbed her arms around herself. "What do we do?"

Well, not retrace. The only possibly clear route was the tunnel that led to the chute of death that led back to the lake.

"Hey!" Gia said. "It's not completely caved in!"

We crowded next to her in the narrow space. She shone the penlight so that we could see that the wall opened up at the top of the pile. It was small—probably barely big enough for us to wriggle through on our stomachs. Easy for me, harder for Devon, but doable.

Except . . .

"Gia—"

"I can do it." She thrust the light at H, visibly clenching her jaw. She hobbled forward, put a foot on the lowest bit of rock that could be used as a foothold, and pushed upward, reaching for a handhold. She went clumsily, painfully, exhaling sharply, but in moments she was up and wriggling through. She let out a primal scream of determination as she pulled herself out of sight, her thighs scraping over the last bit before her boots disappeared. "Come on!" She sounded exhausted, but excited. "I can see daylight!"

H needed no second invitation. She passed me the penlight and scrambled up the rock. She ducked into the tight space, wriggling and clawing her way through.

I looked at Devon. "You'd better go next," I said.

She winced, and her hand went to her arm. "I'll get the passage all bloody. You go."

I got to the top quickly, though the handholds were tricky, and it was obvious H had far better upper body strength. And Gia was clearly fueled by an inhuman determination now.

I was at the small passageway and about to worm my way through when a sound like thunder echoed in the cavern. I froze.

It came again, and Gia screamed. Something rained down on the far side of the hole.

"Amelie, watch out!" Devon hollered.

I looked up to see the rock splinter above me. I threw myself backward, half sliding, half falling with the rock pile as it crumbled. I felt Devon grab me around the shoulders with one arm and wrench me out of the path of raining debris.

There was another ear-splitting rumble, a rending of rock that sounded like a wail.

Then silence, punctuated with a soft clattering as small rocks settled.

"Are you guys okay?" Gia called, her voice muffled.

I pulled myself free of Devon's grasp and shone the light back up the rubble. The hole remained, but it was significantly smaller now. The rock that had crumbled above had blocked a large portion of the hole.

"What happened?" H's voice.

"The hole caved in!" Devon called.

We could hear H and Gia talking, indiscernible but frantic murmurings.

I looked at Devon. She was a bloody, dusty mess. I probably looked as bad. But she'd done what she said she'd do—she'd shown us the way out.

Tricking something into destroying itself by caring for you? H had said that, just outside this wall, a lifetime ago.

It's actually genius, Devon had replied.

She and I were two sides of the same grimy coin. We'd manipulated people with our suggestions because we'd both wanted the Sublime to exist. But Devon had been seeking the truth; I'd been burying it. And Devon had saved us, in the end. What had I done?

"Amelie," she said. "What are you thinking?"

"You said we were all the butterfly and the ants, at different points." Butterflies: coercing, manipulating, influencing.

Ants: coerced, manipulated, influenced. "But I've been the butterfly, too often."

Devon looked at me.

"H is going to kick at it!" Gia called. "Stand clear, okay?"

It didn't seem like a particularly good idea, kicking at an obviously unstable bit of the cave, but a resignation was sweeping me and I didn't argue. A bit of debris tumbled toward us as H started in. The thud of her boot against the rock wall became a kind of rhythmic refrain. Finally, a sizable chunk rocketed down at us.

"How is it?" H called, sounding exhausted.

Devon swept her good arm to the side in an ironic gesture, inviting me to look. I climbed to the top of the rubble. The hole was only marginally bigger. I pulled at some chunks of rock, but it was no good. They were stuck fast.

The hole wasn't person-sized anymore. Well, not normal-person-sized. I slid back to Devon. "It's too small."

She raised an eyebrow. "You sure about that?"

"It's a small space."

"You can do it."

I thought about our trip in, how she'd gotten stuck in the crevice momentarily. "So can you."

"You still have my knife?"

Knife? I fumbled in my hoodie pocket and pulled it out, offered it to her.

She didn't take it. "Right. Like I said: last one standing. Those other two are wrecks."

"I don't want to be the—"

"It'll be okay. I'm not afraid."

Was she trying to give me permission to leave her here? "That isn't true. I saw your face when H looked like she was going to jump. And then when Gia was hanging over the abyss. You were scared."

"But that's why I know it'll be okay."

I squinted at her.

"I was scared for them," she said. "For you. Watching the three of you come apart down here—well, at first, I was kind of relieved. It meant the lore was real. But then I realized I really wanted to help you. I wanted you to make it out. I think for the first time, ever . . ." She trailed off, tilted her head and looked at me thoughtfully. "I've been so fixated on figuring myself out, I've measured myself in situations against other people, but I've never really thought about them, their realities."

I could relate, in the reverse: I'd spent so much time and energy worried what others thought of me I'd constructed my own truth. Sasha had seen through it, had wanted me to let go of it, but I'd doubled down instead.

"And then, after the abyss, I saw something," she said. Her eyes were bright with hope, but there was something else there. The smallest flicker of fear.

"What?"

"Someone. Maybe my brother. I have to go back," she said. "I have to see."

"But—"

"It's okay," she said. "The Sublime changes things." She peered at me. "Can't you feel it?"

I could. Devon was different. But she wasn't the only one.

That thing about my lungs, faking my condition at Dissent, it was something I never would've admitted before we came here. Not even to myself.

"Something's going to change for you," she said.

A spark of hope lit in my heart then. It was crazy, but looking into Devon's earnest eyes—she was so convinced—I could almost believe it. That undercurrent of despair was still running through me, dark and insistent.

Sasha, so still and small in that hospital bed.

What are you afraid of?

"What I want to change is impossible."

"Why?"

The darkness unfurled, washing me in anguish so deep my knees wanted to buckle. My voice caught. "Sasha . . ." I couldn't continue. My heart was a painful kaleidoscope of guilt and need, and I didn't know what to do with it, how to explain.

Devon watched me a long moment. When she finally spoke, I realized it wasn't a revelation; she'd known all along. "It was your suggestion," she said. "The Dissent challenge."

I gripped my hands into fists, feeling the knife handle dig into my palm, and nodded. She didn't try to console me with empty platitudes, assurances that the accident wasn't my fault. "I didn't mean for it to end that way," I said.

The cave rumbled again, and my mind zeroed in on a terrible truth: If I hadn't been so determined to flee from what I'd done, we would've escaped before all of this. Before fighting with Devon, before destroying the path across the abyss, before the cave collapsed around us. All I wanted now was to take responsibility for my choices. But how? What consequences would I face?

I looked at Devon desperately. "What do you think Sasha wanted from this place? Why did she want to find the Sublime?"

Devon looked at me a long moment. Then she said, "There was a wasp in the ants and butterfly story, too."

I blinked. It was a weird non sequitur, but . . . that was Devon. I nodded. The wasp, who destroyed the butterfly and all of its efforts. "I remember."

"You could try being that, sometime."

Trying being the wasp. But if I was the butterfly . . .

She extended her bloodied, injured arm. "Here," she said. "Make yourself slippery."

I blinked. "I don't need it."

"Don't you?"

"Guys?" H's voice came. "I think Gia's blacking out!"

Devon raised her eyebrow. She pointed. "They're waiting for you."

I blinked again. "But—"

"Amelie. Go."

"We'll send help."

She smiled. "You know that won't matter."

I searched her face. Was she saying it wouldn't matter to her—to what would happen to her? Or to me? "This is going to look bad," I said.

"I know," she said. "So you have to tell the story from the very beginning. As soon as you can."

"What—"

"Promise me?"

I swallowed. Nodded.

She relaxed. "Okay," Devon said. "You know how this ends."

I looked at the knife in my hand. I did know.

WEDNESDAY, JULY 26, 3:32 P.M.

SHE PROBABLY KILLED HER.

Vargas's thoughts whirled back to Soustracs's text as the girl paused. She squinted at her still-dark phone—nothing further.

Hadn't Amelie just said *she* was responsible for everything? That it was her unwillingness to face her role in Sasha's accident that had made things go so wrong? That her tendency to manipulate people had placed them all in harm's way?

It was, by all accounts, a revelation that had occurred to her in the cave. Something she realized down there, when the dark crept in and her fears seemed so real she could touch them. She'd admitted that she'd manipulated the girls, that she blamed herself for bringing them here. For the accident. Everything.

Why say that? Unless . . .

Unless that, itself, was a manipulation. A way to deflect from the actual truth: She'd injured Devon, killed her even, and left her there. Maybe out of fear—she'd come undone in the cave, had done something she regretted. Or maybe it was something more premeditated.

A dizzying rush of emotion hit. Vargas put a hand to the tree beside her. Looked at the girl with effort.

"Amelie," she said. "What happened to Devon?"

"Devon needed something to change. So she made a choice."

EMERGE

I RAN MY HANDS OVER MY ARMS, COATING THEM IN DEVON'S blood, making myself slick, so I could get through that small space. I scrambled up the pile of rocks, thrust my arms in, and wriggled my body. My shoulders slid in easily, and I kicked, writhing and worming my way through the space, face to the rock. I was making progress; I could feel different air cooling my slippery skin. I reached and squirmed. The rock gave way, and I clawed with one hand—the other holding the knife tightly—pulling my shoulders through and reaching forward again.

Hands closed around my wrists, and then I was being dragged through the space. Rock and debris scraped along my torso and then, all at once, I was free. H helped me scramble to standing. Gia was leaning on the wall, breathing shallowly.

H was staring at me. "Where's Devon?"

"She's gone. I—" The words died as I noticed something at the end of the tunnel before us. Daylight. It was the first chamber; we'd been down here so long that the small bit of light emanating from outside was bright, practically glowing.

And then a rumble sounded from somewhere overhead. I locked eyes with Gia.

"Gone?" Gia asked.

"She saw something, back there. And she was talking about the Sublime and she . . ."

They were staring at my arms and neck, covered in Devon's blood. At the knife in my hand.

A rumble sounded again, and debris tumbled down behind me. The passage we'd crawled through was trembling again.

"We have to go!"

We scrambled toward the gray glow of the exit. Daylight, so obvious now after hours of dark, was pouring in through the small space. Twenty feet away now.

Fifteen feet.

The sound came again. A thunderous roar.

And the ceiling began to rain on us. Chunks of mud and rock.

Gia screamed. We turtled, pulling our hands over our heads as we ran the last steps, dodging chunks of debris as the cave began to collapse around us.

Eight feet.

"Hurry!"

Five feet.

H was gasping audibly.

Daylight. I dropped to my knees, felt the other two collapse behind me.

They were here. They were with me.

H pressed at my back. "Go!"

I went. Face-first, worming out into the blinding light with H right on my heels. We squirmed through the gap and turned, reached our hands inside, and grasped whatever part of Gia's clothing we could, straining, pulling her violently through the space. She screamed in pain, and the sound of the cave collapsing echoed her with a banshee-like wail. We tumbled away from the entrance as a deafening boom sounded from within.

We pushed to our knees, scrambling away as debris crashed. Then, silence.

Absolute.

We were out.

Three of us were out.

WEDNESDAY, JULY 26, 3:34 P.M.

THE GIRL HAD HER HEAD BOWED. HER DARK CAP OF HAIR was shining in the afternoon sun. She blinked several times, lashes fluttering against her pale cheeks, and glanced up at Vargas.

She was clearly at the end of the story, but it took Vargas a moment to realize it. She was busy reliving those last few moments, as Amelie had told them. "The cave collapsed," she clarified, unnecessarily.

Amelie nodded.

"You said you promised Devon you'd tell the whole story exactly as it happened."

"Yes."

"And Devon chose to stay because . . ."

"Because of the Sublime."

Vargas searched her face. "Amelie," she said. "You've just described a journey that took several hours."

The girl nodded.

"You've been gone five days."

Amelie spread her hands, like she couldn't help it. Then she raised her eyebrows, waiting for Vargas. To . . . suggest an explanation? Cuff her?

Vargas looked at the path beyond the trailhead sign. She

pressed at her phone, scrolling for that text about the monster . . . there: *It was with us all along.* She thought, again, about how Devon had said Amelie would carry the evil out with her.

Unease crept up Vargas's neck. The wind stirred the tops of the trees.

Don't be stupid.

There was no supernatural lake. The girl was lying about the timeline, obviously. As to the rest, well, maybe she'd made a mistake; maybe she'd done exactly what she set out to do in the cave. When Draker came back, they'd take her in and find out.

If Draker came back.

Vargas scanned the trees, anxiety a tight ball in her chest. Where was he?

"Draker," she spoke into her walkie-talkie again, scanning the trees. *Come on.*

"That Nietzsche quote you recognized."

Vargas stilled.

"You remember?"

Vargas turned. "'There are no beautiful surfaces without a terrible depth.'" It was after that quote that Amelie had snapped out of her reverie, agreed to tell the story.

"The opposite can also be true. Underneath the surface of the ugly can be something so sublime."

Vargas studied her. A transformation had occurred in the girl during the course of her storytelling. Her blood-spattered skin and gore-smeared clothes contrasted starkly with a new and palpable relief; she was like some grimy, ethereal creature that had been unearthed and pulled into the light. And she was grateful for it.

A flurry of movement in the trees caught the corner of Vargas's eye and burst the strange spell blanketing them. She spun to find Draker hurrying down the path toward her.

"Dray!" Vargas scrambled toward him, forgoing composure in her relief.

He was sucking air, looking peaked and sweaty. Dark sweat stains had formed rings on his uniform in unaesthetic places, and his face was an alarming crimson.

"Are you okay?"

He arrived, breathing hard. "Been better."

"Find anything?"

"This." Vargas had been so relieved to see him she hadn't noticed he was wearing nitrile gloves again. In one fist: a Swiss Army knife. Crusted with blood. "It was sitting on the Elk's Peak sign." Hadn't Amelie told him to look there carefully? Why—"But hell if I know where that ravine could be." He winced.

"You okay?"

"Thought I saw someone in the woods. I pursued but . . ." He put a hand to his chest, forced the words out. "I think it was a deer."

Alarm spiked in Vargas. "We need to get you to the hospital."

The sound of approaching vehicles drew their eyes to the gravel road. The sheriff's white truck pulled into the parking lot, followed by three other vehicles—all off-road-worthy rigs. Search and rescue had arrived.

There was a flash of relief in Draker's eyes. Yes, he was definitely unwell.

"Come on." She put her shoulder under his arm, only slightly surprised when he didn't protest, and turned.

The girl had been watching them from her perch. She moved then, extending her arms wide like fragile, blood-encrusted wings and stretching her toes toward the ground. She stood, petite frame dwarfed by the pine trees, the large expanse of sky. Crimson-streaked and mottled skin; she twitched, like some kind of beautiful and bizarre insect.

Behind her, doors slammed and bodies moved to the backs of the vehicles, collecting gear. A German shepherd leapt from one cab, following its handler.

The sheriff met them at the patrol car, took one look at Draker. "Goddamn it. Heat stroke?"

"I'll take him to the hospital straightaway." Vargas pulled open the passenger door. She jerked her head to the woods. "You know where you're going?"

"We'll do a wide sweep, ground search." The sheriff scanned the dense forest. "Holding off on the chopper for now." His eyes went to the girl, who was midway across the lot, distracted by the cacophony that was unfolding. "That the witness?"

Vargas pulled her head out from under Draker's arm, let him sink into the passenger side. She shook her head, kept her voice low. "Suspect."

The sheriff's eyebrows rose. "Right." Then he turned, his voice rising above the clamor, ordering the team into a close circle to hear instructions for the sweep.

Vargas closed the passenger side on an ashen-faced Draker and opened the back door. She turned to the girl.

The girl was looking at the trailhead, her gaze tracing the path to where it disappeared into the dark forest. She turned and made her way to Vargas.

"Thank you," the girl whispered as she ducked inside.

Vargas knew the girl wasn't talking to her.

NOW

Subject: re: Surfacing
To: Amelie.d@gmail.com
From: henrik.noved@gmail.com

Amelie,

Don't worry about using the contact form. That account was the first thing I checked when I got back. Your messages were nice to surface to, in a weird way. Like a stroll down memory lane . . . a dark, damp, dangerous memory lane.

The deal was directions for details; you honored that. And hearing the story—the way you told it to that cop—was enlightening. For what it's worth, I don't blame you, either. We are all ants sometimes, too, right?

It must've been wild that day, emerging from the woods, calling for help. Bloody and dusty and scared. Incoherent, maybe? You saw some shit down there, you say. Or maybe you were weirdly calm. Seems like you figured something out for yourself in the telling: a way to atone for what you'd done.

You told the story as it happened, knowing no one would believe you—*because* no one would believe you. You struggled to tell the truth, but you got there. You became the wasp, destroying that manipulative little butterfly inside.

I've cobbled together my own picture in the aftermath of your story: I read about the media circus, the speculation and theories, the police investigation.

The surfacing reveals the truth to everyone, whether or not they'll admit it.

What happened when she surfaced, you ask? I can't be sure, but I like to imagine it this way:

> Vargas has made the call. She is standing on the shore, waiting for the forensics team to arrive.
>
> She waves her hand reassuringly at the dispersing crowd of Upward Junction, population thirty-eight, and scans the top of the reservoir again, hoping, illogically, to see a white van. It won't arrive for another half an hour, at least.
>
> Her initial shock has dwindled, dissipating into a creeping unease that is pierced with doubt. She needs the team to corroborate this. Needs someone to tell her if it's her.
>
> *It's her.*
>
> She turns and looks out over the glassy surface of the reservoir, ignoring the body at her feet.
>
> Low, spruce-covered mountains rise in the background, their slopes angling toward the water in a tangle of dark forest that halts before low, granite cliffs, which plunge into the water.
>
> Enormous fish lurking in the depths, one of the

local boys told her a moment ago. Vargas pretended
not to notice his waders, the pair of pliers tucked
in the bib pocket. The boy had been out for some
early morning boating, and who could blame him?
The place was beautiful, serene. A perfectly crisp
autumn day, no mosquitoes, mirrorlike water.
The unseen, the unimagined, below the surface.

People in the serve-and-protect line
of work talked a lot about gut instinct.
Vargas had always trusted hers.

It was what had guided her in the weeks
following the incident, the places she'd ended up
during her search. The whole thing had lodged in
the wider public consciousness the way a black
widow story might, except in this case it was
no heartless wife disposing of her husband; it
was a few young girls with an ill-conceived thrill
quest that had gone terribly, criminally, wrong.

At least, that belief was what had led
her to arrest the Desmarais girl.

What the public knew: The girls had been
gone from the parking lot almost five days,
were dehydrated and incoherent when found.
There were rumors one of them had mumbled
about hallucinogen-laced candy to the hospital
staff; another had admitted something about
"being lost on purpose for attention." And
then there was the lore of the Sublime, the
Desmarais girl's insistence it was real.

What Vargas knew: The other two girls initially offered far-fetched accounts of monsters and rabid-animal ghosts but, when pressed for details, had had to retract. No, they couldn't be sure. Yes, their imaginations could've run wild. They'd said Amelie was sure the Kirneh girl had lured them there to toy with them, had insisted she had something to do with her cousin's accident. Amelie thought Devon had drugged them, knocked them unconscious. And maybe she had: None of them could account for the strange time lapse. They said Amelie had been coming apart down there, had admitted she'd lied about her health, about the danger in the caves. Yes, they'd all saved the Kirneh girl from an abyss, but Amelie had been caught in the rope at the time—not exactly an active participant. No, they didn't know what had happened between the two girls in those final moments, but was it so implausible that Amelie had taken revenge?

It was a convoluted mess, and the only thing the three agreed on was that the cave had collapsed, and there was no way Devon Kirneh had survived.

But ... what cave? Even using drones and sonography and explicit directions, emergency crews haven't located it, let alone an entrance.

Amelie never did say she hadn't killed Devon. Outright refused to say it, actually. But ... no body, no crime.

Her parents had insisted on a psychiatric

facility. Is the girl still there? Vargas wonders.
Is she languishing? Scheming?

Vargas raises her gaze from the still
waters to the mountains again.

Some people said the girls had simply
become hysterical with fear in the woods, and
three of the four of them had found their way
out of the wilderness by sheer dumb luck.

But her digging, these past three months, revealed
a different take: Luck had had nothing to do with
it. Locals didn't doubt the existence of the cave,
even if that place was, in their opinion, going to be
impossible to find. The Sublime and its river system,
they said, spidered far below the vast wilderness,
winding unseen for miles beneath these hills. The
lore of the one-eyed witch was well known. And
whatever had happened down there, they said, the
fourth girl would surface when "she was released."

Vargas looks at the body, lying peacefully on
the pebbly beach, stringy auburn hair drying to
a moss in the afternoon sun. Delicate wrists that
had somehow come to rest folded one on top of
the other. Lips together in a repose that suggested
satisfaction. Autumn sweetness, crisp apple smell
combined with that stench of decay. But not the
decay of ages; this decay is months-old at best.
The flesh, bound by the slimy feathers of the lake
weeds, is too young. Not "taken too soon" young,
too young because the corpse itself should've been

over a hundred years old. Should've been long disintegrated into something unrecognizable.

"It's not the Kirneh girl," she'd said to dispatch.

"Yeah? You got an ID?"

She doesn't. She doesn't need one.

That one, scarred eye—a blight upon an otherwise serene face, like a barnacle upon a pristine, luminous shell—is enough.

She was of the Sublime, released.

Not that Vargas is going to utter such a thing. No, she'll wait for forensics, not say anything at all. Must be some kind of improbable preserving agent in the caves. Like those bog people, in Scotland.

Her phone buzzes, snaps her from her reverie. She stands, pulling it from her pocket and shading her brow.

"Vargas? Veronica Soustracs here."

Soustracs is the deputy in Rifle who met the ambulance and questioned the hospitalized girls. *Word travels fast in these parts*, Vargas thinks.

"The Kirneh girl's surfaced."

Vargas sighs heavily and looks skyward. "It's not her," she says. "Don't have an ID yet, but I—"

"I don't mean at the reservoir. I mean here, in Rifle."

A pause.

"Come again?"

"Walked into a pasture north of town this morning, intact, unhurt, calm as anything."

Another lengthy pause.

"Are you there?"

The forensics van pulls up at the top of the ridge. "Yeah," she says.

"Thought you might want to know."

"Thanks."

"We'll keep you posted."

She hangs up. The crunch and shuffle of the crowd has quieted. From the top of the incline, doors slam, signaling both the departure of the crowd and the arrival of the team.

A breeze stirs the branches of the distant spruce, and the sun glints off shining water, lapping gently at the figure. She peers at that scarred eyehole, a violent tear upon an otherwise pristine canvas. Whatever was in those caves was one hell of a preserving agent.

She straightens up.

What had the Desmarais girl insisted during her many hours of questioning? Something about terrible surfaces and beautiful depths. She considers the hills, stoic in the midday sun, and pictures the dark arteries winding beneath. Unseen, unknown.

She turns and starts up the bank.

That's what happened, Amelie. Like you, I can't be sure, but I like to picture it that way. I like to picture her, released. Allowing *me* to surface.

But maybe that's what you can't picture. Maybe you were asking about what happened *next*. How was it that I walked out of the pasture, unhurt, intact, calm as anything? Maybe you want to understand that.

That's harder to explain.

As you know, one minute down there could be an hour, a day. But that isn't the important part. The important part is that I told you the Sublime would change something for both of us, and it did.

I heard that Sasha came out of her coma, no residual complications.

I'm glad. I liked Sasha. I didn't know her well, but I think she felt safe; I was just some anonymous urban-legend junkie, a kraken avatar, a place to put her thoughts. We talked about the Sublime—just like you and I had. But whereas you'd just wanted directions, she wanted to know it was real.

Why? What did she need to change so badly? You asked me that in those last moments.

My best friend. I want her back. I want her to be honest with me.

I could tell you were struggling with that, in the cave. We all were, maybe. But I think we got what we needed, in the end.

Maybe we can meet up, when they let you out of there. Should be soon, now that you're no longer responsible for my murder. Of course, you might need to explain why you never said you weren't.

Maybe it's a bad idea. I doubt Gia will be into a Sublime reunion, just yet. And H must be disappointed: This is nothing like a horror movie.

You're not the last one standing. And nothing was carried out with either of us.

At least, nothing that we hadn't carried in.

—Devon

ACKNOWLEDGMENTS

Heartfelt thanks to . . .

My incredible author friends who read versions or offered suggestions or commiserated generally as I unearthed this book, including Dana Alison Levy, Rachael Allen, Alina Klein, Laurie Devore, Liza Palmer, Natasha Deen, and Nikki Vogel.

My agent, Michael Bourret, for continuing to be the best human I know in this biz.

The team at Holt, including my kind editor Mark Podesta, Christian Trimmer, brilliant designer Rich Deas, publicist Morgan Rath, and everyone paying attention to the many production details, including Lelia Mander and Susan Bishansky.

Constable Brady Dryer, for generously answering my procedural questions.

Mieun Kwak, for the helpful thoughts and years of friendship, and my joka Seojun—for lending H your last name!

Marcel, Matias, and Dylan . . . for everything.